Forgetting Ophelia

a novel

JULIE C. GARDNER

Lavender Press

Published by Lavender Press

Previously published by Velvet Morning Press in 2018.

ISBN-13: 978-1-7977-4460-5
ISBN-10: 1-7977-4460-7

Cover design by Ellen Meyer and Vicki Lesage
Author photo by Ana Brandt Photography

Read more from
JULIE C. GARDNER

To Nancy and Di, who keep me afloat

One

I should've known better—I thought I did—but I asked one innocent question and was permanently haunted. Afterward, whenever I logged onto Facebook, I had to scroll past ads that didn't apply to me. Beautiful infants in Baby Gap onesies, their Michelin-tire thighs poking out. This one boy who kept popping up had feet like mini potatoes. They were so tiny I was sure they'd fit inside my mouth. That was what I actually thought the first time I saw him: *I could fit those in my mouth*. I tried erasing the browser history, but my curiosity trailed me like a cat you just fed tuna. And all because I was stupid enough to Google *how old is too old to adopt*.

According to the sites I clicked on—and I only clicked a few—thirty-five wasn't too old. Unless you were single. Which I wasn't. But Jake and I weren't looking to adopt, either. In fact, we'd both often wondered out loud how Danny and Maren managed any romance with Nora in their bed. I pictured her small body horizontal, legs pressed against one of them, head upon the other. Sure, she probably smelled like baby shampoo. Sweet and warm. But I was also sure it got too hot all tangled up in those sheets. How did the three of them get decent sleep? They didn't.

That was the right answer.

In any case, my Google search meant nothing. It really didn't. I was home alone—Jake was working a weekend flight to Maui again, I think—so I was killing time reading through a stack of student journals from my sixth period class. Tori Zilkin's was the last one. Her entry on Milestone Moments was about her mother helping her find her birth parents. Honestly, that punched me in the gut. I couldn't stop thinking about Mrs. Zilkin, how brave she must've been, letting her twelve-year-old daughter look into the past like that. What if Tori met her bio-mom and loved her more than she loved Mrs. Zilkin? Because I for one would've been thrilled to learn someone other than Regina was my mother.

Anyway, that got me guessing how old Tori's mother was. If she'd always wanted to adopt and started early, she still might've been relatively young. But I figured it was more likely she'd had trouble getting pregnant. And if it took her years to take the adoption route, she could've easily been in her forties. Fifties, even. So that's all I was thinking when I Googled *how old is too old*. I was thinking about Tori Zilkin's mom. Not adopting my own kids.

But clearly Amazon didn't know that, because their next ad suggested a Bugaboo stroller that cost more than the rent for my first college apartment. In the seat was a little girl with a swirl of black hair that reminded me of Jake. But Jake and kids would never happen, so I clicked over to La Perla and ordered a bra and panty set. Because lingerie and Jake could still happen. And April 1st was only one week away.

We'd be celebrating my thirty-fifth birthday and our fifth anniversary that day so everything had to be extra-special. It's what Jake and I had promised each other practically forever ago. Yes, on April 1st, I'd finally get my diamond ring, then Jake would be whisking me away on a spring break honeymoon. He hadn't even told me where yet. He said he wanted it to be a surprise. Of course an engagement ring and honeymoon five years *after* the wedding was unconventional, but we'd talked it through before Jake proposed. Engagement rings were just props, right? One carat. Two carats. Platinum vs. gold. It was a competition, not real commitment, and we were above entering the race. Besides, we already owed Jake's parents for the down payment on our bungalow—a two-bed, two-bath foreclosure in Manhattan Beach. Jake and I had love, and a place to live just three blocks from the ocean. As far as we were concerned, a diamond and honeymoon could wait. When Jake suggested a five-year timeline, I agreed with him. After all, there wasn't one way to be in love. We'd be set apart. Extraordinary. *Jake and Lia do life differently*! This was all part of The Plan—one I'd capitalized in my head.

When the package from La Perla arrived, I stood in front of our full-length mirror in my new purple panties and matching lacy bra. They weren't the most comfortable things, but I still managed to shimmy and smile at my reflection. I imagined Jake smiling at me too. Then I had one more crazy idea to try, but it would require Maren's help.

My phone was charging next to the computer, so I sat at my desk to call her. I was still half-naked, but the curtains on our bay window were pulled, so even if Harold from next door were trying to see in, he couldn't. At least I hoped not. When Maren answered on the first ring, I wondered for the millionth time if my best friend had a sixth sense.

"Lia?" she gasped, breathless. "Nora, it's Aunt Lia. Say hi." Nora called out "Hi, Mimi!" and I guessed they were at the park, Maren pushing Nora on the swings. Nora's my goddaughter, and she's almost four, which I would've assumed was old enough to pump for herself. But how would I know?

"What's up, buttercup?" asked Maren.

"Not much. Just hanging around in my underwear." Out of habit I glanced at my computer and saw an ad for an all-white high chair. The model posing as a mom was wiping the tray and grinning. Cleaning sure made her happy. "Where are you?" I asked.

"Park."

"When you get a minute, could you send me the contact for your wax place? What's the guy's name again? Frederick?"

"No!"

"*No* you can't send his number to me? Or *No* his name isn't Frederick?"

"No. I mean yes. That's his name," she said. "And yes, I can send you his number. I just can't believe you're actually going to do it. I've been telling you for years!"

"I'm still at the considering stage," I said. "But Jake's probably taking me somewhere tropical, don't you think? And if I'm going to be in a bathing suit—"

"You should get some of that plumping lip gloss too," she interrupted. "Or you can borrow mine. It would play up the whole Scarlett Johansson vibe you've got going on. Plus, it's tingly!"

"Nah, Jake hates lip gloss. Too goopy. Anyway, I think the wax job will be enough of a shocker."

"Oh my God! Are you going full-on Brazilian?" By the end of her question, Maren was doing her loud-whisper, probably so Nora wouldn't hear and ask for details. *Mommy? What's a bazillion?*

"I don't want to overthink it," I told Maren. "I'm afraid I might chicken out."

"Want me to go with you? I'll have time on Monday while Nora's at preschool."

"Thanks, but I was hoping to go today. Besides, there's no way I'd let you hold my hand while I'm getting waxed."

"You wouldn't be able to, anyway. For a Brazilian, Frederick will have you up on all fours. He really gets in there and—"

"Mare! Please stop talking, or I won't be able to go through with this."

"You'll be fine," she said. "Just remember to take Advil first."

"Ouch. It hurts that bad?"

"Trust me," she said. "And take pictures."

"This surprise better be worth it."

I met Frederick that same afternoon. For confidence I wore my second-best pair of underwear, the silky blue ones from Victoria's Secret I got for our wedding night. At the time, Jake was a new-ish pilot whose schedule shifted every month. He'd be gone for long stretches at a time, often with little notice. And as a teacher with a hundred students, I couldn't just join him on a whim. So we made his returns home a celebration. He'd pick up take-out on the way from the airport, and I'd fill our claw-foot tub. Afterward, we'd lie in each other's arms while he threaded lengths of my hair through his fingers. *It's like melted caramel dipped in honey,* he told me. *You're a goddamned candy apple.*

That sounds sticky, I said.

I'm thinking sweet.

Messy?

No, delicious.

Fine. I grinned. *You win.*

Yes, he said. *I do.*

After the waxing, I strolled the mall for a while, avoiding Baby Gap. Then I ate an entire Cinnabon as a reward. Honestly, the whole ordeal was less painful than Maren had prepped me for. Maybe being a natural blonde made a difference. But I wouldn't ask Google. Not a chance.

Later that night, when Jake and I were at Maren and Danny's, Maren dropped her own surprise. The men had assumed their usual positions on the couch, riveted to the Clippers game. Maren and I were at the kitchen table, splitting a bottle of pinot and a bowl of Ruffles. That's when she brought up the idea of the four of us driving to Napa for my anniversary.

"Wine tasting, huh." I glanced at Jake. "A couples trip."

"How much fun would we have?" Maren grinned that toothy Maren grin. Her hair was a riot of strawberry. "I know it's last-minute, but a little spontaneity never killed anyone. Plus, you two don't exactly need alone time. Your whole *lives* are alone time."

"Wow," I said, to stall her. Maren had really thought this through. "Napa does sound good." I nodded as if I were actually considering it. "But maybe another time? This isn't that big a deal."

"Lia, Lia, Lia." Maren clucked like a red-haired chicken, if red-haired chickens wore plumping lip gloss. "It's your thirty-fifth birthday *and* your five-year anniversary. We're practically obligated to splurge." She shoved a handful of potato chips into her mouth and kept talking while she chewed. "You *have* to go all-out every five years," she said. "It's the law."

I smiled. Maren meant well, she was just a bulldog with a metaphorical bone. Or maybe a Chihuahua. Maren was tough, but a little too scrawny to be a bulldog. "Last I checked," I said, "your law-of-every-five-years wasn't in the Constitution."

"Last time *I* checked, I wasn't a social studies teacher. So save the history lessons for your classroom." She patted my hand. "I'll take it from here."

"But—"

"Hey, menfolk," Maren announced, loud enough for Jake and Danny to hear. "Are we doing this, or what?"

Jake glanced up, his black hair swooping in his eyes. "Doing what?"

"Nice try, Jakey," Maren said. "Don't pretend you weren't listening."

He took a swig of Sam Adams. "You couldn't be more wrong."

"Mare has an idea," I said.

"I have a fabulous idea," she told him, with an emphasis on *fabulous*.

"She thinks we should go to Napa," I said. "For the whole birthday-slash-anniversary thing. She also thinks she and Danny should come with us." Jake looked at me, and I raised an eyebrow, silently begging him to say no.

"Sorry, Mare." Jake shifted his jaw. "You know I've got something planned."

"*Something?*" Maren wrinkled her nose. "You've got *something? Something* doesn't sound awesome. And Danny's way behind on vacation days. Plus, my parents agreed to watch Nora."

I choked on my wine. "You already asked them?"

"What can I say? I'm basically desperate." She widened those big Chihuahua eyes. Begging. "Danny and I haven't been away since we got pregnant."

Jake cringed. He hated when women said, "we're pregnant." *Did Danny grow a uterus?* "Four years is a long time," he said, with an emphasis on *is*. "Maybe you should register your complaint with this guy." He nudged Danny who was sprawled beside him.

"Huh?" Danny's hair poked out from his ball cap in straw-like thatches. With his long legs and skinny arms, he looked like a scarecrow in a Clippers jersey. "Who's taking what up with who?"

"I was just telling your wife here that you need to step it up, man. Take her away somewhere. According to her, you guys could use a vacation."

"I can't wait to have that conversation," Danny said, with an emphasis on *that*. "Thanks, brother."

Maren smacked the tabletop. "This isn't about me, Daniel Hollister. Or you either, Jacob Townsend. This is about Lia and her double-duty day."

"Ummm… Hello? Hey, there." I waved to get Maren's attention. When she noticed me, I smiled. "It's Jake's anniversary too."

"Exactly." She beamed as if I'd just made the point for her. "And I don't want you both looking back someday thinking 'Damn! We could've had the most awesome time with Maren and Danny, but instead we did… *something*'." She put air quotes around "something," and I had to laugh. Her pout made her look like Nora.

"You're sweet to worry about us, Mare." I leaned over to wipe a shard of potato chip off her plumped-up lips. "Don't be sad."

"I'm not sad." Maren shrugged, a total Maren shrug—the higher her shoulders, the more she cared. "I'm just surprised. We're the ones with a kid. When did you two get so predictable?"

"Hey!" I set down my wine, prepared to defend myself. To defend us. "What about the hot yoga class I took you to last month? It was super… hot. And who suggested that new sushi place in Long Beach?"

Maren snorted. "I stand corrected. You're truly living on the edge." She slid off her chair onto the rug and began corralling Nora's Legos into piles. "Anyway, I just thought it would be fun to—"

"Whoa, ho, ho!" Danny jumped up from the couch, and Jake followed suit, both of them whooping loudly. The two high-fived each other, then drained their beers while the fans at the Staples Center roared.

"What happened?" Maren asked.

"What happened," Danny said, "is we need more beers." He ambled to the kitchen and clanked around in the refrigerator. Jake came to the table, put a hand on my shoulder.

"Napa is a great idea, Mare," he said. "You and Dan should go."

She looked up and chucked a Lego at his face, but her mouth was crooked. Almost a smile. "Yeah, yeah, yeah," she said. "I might forgive you for choosing a boring honeymoon over us if you top off my wine."

"That I can do." Jake filled her up first, then me. He lifted his empty beer bottle and tapped the neck against my glass. "To us," he said. "To The Plan."

My cheeks warmed. "To The Plan."

∽∾

One week later—finally April 1st—Jake and I were enjoying osso bucco at our usual table in *Mangiamo*. Between us a candle flame flickered. Two flutes of Veuve Clicquot sat bubbling beside our plates. My stomach felt like the champagne looked—liquid giddiness, if that were a thing. I was glad my wax job had finally stopped itching. As for the new bra and panties, they were another story. But I wasn't going to let scratchy underwear bring me down. Not when I was about to get my first-ever diamond. Definitely sized. Probably hidden inside the crème brûlée.

After our waiter cleared the dinner plates, I realized Jake and I hadn't made a toast yet. "Should we ask Emilio to bring more champagne?" I glanced at the two inches still remaining in our flutes. "Or something else…" My words trailed off, and I wondered if Jake had slipped the ring to Emilio when I wasn't looking. Or maybe he'd dropped it off earlier in the day? My insides fluttered. Hummingbird wings. I wanted to be in the future, wearing my ring, listening to Jake explain how he'd pulled it off.

He cleared his throat. "I just want you to be happy," he said.

"Mission accomplished, sir." I saluted him and smiled. "Tonight's been wonderful, so far." I scanned the restaurant, and a couple, leaning on each other, slipped out the glass doors. Obviously, Jake was waiting until we were practically the last ones in the dining room.

Perfect.

"Lia." He leaned forward, and his hair brushed the tops of his ears. *The man always needs a trim*, I thought, and I loved knowing that about him. "I hope you know how much I love you," he said. Emilio approached again, and I held my breath, but he continued past us through the swinging doors into the kitchen.

"Jake." I reached for his hand. "Did you forget to order the crème brûlée?" He turned his head toward the kitchen. "Don't worry," I said. "I'm not in a hurry." Actually I was, but I'd waited five years for this moment. Another ten minutes wouldn't kill me. "So." I thought he'd summon another waiter. When he didn't, I peeked over my shoulder.

Were we being filmed or something?

"You're so damn beautiful," he began again. His voice was gravelly. I loved when Jake got emotional. "So smart and strong," he added.

"You are too." I grinned. "I mean you're smart and strong and handsome."

"Let me finish." His dark eyes were shining in the candlelight. He must've prepared a speech. "I know you're expecting a ring," he said. "But—"

But?

From inside the kitchen came a clatter of dishes. Jake held my gaze, and I bit my lip, hoping my face didn't look too disappointed. I told myself to get a grip. Smooth out my forehead. Jake must have a plan. Jake's a planner.

Yes. That was it.

"I get it," I said, nodding to show him I understood. "You'd never pick out a ring without taking me window-shopping first." I squeezed his hand. The skin of his palm was warm. "You're always saying Maui has great jewelry shops. So. Is that our mystery destination?"

"No." He shook his head.

"Right." More nodding from me. "I should've known you wouldn't pick Hawaii. You'd feel like you're working the whole time. Is it Cabo, then? You haven't flown that route for a while."

"I don't think—" he started to say, then cut himself off.

"Come on, Jake." I kept my tone bright. I wanted to prompt him without sounding irritated. "You can tell me where we're going now. Spring break's coming up, and I want to be prepared. It's my honeymoon. Please."

"Lia."

"OK." I pressed my lips together. "We can stop calling it a honeymoon if that feels too weird. As long as we get to go away somewhere. Anywhere." I laced my fingers more tightly in his. "It's The Plan, remember?"

"I remember." He pulled his hand away, picked up his glass. "And I'm sorry." He downed his champagne, then wiped his mouth on his sleeve. "But I have to leave."

"Ha, ha. You're hilarious."

Jake just stared at me, and I realized he wasn't kidding. I mean, I was used to him picking up last-minute flights when other pilots called in sick or had some other kind of emergency. He used to say yes all the time because he was the new guy; then when he wasn't new anymore, the money was a bonus. So we lived with the spontaneity. But I couldn't believe he was seriously considering it now. Tonight?

"No. No way." I swallowed my frustration. "Not this time."

Jake held my gaze.

"It's our anniversary. It's my birthday." My voice trembled. "It's not fair."

"I know it's not."

"Anyway, you've been drinking," I said, a little too loudly now, but oh well. "You can't fly tonight. Tell them. Or I will."

Jake looked at his lap. "I'll leave in the morning."

I blinked once. Twice. "You're picking the airline over me," I said. "Your job means more to you than I do?"

He lifted his head again. "Jesus, Lia. Don't make this harder than it is." His eyes were watering, and my nose began to sting. I told myself to *Stop it. Just stop.* We could still enjoy ourselves until tomorrow. I could be strong, like Jake said. I could be the woman he believed I was. Still, my throat ached. I wanted to scream. *What about The Plan?* I didn't scream though. I smoothed the tablecloth with my thumbs.

"Fine." Inhale. Exhale. "Where are you flying to this

time?"

Jake sat back in his chair and gave me the only surprise of the night.

"I'm not flying anywhere," he said. "I'm leaving you."

Two

I called Maren the next morning, and she yawned into the phone. "Not funny."

"This isn't a joke, Mare."

Jake left me.

It was only the second time I'd said the words out loud. The first had been a dry-run in the mirror while Jake dragged his luggage into the living room. After that, it took me a while to get control of my sobbing. So much for being strong. Jake had been gone more than an hour before I found my phone charging in the kitchen. He must've made sure to plug it in for me on his way out.

"I don't know what to do," I said.

"Wait. You're serious?"

"He had his bags packed. Shoved under the bed. I didn't think to look."

"Holy shit!"

Face in my hands, I braced myself for a string of questions, but Maren's voice grew muffled, like she'd dropped her phone onto a pillow. I tried to hear what she was saying, then realized she wasn't talking to me. After half a minute, she came back sounding clearer now, but no less confused.

"Danny says he had no idea. What the hell? I'm coming over."

"You don't have to," I said, although both of us knew she would.

"Hold on. I'm not hanging up. I'm just getting dressed. One-handed." I listened while she threw on her clothes, ticking off instructions about Nora's breakfast. "No, Danny, we're not going to church!" she shrieked. "Are you crazy? Jake just walked out on Lia!"

"Mare," I said. "Mare!" I repeated her name, louder and louder, but my head felt stuffed with cotton.

"I'm still here," she said. There came a fumble and a thump. "Talk to Danny while I pee." *Oh God. Was she handing her phone over?* The only man I wanted to talk to now was Jake, begging to come back home. I'd listen patiently while he cried into the phone, telling me last night was a terrible mistake.

Good luck with that, Lia. Jake Townsend doesn't make mistakes.

My vision swam, and I crumpled to the floor, my skirt snagging on a hardwood plank. The fabric was a stretchy knit, sheer and clingy. Maren had helped me pick it out, along with a new silk tank top and a draping necklace. Below the hemline, my toes winked up at me, ten dots of pink.

What happened to my shoes?

"Hey, Lia," Danny mumbled. I could almost hear his bedhead through the phone. I opened my mouth, but what could I say?

You sound sleepy. Yesterday was my birthday. I wish I were dead. How are you?

"Are you all right?" he asked. "Lia?" He sounded fully awake now and worried. Of course he would be. I'd known Danny Hollister almost as long as I'd known Maren. He was the brother I'd always wished for. The father-figure too. In this moment, the kindness in his voice would've brought me to my knees if I hadn't already been on the floor. "Lia. You there?" he tried again. "Mare was tearing around the house like a hurricane. She ran to the car without her phone."

"Promise me you didn't know," I said.

There was a pause, then Danny blew out a puff of air. "That Jake was planning to walk out? Hell, no!"

"But you knew something?"

He waited a beat too long to reply. "Maybe he's been acting kinda strange lately."

"Lately." I choked a little on the word. "Lately is good,

right? Lately means we can still fix this. I just need to know what I did wrong. Whatever it is, tell me. Jake and I can work this out. You—"

"Lia." Danny interrupted. "I'm not the one you should be talking to about this. You understand that, right? You get it?"

I took a breath. "But… you're my friend."

"Yeah," he said. "I am. And I'm Jake's friend too."

"Right. Right." My tongue popped against my teeth, and I almost gagged. "Thanks, Danny. I'll tell Maren she left her phone at home when she gets here."

"Lia, wait. Let me—"

Before Danny could say something I might not be able to forgive, I switched off my phone and shoved it into the drawer above my head. The only person I trusted right now didn't have hers with her anyway.

∽∾

Maren Hollister and I met seven years ago after we'd both joined a local book club. At the time she was a designer for LeBlanc Interiors, and I was a new-ish teacher at Manhattan Beach Middle School. Our club, we soon discovered, favored *classics*, the dustier the better. While everyone else dissected the books—Themes! Symbols! Motifs!—Maren and I would kick each other under the coffee table.

One night about six months in, while Jillian Huang labored through an analysis of *Don Quixote*, Maren bent her head to mine. "When there's a break," she said, "I'm getting out of here."

I whispered, "Right behind you."

At the next lull in conversation, we made excuses to the hostess. I felt so free, I practically skipped. When we reached my car, Maren stopped too. "That's it," she said. "I'm done."

"Done with what?"

"I can't slog through another 800-page monstrosity only to find out everyone else is just pretending they finished."

"I finished," I told her. "And I'm sure Veronica did." Veronica Stinson was our group's founder, a distinction she liked to mention often. Her brow was furrowed—

permanently—and she licked her lips before speaking. Every time.

"I would've known that if she and Jillian ever let you get a word in edgewise." Maren smirked. Her face was pale like the moon. "Anyway, consider this my official heads-up. I'm telling Veronica I enrolled in a Wednesday night pottery class."

"Did you?"

She cackled.

"I'll take that as a no."

"If you quit, Veronica won't be happy," I said. "Honestly, neither will I."

Maren shrugged. "Then I'll tell her you're taking pottery too."

"That might put her over the edge."

"I don't much care."

"Why lie to her about a class, then?"

Maren grinned. "Well, I'm not a total bitch." We both laughed, and I soaked up the feeling of being with Maren Hollister. She liked to tease, but the edge of it was warm. I was already missing our once-a-month friendship. "Thanks for the offer," I said, "but I think I'll stick it out." I glanced around, even though the street was empty. "I kind of like book club."

"Ha! You're such a nerd!"

"Absolutely. But keep that to yourself."

"Your secret's safe with me, Sancho Panza." Maren stuck out her hand, and I shook it. "Well, it's been real, Lia."

"Yeah. It's been something, all right." When she began walking toward her car, I called after her. "Hey, Maren!" She turned back. "I'll miss rolling my eyes at you whenever Veronica starts a comment with '*Actually*.'"

She laughed. "I'll miss that too."

"Maybe we could meet up sometime," I said. "For coffee? It would be easier than reading Cervantes."

"I like Peet's near Highland."

"Does next Wednesday work for you?" I asked.

It did.

Now my front door banged open, and there was Maren, wild-haired and wide-eyed, barging into the kitchen with a big paper bag. I sat hunched against the cabinet where I stored our pots and pans. They were Calphalon and pricey, a wedding gift from my mother-in-law. When I explained to her that Jake and I already owned two sets between us, Ivy Townsend told me this: *Those are His pots and Hers pots. You need Yours pots.*

Maren set the bag on the counter. "I brought salt bagels."

I sniffed. "You hate salt bagels."

"True, but I love you." From the bag, she pulled a tub of plain cream cheese and six bagels, which she arranged on a serving plate. She brushed both hands along the sides of her cardigan, then hauled open the knife drawer. "What the hell is your phone doing in here?"

"I have no idea." I wiped at my swollen eyes. I had to squint to see anything more than two feet away. "You're wearing slippers?"

Maren pulled a knife from the drawer. "I didn't have time to put together a complete ensemble this morning. Blame Jake." She sawed apart two bagels and placed them in the toaster oven. Then she slid onto the floor next to me and folded her hands in her lap. "Now," she said. "What's the plan?"

The Plan.

"Well." I rested my head on Maren's shoulder. "I have projects I need to finish grading before spring break."

"Lia."

"I'm almost done," I continued. "But filling out rubrics on Mesopotamia puts me to sleep."

Maren drew back, and I lifted my head. She shifted her whole body to face me. "You're kidding, right?"

"No. Mesopotamia is really boring."

"Lia," Maren repeated. Her voice was so soft, it cracked me wide open. I threw my hands up over my face and shuddered. Maren put an arm around me but said nothing. After a minute, she shoved a tissue into my hand. My best friend hadn't bothered to put on shoes, but she'd managed to bring Kleenex.

I gulped, swallowed, choked. "I don't know what to do."

"Then we'll figure it out together," she said. "You are not alone."

Three

The first time I laid eyes on Jake Townsend, his face was in shadow. I glanced up from my chair, a hand cupped over my forehead to block the glare. He stood above me in red swim trunks, his black hair slicked back and dripping. The air was ripe with coconut lotion and spilled beer. Around us a pool party hummed. Katy Perry's "California Gurls" was playing for at least the fourth time, but all I heard was his voice.

Can I sit here for a minute?

I adjusted my legs to make room for him, and we talked until the sun went down. Until I no longer cared how crowded the deck had become. Until I didn't mind that I'd been ditched by the friend who'd brought me to the party. Pauline Herrera, my co-worker, had convinced me to come with her. It was her cousin's birthday, but she'd left with some strange guy.

Jake told me he was a pilot, and I admitted I'd never been on a plane. Someday he'd take me on a flight, he said, firing off destinations. At some point, he gave me his towel although he had goose bumps on his arms. The following week, on our first official date, I asked Jake why he'd chosen my chair.

You were by yourself, he said. *And too pretty to be alone.* He tucked a strand of hair behind my ear and kissed me.

God, I loved that story.

As I recounted the details to Maren again, she fed me bites of bagel. Later, after I'd retched that up, she dragged me to the shower and started the water. While the water heated, she found a clean pair of leggings and a sweatshirt and laid them on the bed.

"Will you be OK if I go call Danny?"

I nodded. *OK? Really?* I peered into the mirror. My hair was dull and stringy, the blue of my eyes shot through with red. I stared at my reflection until the glass fogged, then I peeled off my clothes. The new purple underwear and bra landed in a heap. Sheer and empty like a chrysalis.

I stepped into the spray.

Opening Jake's body wash was a terrible idea, but I couldn't help myself. I wanted to smell him, to conjure up his presence in the wake of this too-bright absence. I reminded myself I was used to his being gone. After years of frequent separations, I no longer felt sad when he left. But this was *separation*. The intent was completely different. *His* intent.

I hadn't seen this coming.

Before he left, he'd stood in our doorway, a suitcase in each hand. I asked him when he thought he'd be back. "I can't," he said. "I can't." His gaze traveled the living room, like he was videotaping with his eyes. "You can keep it all," he said. "Everything."

"What does that even mean?"

His shoulders sagged. He looked resigned. "It means I won't be back."

Hot water pelted the top of my skull now and dribbled off my nose. I breathed in the scent of Jake's body wash. Pine trees and the ocean. Like Santa Cruz, my childhood home. *Thirty-five years later and I'm alone again.* I poured the rest of the bottle down the drain.

As it turned out, I didn't grade projects that day. I didn't do much of anything except sit on the couch cradling my phone like a baby bird in its nest. I wanted that damn phone to chirp more than I'd ever wanted anything, but it didn't, and the silence echoed. I felt sunken underwater.

Time to wake up. Time to wake up. Time to wake up.

I parroted the phrase in my head and kept my eyelids shut. This was all just a horrible nightmare, right? In the next second, I'd roll over and discover it was April 1st . And Jake would be beside me, black hair mussed, dark eyes crusted by dreams. He'd smell like sleep, his skin warm and spiced with sweat. That was my real life. What I believed in. All I knew.

Someone pressed my hand then. The fingers were small.

It was Maren, and Jake was still gone.

She stayed beside me the rest of the day, speaking softly, weaving my damp hair into a braid. I turned down her offers of coffee. Soup. A Xanax from the stash in her purse. Just before six o'clock, my phone finally rang, but it was Danny, asking if he and Nora could swing by our house with dinner. Our house.

My house.

You can keep it all.

"It'd be good for you to see Nora," Maren said.

"No," I told her. "I don't want to set a precedent of being your third wheel."

"Doing something once isn't a precedent, Lia."

I almost laughed at this, a small hiccup. "That's exactly what a precedent is."

"Then think of it like this. You're not a third wheel, you're our fourth. And everything runs better on four wheels."

"Nice try," I said. "But you should go. Be with your family."

"I'm staying right here until Jake calls. You know he will." I nodded, and that's when it hit me: When Jake did get in touch, I wanted to be alone. Whatever we needed to say to each other, whatever I had to do to get Jake back, I didn't want an audience.

"I'm fine," I told her. "I'm sure. You can leave now. Please." I squeezed Maren's hand. "I'll feel better if you do."

Maren frowned. "I'm worried about you."

"Don't be." I swiped at my cheeks with the back of a hand. "See? I'm good."

"OK." She sighed. "I'll call you in an hour." She left one Xanax and a glass of water on the coffee table, then kissed me on the forehead. As soon as she was gone, I hurried to my computer. Maybe Jake was afraid to apologize over a phone call. And a text might be too limiting, right? It wasn't impossible to think he could've sent me an email. For all I knew he was already asking permission to come home.

Please, Baby. Yes. Make this go away, or tell me why.

I refreshed the page, but the only new message in my inbox was from a parent of one of my students.

My students.

I couldn't face them yet. I'd seen myself in the mirror. I was a horror show on legs. So I requested a sub for the next day, then returned to the bathroom and filled the tub—as hot as I could stand. The tap was leaking, and each time a new drop hit the water, I surveyed the bathroom, indulging in dark thoughts. What would bring Jake home?

My hairdryer dropped in with me.

A razor up my wrists.

Doses of sleeping pills and a slow slip under water.

Drip drip drip.

Lia, you're awake.

Jake

I'm a better liar than she is, plain and simple. Sure, she managed to hide her feelings for a while. But I wasn't looking for the truth. I saw what I needed to see. Heard what I wanted to hear. She still doesn't know how I feel about her. How much I'll always love her.

The day we met, I would've said just about anything to get her in bed. I'm human after all, and she was gorgeous. Drop dead. The fact that she didn't know it made me want her more. That hair falling over her face. And those eyes. Blue as the water. She was on a lounge chair, curled up like a conch shell. Jesus, she was magnetic. And alone.

I couldn't stay away.

She tried acting tough—teeth set, head cocked—but I could tell she was nervous, felt it the second I sat down. She could barely make eye contact. I thought she might bolt, but she stayed. All damn day. When the sun set and she started shivering, man, that was it for me. Here was a girl I needed to keep safe. All I wanted was to tuck her away. Shelter her. From the world at first, and later, from Regina.

I asked to see her again, right there on the pool deck. I could already feel myself wrapped around that body. But what I wanted most—what I needed from her even in the beginning—was beyond physical. I wanted support. Trust. Unconditional approval. I wanted to hear *yes,* and hell if she didn't say it every time.

She was a goddamned miracle.

When I pushed, she never pulled. She'd step backward, absorb my weight. And I loved it. Loved the damn control. No matter what I said, she agreed. Everything I asked of her, she accepted. And I asked a lot.

No diamond ring? No honeymoon?

"They can wait."

A house by the ocean?

"I love the water."

No kids?

"You're my family now."

She actually said shit like that. And for a long time, I believed it. But like I said, we both figured it out. Years later, after the pool deck was just a memory, after I could barely remember that first taste of her mouth. I knew she wasn't happy.

Then everything changed.

Look. I'm a selfish bastard, let's get that straight. Anyone who tells you they aren't out for themselves is delusional. We all want things from the people around us. That's why we choose them. It's in our nature.

Even hers.

That's right. She had her goals too. She was looking for a way out of her old life, and becoming a Townsend was it. I'm not sure she even minded all the compromising. At least not at first. But then we both did. We both minded a lot.

If I'm being honest, I always knew she needed more than I gave her. A larger life than we had. But for me, Lia stayed small. She shrank so much I could barely see her anymore. And that was the worst part. Because damn, Lia Lark was beautiful. Even now I can't imagine living without her. But I have to. I will.

For all of us.

Four

In the months before my grandmother died, dementia began to claim her, stealing chunks of memory as she faded in and out of time. She'd wake up asking for my grandfather. I can still hear her. *Where is he, Ophelia? Stop hiding him.* I'd stare into her eyes, terrified, watching as the truth crept in. I could actually see her remembering he was gone. And when she'd start crying, I'd huddle in a corner, frightened and alone. Rocking. Waiting.

All these years later, I was a little girl again, waiting to hear from Jake. I hated feeling desperate, hated him for making me that way. But I loved him even more. So I called him. Three times, in fact. Once each night after calling in sick. All my attempts went straight to voicemail. I never left a message. What was there to say? He'd see that I'd tried to reach him, and the calls already felt too much like begging.

On Thursday, at the end of my first day back at work, I sat at my desk sipping cold coffee. Afternoon sunlight shone in squares on the linoleum. Across the room, the wall clock ticked softly. Minutes before, I'd been surrounded by students, but I'd never felt more alone.

Jake used to visit me here, showing up unannounced when he'd caught an early flight. I'd spot his pilot's hat through the window, then he would fill the doorway. All at once. Broad shoulders and white teeth. A brush of stubble darkening his jaw.

"Hello there, Mrs. Townsend." He'd grin at me and bow, then slide into a desk, a full-grown man among the tweens. While the students giggled, I'd grin back at him, completing a mental inventory. *When was the last time I shaved my legs? Did I put on lipstick after lunch?*

The door to my classroom opened now, and Pauline Herrera poked her head in. She was a good, warm bluster of friendliness who taught pre-algebra across from me. Her voice was so loud, I could hear her teaching. A lot. I sometimes wondered what that would feel like, my words booming overhead.

"Hey, Pauline." I straightened and tried to smile.

She came toward me, and her chin went double. "You still not feeling better?"

Right. Everyone knew I'd been calling in sick this week.

"Allergies," I told her.

"Take Vitamin C when you get home tonight, just in case."

"Good idea." I nodded. *Of course I'll take care of myself.*

"Eddie and I were thinking about grabbing an early dinner before Open House. Want to join us?"

My nod switched to a shake. I couldn't stomach a meal with anyone else yet—not even Pauline. "I have to get these projects displayed before the parents show up," I said. I pointed at the table in the back stacked with shoebox dioramas.

"Mesopotamia?"

"Everyone's favorite."

Pauline stalled, examining my face. "What can we bring back for you, then? A burger? Fries?" *We.* Right. For a while now Pauline had been hoping something might happen between her and Eddie Lundgren. Even more reason for me to stay away from them. Happy couples would be torture right now.

"Thanks, but I'm not hungry."

"Work or no work, a girl's gotta eat." When I didn't respond, Pauline came over and hugged me. The press of her was soft, and I bit my lip to keep from crying.

"If you change your mind…" Her voice trailed off.

"I won't. Have fun with Eddie."

༙ॐ༙

A few minutes before six o'clock, the first eager parents started peeking in the windows. I'd lined the counters with our Mesopotamia dioramas. On the screen up front, a PowerPoint presentation scrolled. The space smelled of Windex and white board markers, with a whiff of preteen hormones. Smoothing my skirt, I unlocked the door, and began to greet the line outside.

Hello. Welcome. So glad you could come.

A blur of handshakes followed, a series of faces I recognized, but only indirectly. These were adult versions of my students, their familiarity both odd and thrilling. A tallish man approached, with broad shoulders and a tilt to his head. His sandy hair was tousled—like he'd just run two hands through it. He carried a suit jacket over one arm, and the knot of his tie was already loose.

"Nice to meet you, Ms. Townsend." He had to duck to catch my eye. His own eyes were so bright, I couldn't figure out the color. Blue. Green. Maybe both. "Long night?" he asked.

"The longest." I arranged my mouth into a smile. "Only ten minutes to go. Not that I'm counting."

"Of course you aren't," he said. When he grinned, I noticed his bottom teeth were slightly crooked. But he had a strong jaw and a cleft in his chin. "Spring break was scheduled so late this year," he said. "You must really be ready for it."

"You have no idea."

"I think maybe I do." His laugh was choppy at the end. "My wife was a teacher."

"Ah. So you *do* understand." I forced another smile just as the woman behind him stepped up to take her turn.

"I'm Jennifer Zilkin," she told me. "Tori's mom?"

I thought of Tori's Milestone Moment journal, the search for her birth mother. "I'm glad you could make it, Mrs. Zilkin."

"Please call me Jen," she said. "You're Tori's favorite

teacher." Then she whispered, "Don't tell her I told you."

"I won't," I said. "But you can tell Tori I love having her in class." After another half-minute of small talk, I directed Mrs. Zilkin to Tori's diorama. Only then did I realize the sandy-haired man had left without telling me his name.

After the last of the parents had gone, I sat at my desk, phone in hand, tapping my foot. I'd been avoiding this call since Jake left, and my classroom seemed like the most neutral place to do it. When I got Regina's answering machine, I smiled. My first real one of the evening.

"Hello! Hi there." Even in my own ears I sounded falsely cheerful. An actor in a Hallmark commercial. "I just wanted to let you know Jake and I won't be coming up for Easter. Sorry about the late notice, but—" The line clicked, and Regina picked up.

"Lia? Is that you?"

"Oh, hey," I said. "You were screening?"

"No, my hands are covered in dirt."

"Dirt?" I played dumb, but I was aware of Regina's schedule. It's why I'd waited until almost nine o'clock to call her.

"You know this is the best time to garden, Lia. Just the best. In the dark, you have to rely on your sense of smell and touch. I listen to my plants. I do. Each one tells a different story."

Once upon a time, I thought, *I was Regina Lark's carrot.*

"Anyway, I've got potting soil and fertilizer all over me," she said. "Can you hold on a second?" Before I could answer, she set down the phone, humming over the sound of running water. While she washed up, I scanned the *Parts of Speech* posters on my wall. Which combination of noun + adjective + verb would help explain what happened between Jake and me when I didn't understand it myself?

"Are you still there, Lia? Did you get my cards? Weren't they wonderful? It's a gift really, being able to make your own."

"Yes, thanks. I got them both," I said. Regina always sent homemade cards for my birthday, praising herself for her gifts before I could. This year, for the first time ever, she'd made one for our anniversary. On the back of the envelope she'd written *Guess I was wrong!* The irony made me queasy.

"I hope the paint didn't stick to the envelopes," she said. "Were they sticky?"

"No. They're great. But I haven't had time to—"

"And I've convinced Uncle Quentin and Simone to join us for Easter," she interrupted. "You know they can't say no to me. I'm very convincing when I want to be."

"That's why I called," I said. "It looks like Jake and I can't make it up there next Sunday."

"What?"

"We have to postpone our visit." *Postpone?* Why had I picked that word? Unintentional hedging? Purposeful self-preservation? Either way, this wasn't the time to examine my motives. "Jake had to leave again," I told her, making it sound like another work trip. "But don't worry."

"Why would I worry?"

"I said you *shouldn't* worry." I took a breath. "He'll be back. I'm not sure when, but he will be. Soon." As I spoke the words, I found myself believing them. First a little bit, then a lot. Jake would return, right? He'd miss his house. He'd miss me. He was coming home, and I'd be there to meet him.

"Lia. Have you been drinking?"

"I'm at school. Tonight was Open House."

"Well, there's no law against drinking at work."

"Actually, there is."

"Well, there's no law against daughters visiting their mothers just because their husbands are out of town."

Out of town. Sure.

I thought back to that moment in *Mangiamo*, after Jake said he was leaving. The room had started buzzing, a beehive in my head. I thought I'd misunderstood him. After all, it was my birthday. Our anniversary. This couldn't be happening. I stood up and slipped out of my shoes, as if the chill of the floor might help me hear better.

What did you say?

Jake didn't repeat himself.

But Regina's expecting us for Easter.

It occurred to me now, this first reaction was absurd—the

least of all the losses I stood to suffer. Jake had always hated our Easter visits anyway. Every year on the drive up to Santa Cruz, he'd point out that celebrating with Regina was ridiculous. *You don't believe in that crap, and she's a total atheist. Also, what kind of twisted vegetarian cooks ham?* Still, that night when I brought up Easter, Jake didn't argue with me.

He cried.

It's OK, I said. *It's OK.* As if he was the one who needed comforting. *We can tell her later.* Jake had reached for my hand then, but I stumbled out of the restaurant and walked home alone in my bare feet.

"So you'll come, then?" Regina asked. "To Easter?"

"What?" I shook my head, jarred back to the present. "No, I can't."

"Because…" She drew out the second syllable, waiting for me to complete the sentence.

Because I am barely holding myself together. Because I'm going through the motions. Because I'm losing my mind.

"I just can't," I said.

"Lia, you sound exhausted. Why don't you come up here and let me take care of you?" I stifled a laugh trying to picture that. Regina poised over a stovetop, her auburn ponytail streaked with silver. A cluster of bracelets jangling above the spatula. Both sleeves of her caftan draped into the bacon. *I didn't see the flames,* she'd say. *I was composing a new opera in my head.*

"Because I'm going to Maren's," I blurted out. "Yep. Maren and Danny's." The excuse wasn't true, but then again, why shouldn't I go? Being with my best friends would be a distraction, and I'd be close to home when Jake showed up.

"Please, Lia. You must come." She paused then. A long one. "The truth is," she said, "I could use your help."

Right. I should've expected this, her ricochet from taking care of me to needing me. Over the years, Regina Lark had claimed to be many things: undiscovered painter, tortured poet, talented sculptor, unpublished author. What she'd never been was any kind of mother. "What's going on?"

"Well, your uncle's finally arranged to have a few things fixed up around here, and it's about time. The sink's been leaking forever, and the flooring's awful in the kitchen. Some of the tile on the counter is—Didn't I tell you about this? I'm sure I told you."

"I don't remember a—"

"And as you know, I have an excellent eye for design. Truly excellent. But I get so caught up in the beauty of things—in the art of it all—and you're so practical, Lia. Not at all artistic. You're able to say no to loveliness."

"I am?"

"We'll discuss all the details when you get here," she said. "Just don't be late. You know I like to serve dinner early on Easter. Say, four o'clock? Did I tell you I'm making a ham?"

"I'm sorry," I said. "But I promised Maren."

"Then let me talk to her," Regina said. "It's a gift, really, being able to persuade people." For the next ten minutes, I listened to Regina's reasons, standing my ground despite her *gift* of persuasion. I didn't like lying, but in this case, it was necessary. No matter how much Regina thought she needed me, I needed to stay close to home more.

The next morning, over a couple of Peet's lattes, I relayed the whole conversation to Maren. Danny had offered to drop Nora at preschool so she could meet me for coffee before class. While I imitated Regina, Maren smiled in all the right places, and I felt hopeful for the first time since Jake left. At the end of my story, I said, "Anyway, I hope it's OK I invited myself over." I laughed and waited for Maren to laugh too. She tucked a strand of hair behind her ear.

"You mean you're not going to Santa Cruz. For real."

"I want to be here when Jake comes to his senses. He's going to wake up any day now and realize he made a huge mistake. Right?"

"Of course he is." Maren stirred the foam leaf on her latte. "But if you think Regina needs you…"

"So she can tell me again that I say no to loveliness? That I don't see beauty in things?" I snorted. "No thanks."

"It's just that we figured you'd be at Regina's," she said. "Danny figured, anyway."

"Why would Danny care if I come over?"

"He doesn't care," she said. "I mean, he cares about you.

He loves you. We both do. It's just…"

"Maren. What's going on?"

She cleared her throat, shifted in her seat. "We can cancel. That's it. We'll just cancel the whole thing. Leave it to me. I'll call Danny right now and tell him."

"Cancel what?"

Maren let her spoon drop, a clatter on the saucer. "Jake."

"What about Jake?"

"He's coming. To our house. For Easter."

"Oh." A slideshow flashed in my head, memories of the four of us sipping margaritas in the Hollisters' backyard. Playing cards at our kitchen table. Nora smearing pink frosting across her one-year-old face while we all sang and clapped.

"I'm so, so sorry," Maren stammered. "When Danny told me, I didn't know what to think. I should've said no."

"Oh," I said again. A sliver of truth stabbed my gut. Maren and Danny loved Jake too. I'd been a fool to think I could keep the Hollisters to myself. He'd already gotten to them. First.

"Lia?" Maren stared at me. "Say something." She waited.

I opened my mouth and said, "This changes everything."

Five

My phone chirped next to my computer. Probably Maren again. She'd left me messages all weekend. I'd spent most of the weekend in bed. Every time she called, I stared at the phone, waiting for the signal that I had a new voicemail. Then I erased each one without listening. It may have been cruel, but I couldn't help myself. I wasn't angry with her.

I was gutted.

A part of me had forgotten Maren and Danny were Jake's friends too—that the shock of our breakup might be hard on them, maybe even devastating. Still, Jake had *chosen* to leave me. I was helpless. At the edge of an abyss. I expected Maren and Danny to drag me back, to support me first and only. Selfish or not, I couldn't set aside my own pain right now to consider what they might've lost.

Chirp. Chirp. Erase.

On Monday I picked up take-out from Wahoo's after school with a plan to grade papers all night. I wanted to finish everything before spring break. But no matter how hard I tried, I couldn't focus. Midway through a paragraph, my thoughts would wander, and I'd find myself at the end of a page without absorbing a single word. Jake was all I could think about. Had Danny called him yet? Was Jake mad at me? Whatever. Let him be mad.

Try not to care.

Dammit, I cared.

I gave up on grading and checked my email. Maybe Jake had finally reached out to me. But he hadn't reached out. Not by email. What a stupid idea. The only new message was from the mother of one of my students.

Dear Ms. Townsend,

Thanks for your quick response. I told Luke what you said—that he should come talk to you during lunch or after class today—and I'm just checking in to see if he followed through. Full disclosure: He told me he did, and if he lied, there will be consequences. But no pressure. And don't feel bad either way. Believe me, he'll be just fine without video games and YouTube over spring break. Please let me know.

Thanks,
D. McKinley

I shook my head. Poor Luke. The truth was, he'd barely made eye contact with me today, then hurried out of class the minute the bell rang. He'd gotten a D on his Mesopotamia project, and his mom was right to be concerned. Not only about the grade, but about the lying. Still, I knew from experience that telling mothers the whole truth could be tricky. I kept that in mind when I replied.

Dear Ms. McKinley,

I know asking a teacher for help can be a little intimidating for middle school students. If I'd asked Luke directly to see me after school, I'm sure he would have stayed. He is always well-behaved, and his performance has been good all year; it's only recently that I've noticed his grade slipping. If you give me the go-ahead, I'll send a note to him in homeroom tomorrow saying I need to speak with him at lunch. Assuming he shows up, I will let you know what we discuss.

Best,
Lia Townsend

As I typed the word "lunch" my stomach growled. I felt

absurdly betrayed by my body. How could any part of me want food now? I had no appetite, but it was six o'clock, and my insides knew that meant dinnertime. So I dug a fish taco from the Wahoo's bag.

Just eat. You don't have to like it.

Ordinarily I loved their tacos, but today they tasted like sand. I forced myself to swallow and wiped my mouth on the sleeve of my T-shirt. Actually, it was Jake's. A souvenir from a 10K fundraiser he ran for the City of Hope. The day of the race, I'd waited for him at the finish line holding a cup of Gatorade. He didn't want the drink. In fact, he was barely sweating.

"You should run this with me next year," he said.

"Sounds good," I told him, knowing I wouldn't.

The shirt had been in the laundry when Jake packed, so it got left behind. Like me. I'd been sleeping in it every night since, holding on to the scent of him. But now the sleeve probably smelled like fish taco. So I tossed the shirt back in the hamper. I'd do laundry tomorrow.

I took a hot shower and threw on an old Manhattan Beach Middle School sweatshirt—one with no romantic associations. Back at my laptop, I had a new email. Not the one I'd been hoping for.

Dear Ms. Townsend,

First of all, thanks for caring so much. Second, when I met you at Open House, you didn't seem intimidating. But I appreciate your thoughts on Luke and therefore invite you to do your worst. (Or your best. Either way.) Good luck tomorrow, and please let me know how it goes. Third, call me Declan.

D. McKinley

Oops. I'd been assuming D. McKinley was Luke's mother. Most emails about my students came from their moms. It was great that Mr. McKinley was so involved with his son and also sad that this was such a rarity. I was writing a quick reply to him when someone started fiddling with the doorknob. Twist.

Turn. Locked.

Jake!

My heart leapt into my throat.

I took a breath and reminded myself begging hadn't worked with him before. Showing strength was my only option now. Jake would see I was surviving just fine without him and be impressed. Maybe even a little jealous. Thankfully I'd showered and wasn't wearing his 10K T-shirt. But what would I say once we were face to face again? I'd practiced the speech in my head countless times, but now I couldn't remember a single word.

"Let him do the talking," I said out loud. Then I peered through the curtains and saw Maren. She was holding Nora's hand.

Nora spotted me and crowed, "Mimi!" She still couldn't get her tongue around the L in Lia. Hearing her nickname for me made my nose sting. Damn, Maren knew my weakness. No matter how hurt I was, I couldn't disappoint my goddaughter. When I opened the door, Nora pounced on me.

She hugged my knees, then scampered across the room to the television cabinet. Jake and I kept a basket of toys in there for when she was here. Along both sides of the cabinet, my book collection loomed, some on shelves and the rest stacked against the walls. I'd installed the shelves myself after Jake convinced me to make our spare room a guest room rather than an office. I painted the shelves my favorite color— robin's egg blue—as part consolation, part reward.

Nora dragged the basket to the edge of the rug and flopped on the floor. "You might find something new in there today," I told her.

Nora grinned. "I hoped it!" She'd be four in August, less than four months away. I tried to picture all of us together, gathered around Nora and her cake. Would Jake and I stand in opposite corners this year, me shifting my weight, him averting his gaze? I couldn't stand it. *I won't go,* I thought. *I can't. I can't.*

"Mimi!" Nora was looking up at me. "Where?"

"It's there. I promise."

She dug in again, sorting through a stack of board books. "Anna!" she shrieked, pulling out a new coloring book with pictures from *Frozen*. I'd rented the movie for her a couple of weeks ago. The next day Jake bought the coloring book and a fresh box of crayons. I wondered if he'd known then that he wouldn't be here when she found them.

"What do you say, Nor?" asked Maren.

"Thank you, Mimi!" I didn't tell her the surprise was from Jake. Maren helped Nora open the crayons, then she led me to the couch.

"You wouldn't answer your phone," she said, "but whether you like it or not, you're going to hear me out." She kept her voice low, but her eyes were wide. "This whole mess isn't Danny's fault. Or mine." I looked down at my lap. Maren was probably right, but I wasn't ready to concede the point yet.

"Jake called Danny a couple days after he... well... after. And he asked if he could see us. He said he needed to explain things in person, and we all figured you'd be going to Regina's for Easter." I lifted my chin, and Maren said, "You always go, Lia. Always." My eyes watered. I couldn't argue with her. "Anyway, Danny said—and I agreed with him—it would be a chance for us to tell Jake to his face he's being stupid."

"He is, right? So, so stupid." My nose was officially running now, and I grabbed a tissue from the box I now kept permanently on my coffee table.

"Danny and I just want to help you," she said. "We aren't picking Jake over you. We would never. Never, ever." She stared at me, and her eyes got shiny too. "Please," she moaned. "Don't make me stand here babbling. Say something. Anything!"

I blinked at her. Maren wasn't the one who'd abandoned me. We were in this loss together. "OK," I said. "I like your glitter." For a moment, Maren just gaped at me. Then she reached up to touch her forehead.

"Oh, this." She sniffled. "Nora brought a container of glitter home from preschool today and asked if she could give me a makeover. That's the highlight of my life now. Being glammed up by a three-year-old."

I tried to smile. "She did a pretty good job."

"Whatever. I don't care."

"Since when do you not care about makeup?"

Maren made a small sound—somewhere between a cough and a sob—and we collapsed into a hug. I patted her on the back, even though me comforting Maren seemed strange under the circumstances. Still, I kind of liked the temporary role reversal. This was a chance for me to practice my strength. I could be strong. I would be.

I had to.

"I'm so sorry," she said, when I finally pulled away.

"You have nothing to be sorry about."

"Maybe not, but don't worry. Danny's calling the whole thing off. He's going to tell Jake tonight." I searched her face then—the rings under her eyes, the pale cheeks. Maren was clearly miserable. I didn't want to use her or her guilt, but I had an idea, and I hoped she'd be willing to help me.

"Don't," I said.

"Don't what?"

"Cancel on Jake. Let him come on Sunday. In fact, I want everyone to be at your house."

Maren sniffled again. "What do you mean by everyone?"

"I mean all of us. Nora. You and Danny. Me and Jake."

She grabbed a tissue. "I'm not sure that's a good idea."

"I have a plan," I told her. "It'll be fine."

I almost believed it myself.

᙭᙭᙭

The next day Luke McKinley appeared in the doorway of my classroom at lunch. His jeans hung loose, and he wore giant sneakers on feet he'd yet to grow into. He removed his hat but wouldn't make eye contact. I needed to convince him I was on his side.

"Thanks for coming." I nodded at the chair across from my desk. "Do you know why you're here?"

"My dad," he mumbled, keeping his gaze fixed above me.

"You're here because I need a favor." His mouth twitched, but he said nothing. "You tanked that Mesopotamia project, but it kind of sucked, right?" Another mouth twitch. "I totally get it. I inherited that assignment from the old department chairman. I'm pretty sure he started teaching in the Paleolithic era." I waited, but Luke didn't laugh. "Anyway, I want to change things up for next year, get a fresh start. Maybe, instead of a shoebox diorama, you guys could make videos. Something to post on YouTube?" Luke met my gaze. I was making headway. "The new project would be a big change, and I'm not sure about the logistics yet. All I know is it should be fun, but still challenging, and it would have to be an assignment everyone could do, not just kids with access to expensive technology." Luke nodded, and I smiled. "So. I was wondering if you'd be willing to help."

His eyes widened. "Me?"

"The thing is, I don't know a lot about YouTube, and I need an expert on this." Luke was still staring at me but not saying anything, so I made one last ditch effort to get him on board. "Basically, I need a tutor," I said. "Do you think you could handle it?"

His mouth hung open. "You want *me* to tutor *you*?"

"Pretty much. You'd be making the prototype, working out the kinks for me. I thought you'd be good at figuring out the music, sets, scripts. Then afterward, we could work together to make the rubric for next year. It'd be a lot of work, so you'd get extra credit."

Luke straightened in his seat. "Yeah," he said. "OK." His nod was hesitant, but it was a start.

Declan,

I'm happy to report, Luke did come see me today. And he's going to be too busy over spring break to be playing video games. I'll let him fill you in on the details, but I think everything is going to turn out all right.

Lia

Six

On Sunday morning, I scrutinized myself in the mirror, trying on smiles for size. My hair was down—loose and wavy—the style Jake liked the best. I had on a new sundress, spaghetti-strapped and silky. The print was flowery, but not *too flowery*. As I ran a hand down the smooth fabric, my stomach turned over. Twice. More than any other time since I'd met Jake, I wanted to look beautiful today.

I arrived at the gates to Maren's neighborhood on autopilot. After punching in the code, I drove past the palm trees that lined the curb of their two-story Mediterranean and parked in the cul-de-sac one street over. I didn't want Jake to see my car and drive off before we had a chance to talk.

I hope you know how much I love you he'd said to me that night at *Mangiamo*.

I do, I told him. I did.

What I didn't know was why he left me. But today we'd be face to face again, and I was going to get my answers. Whatever had happened between us couldn't be so catastrophic that we couldn't salvage things. And if I'd done something wrong, I could fix it.

I just had to know what *it* was.

I came through Maren's front door, calling out "Knock knock" instead of ringing the bell. The four of us had always done this, entering each other's houses without knocking first. It began as a symbol of our closeness—their home was our home, and vice versa—but Jake had stuck to the tradition even after Nora was born. When I suggested Danny and Maren might need more privacy with a new baby, Jake insisted, *We're still the same. Nothing needs to change.*

"Hello?" I said in the entryway. Danny emerged from the kitchen, twirling a dishrag in his hand. He'd combed his scarecrow hair and wore a collared shirt. When he saw me, he grinned.

"There she is!" It was Danny's typical greeting. *Nothing needs to change.* He came toward me and gave me a hug. "You look beautiful."

"So do you, Dan." My lip began to quiver. We could all pretend this was just another brunch, but my heart knew different. Today was my first—maybe my only—chance to convince Jake he belonged back home with me.

"Mare!" Danny called out. "Lia's here!"

At the top of the stairs, Maren whisper-hissed, "Shhh!" She wore a yellow tunic top, a white skirt, gladiator sandals, and a glare. She hurried down and shooed Danny back into the kitchen. "The dishes won't finish themselves."

"Aye aye, Cap'n," Danny said.

"Nora was awake at four o'clock this morning," Maren told me, "trying to catch the Easter Bunny. I had to put her down for a nap. You just missed her."

"That's probably for the best," I said. "I'm kind of a wreck right now."

Maren frowned. "Believe me, Nora was too. I couldn't even finish dyeing the eggs. I was hoping you could help."

She led me to the table on their back patio where she'd set up an egg-dyeing station. There were six bowls of dye, and the *LA Times* was spread out beneath the cartons with the eggs she'd already dyed. "Just a dozen left," she said, moving a carton between us. Her smile said *everything's normal,* but the brightness in her voice betrayed her nerves.

"You OK?" I asked her.

"I finally talked to Jake this morning," she said, lowering two eggs into the bowl with purple dye. "He called to make sure you'd be at your mom's today."

"What did you tell him?"

"I told him that was the plan." She glanced up, then away from me.

"You told the truth, Mare. That was the plan. Originally."

"You're right," she said. "It was." She stuck two eggs in each of the remaining bowls. Blue. Red. Yellow. Green. Orange.

"Did he sound worried? About me?"

"He sounded tired," she said. "Like he hadn't slept in weeks. When I asked how he was doing, he told me what he'd told Danny: he needed to talk to us in person. He said then we'd understand."

"See? We're just doing what Jake wants, then. Talking to him in person." I used a spoon to spin the eggs so the shells were evenly soaked in dye.

"I was thinking when Jake shows up, I'll tell him Danny and I need to wake up Nora and get her ready for the hunt. Then I'll ask if he can hide the eggs for us. He won't be expecting you to be out here. You'll have the element of surprise."

"Good. I think. Maybe. I don't know."

We were both quiet then, waiting for the eggs to be ready. When we started lifting them from the dye, one of them slipped off my spoon and cracked on the patio. The shards of shell left a blue stain. When I tried wiping the flagstone with a paper towel, Maren laughed.

"Don't worry about it. Nora does worse with her sidewalk chalk. But let's try to get the rest of them safely back in the carton."

I smiled grimly. "Maybe I need a nap too."

"I can imagine," Maren said. "Actually, I can't." She tilted her head. "Do you know what you're going say to him yet?"

"I have a script in my head. Several scripts, actually, depending on how he answers my questions. I've been practicing in the mirror. Is that ridiculous?"

"No," she said. "I'm glad you're prepared."

"I'm not sure I am."

Maren ran a thumb along the edge of one of the bowls. "The way I see it, marriage is hard. People do weird things all the time."

"True."

"So everyone's entitled to go a little crazy now and then, and maybe that's what happened with Jake. God knows Danny and I have been on the brink of calling it quits before. More than once."

I nodded in automatic agreement, but then her words sank in. "Wait. What?"

"My point is that we always get over it. And Jake will too."

"But—"

"Anyway, this isn't about me and Danny. It's about you. Jake. Your future."

"How come you never said—"

"Lia." Maren was staring at me, serious. "Promise me you won't let Jake be a steamroller this time. You're extra vulnerable right now. He could mow right over you."

"He wouldn't," I said.

She arched her brow.

"OK, you're right. Yes. I promise. I'm pretty much done pretending this whole thing was just a bad dream."

"I think we're all done with that." She glanced at the eggs. "We should give this last carton a few minutes to dry, but we can start hiding the rest."

"I thought you were going to ask Jake to do it."

"That's just the excuse to get him out here. But Nora's going to be ready for her egg hunt when she wakes up. Hopefully by then, you and Jake…" her voice trailed off.

"Right. Hopefully," I said. "Anyway, I need to keep busy, so I'm in."

"Great." Maren stood, picked up a carton. "You're an egg-hiding virgin, so there are a few things to keep in mind." She gestured toward the rose bushes. "We can't hide any in there, obviously, and don't put any up in the tree house. The last thing we need today is a trip to the emergency room. Around all the hedges is good though, and the juniper works. The potted plants too. Even in the orange and lemon trees. Nora likes it when Danny lifts her and—"

"Mare," I said. "Slow down."

"I just want to—"

"Please. You're making me even more nervous than I

already am."

She blew out a breath. "Well, that's not good."

"Why don't you go inside," I said. "Try to relax. Have a mimosa. I can handle the eggs."

"Are you sure?"

"I could probably use a few minutes by myself to get my head right."

Maren sighed. "I could probably use a mimosa."

೨◦ಳಿ

While hiding the eggs, I thought through what she'd said about her and Danny almost calling it quits. I knew they weren't perfect, but to me they'd seemed perfect for each other. Still, the fact that they'd struggled before wasn't what shocked me. What shocked me was that I'd had no idea. Maren was my best friend, and she'd said nothing to me. Was no relationship safe?

Not even mine and Maren's?

Above me, a pair of hummingbirds danced around a red plastic feeder. They hovered in close to each other, then darted out again, wings fluttering too rapidly to see. The smell of roses wafted up, and a wind chime clanged in the breeze. The doorbell rang.

Jake.

But, wait. Jake never used the bell.

Without thinking, I slid into the patio chair closest to the living room window. The glass was open, so the only thing between me and the screen was a row of white rose bushes. I hadn't planned to eavesdrop, but from where I was sitting, I could hear Danny at the front door. How would Jake sound to me? Tired, like Maren said? I scooted closer to the window, and my pulse raced.

"There he is!" said Danny. His typical greeting with typical enthusiasm. Sure, a part of me wanted Jake to feel welcome, wanted everything to be normal again. But the rest of me kind of hoped Danny would've punched him in the face.

"Thanks for having us," Jake said. "Sorry to spring this on you."

Us?

Before I could process the pronoun, Jake said, "Danny, this is Joe."

The wind chime clanged again, and my shoulders sank. Joe Whittaker was another pilot, a good friend of Jake's for years. I liked Joe well enough—he was funny and quick with a joke—but his being here today changed everything. How would I manage to be alone with Jake now? Maren would have to think of something quick. When she came to the door, I craned my neck over the rose bushes to hear better.

"Jake?" she said.

"Happy Easter, Mare."

"Jake?" She repeated, sounding baffled.

"Can we come in?" he asked. "I want you to meet Josie."

Josie?

Bile rose in my throat, and I was sure I would throw up. How could I have been so stupid? I leaned over and gagged into the rose bush. Was this truly happening? I'd been so anxious today but also hopeful about reconnecting with Jake, while all along he'd been planning to introduce some new woman to our best friends. I spit and wiped my mouth with the back of my hand. *Oh God. What do I do?* Then Maren said, "I'll go see if Nora's awake."

I slid off my chair onto the ground.

I stayed there on the flagstone, eyes shut, picturing Nora meeting Josie. Would they be comfortable with each other right away? Would Nora offer up hugs or crawl into Josie's lap? What if someday Nora called this stranger Aunt Josie? No. *No, no!* I tried holding my breath, but my heart kept beating. I couldn't move, and I didn't want to. I was still on the ground when Maren came to find me. I opened my eyes.

"Get up," she said. "Hurry!"

I whimpered, "Make her go away."

"You *can't* let them see you like this."

"I don't care what they see."

"Yes, you do," she said. "You will."

"I feel so stupid." I rubbed at my face, like I could erase everything I'd just learned. About Jake. About me. Us. This wasn't some misunderstanding we'd figure out together. Jake's leaving must've been well-planned. I wanted to dig a hole in the patio and hide underground forever.

"We don't have time," Maren said. "Trust me, you—" Before she could finish, Jake stepped into the backyard with Danny trailing behind him.

"Lia?" Jake's eyes went wide. "I thought you were at Regina's."

"I wish I were."

"What are you doing on the ground?"

Of all the things I'd imagined Jake asking me today, that one hadn't made the list. I knew I looked ridiculous—in a new sundress, my hair done the way Jake liked it—and a wave of rage washed over me. Damn him. Damn the stranger he'd become. I didn't recognize either of us anymore. Gathering what dignity I had left, I pulled myself up, smoothed my dress, and stared Jake down.

"I came here to fight for you," I said. "For us. Guess I'm too late though." He opened his mouth, but I cut him off. "Who is she, Jake? Does she even know I exist?" My voice grew louder, and a part of me hoped Josie was hearing me. "Maybe I should pop inside and introduce myself. Won't your new girlfriend be surprised to meet me."

Maren grabbed me by the elbow. "Wait."

"Why should I wait?" I glared at Jake without blinking. "He didn't."

"Danny," Maren said, "these two need to talk. Now." He nodded, and Maren released me. Then she and Danny went back into the house.

"You've got it all wrong," Jake said.

Wrong? My eyes burned, but I wouldn't look away. "It seems pretty clear, Jake."

"Then why don't you tell me what you think's going on here."

"Oh, I *think* you met someone else," I said. "And I *think* you like being the good guy, so you didn't want to hurt me. I *think* instead of admitting the whole truth, you figured you'd ease into it. Take me to dinner. Tell me you'll always love me. Break the bad news a little at a time. So you start with the leaving first, then the part about *Josie* could come later. I bet you even convinced yourself we'd get through this amicably. You probably thought if you were nice enough—if you let me *keep everything*—I'd come around in time, right? That's so like you, Jake. Always smooth. Never ruffling anyone's feathers. Not even Danny and Maren's. That's why you wanted to see them in person, isn't it? So you could manipulate them? Plead your case? Shed a tear or two? You thought if they saw how hard this was on you, they wouldn't be too mad. But you know what, Jake? I don't care how Danny and Maren feel. I'm angry enough for all of us."

Jake ran a hand through his hair, but he didn't say a word, so I spoke even louder. Not quite yelling but close. "You lied to me. You've been lying for a while, I guess." My voice splintered then, but I couldn't stop. "Long enough to fall in love with someone else while I was still in love with you."

Jake opened and shut his mouth. It looked like he was chewing on my words. Finally, he said, "You're right. I do try to be the good guy, and I'm in a tough position. An impossible one."

"Ha!" It was as much a sob as a laugh.

"I may be an asshole," he said, "but I didn't fall in love with someone else. At least not in the way you think."

"Great. So you're just screwing her, then?"

Jake flinched.

"Oh, I'm sorry. Was that too crude for you? Is Josie already up on the famous Jake Townsend pedestal? Too precious for this kind of talk? What was it about *me* that wasn't precious enough for you anymore? Is Josie prettier? Is her job more glamorous? Is she better in bed?"

"Stop."

"I know I'm just some schoolteacher who hasn't seen much of the world. But if I remember correctly, that's the way you liked it—me at home, waiting in the wings. Did that get too boring? Was I too easy to please? You probably told yourself you couldn't help it. The heart wants what the heart wants, right? Well, guess what, Jake. You don't get to leave me for someone else and still be the *good guy*."

He clenched his jaw. "It's not like that."

"OK. Tell me what *it is* like, then. Tell me I wasn't an idiot to trust you. To trust us. Tell me I wasn't monumentally dumb to believe you'd come back to me. I thought you just needed time. That in the end you were an honorable man." I paused for a breath. "I came here expecting to work things out with you, not to discover you'd already found someone new."

Jake shook his head. "She's not new."

My stomach lurched, an elevator plummeting. "What?"

"Josie. She's not new," Jake told me. "She's my daughter."

Seven

My eyes fluttered open, and I struggled to find my bearings. Along the wall, stacks of magazines tilted at perilous angles. Two dead plants dangled from the ceiling in macramé pot holders. Across the room an easel boasted a half-finished still-life, and on the bench below was a palette crusted with smears of unused paint. The sting of turpentine hung in the air. I closed my eyes again as I remembered.

I was in Regina Lark's art studio.

Years ago, this had been my bedroom, back when my grandparents were still alive and the ranch house belonged to them. Their property—now Uncle Quentin and Regina's—was surrounded by pine trees, the grounds blanketed by needles. I used to pretend we lived in a fairy-tale land where children's wildest dreams came true. In my little-girl mind, all the good fathers were off seeking their fortunes, and all the good mothers weren't too busy or too tired to play.

Regina hadn't asked why I'd shown up unexpectedly last night, and she said nothing about my puffy eyes or sniffling. Instead she pulled a platter of leftover ham from the fridge and opened a fresh bottle of Pinot Noir. Back at the dinner table, Uncle Quentin picked at the ham while his girlfriend Simone finished the wine. I listened to Regina talk about her upcoming project: raising chickens. Soon she'd be an urban farmer, she told us, although she did admit her neighborhood was "actually more rural." Eventually Regina's clucking sounds must've become too much for my uncle because he offered to take Simone to a hotel so I could stay in my mother's guest room. Regina wouldn't hear of it. After all, Quentin and Simone had slept in the guest room the night before, and Regina didn't want to change the sheets.

"My art studio will be just fine for Lia," she said. I nodded then, feeling relieved. I hadn't wanted to sleep alone in the room where I used to stay with Jake. Rolling over on the futon in the studio now, I kicked off the blanket Regina gave me last night. "I made this," she told me. "My knitting's really coming along, isn't it?" Her throat was blotchy from too much wine. "I'd use it myself, but I'll be up for hours while the rest of you are snoring away."

Since I was a little girl, Regina had liked to claim she needed less sleep than average people. "I have to get the good stuff out or it'll die inside me," she'd say, pointing to half-filled journals and unfinished paintings. "You should try it, Lia. Really. The night's too bright for sleeping." Back then I'd been too young to argue that in between her *good stuff*, Regina stayed in bed for days.

She appeared in the doorway of the studio, a cup of coffee in hand. "I can't believe you're my daughter." She shook her head. "I never sleep this late." She peered down at me but said nothing about my swollen face. "Quentin and Simone left an hour ago. He was sorry not to say goodbye, but he wanted to get on the road before Monday morning rush hour. It's always work work work with him, you know. I'll never understand it." She blew over the top of her mug then took a noisy sip. My skull was already throbbing.

"Any more coffee where that came from?" I asked.

Regina shrugged. "I only made half a pot. But you're welcome to brew your own. I can wait." I thought about asking what she'd be waiting for, but instead I stretched into a stand. I was still wearing my sundress from yesterday, the one I'd put on to win back Jake. Regina sat on the painter's bench, and I turned on my phone. Nothing from Jake. Then again, I'd blocked his number yesterday. I did have three missed calls and one text. All from Maren.

We need to talk.

Yes, I thought. *We do. But not until I get some caffeine in me.*

"I'll be back," I told Regina. I shuffled down the hall to make my own half-pot of coffee. Rounding the corner into the kitchen, I found a man bent over the sink with a measuring tape. His hair was more like a shadow over an almost-shaved scalp. The skin below it was creamy brown.

"Hi?" I said. When he turned, his hooded eyes looked familiar. For a second, I thought *haunted.* Then he straightened, and I thought *strong.* "I'm Lia," I said. "Regina's daughter?" He nodded and moved to a yellow legal pad to scribble down numbers.

"I'm sorry," I said. "Who are you?"

Without lifting his head, he said, "Contractor."

"Oh, right. I forgot she's having work done." The man nodded again and added something to his pad. He squinted at the numbers and continued to ignore me. "Anyway, I need to get in there," I said. He looked up, and I pointed toward the cookie jar in the corner where Regina kept her coffee grounds. The jar was supposed to resemble an oversized Oreo, but it came out of the kiln crooked, like someone had taken a bite from one edge. Of all my mother's failed art projects, this lopsided Oreo was my favorite. Not because she made it for me—she didn't—but because it showed the bright side of good intentions. Despite every dreadful outcome, Regina Lark kept trying. Trying. Trying.

The man stepped aside, and I slid past him, moving the jar to the opposite counter. Why Regina kept her grounds so far from the coffeemaker was beyond me. I smiled to myself.

It's probably beyond her too.

"I'm making a fresh pot," I said, waiting a beat. "You want some?" He shook his head and began flipping through an appliance brochure, pausing to bend the corner of one page. I leaned forward to see what it was in the brochure that had caught his interest. "Anything good?" I asked.

"Maybe." He turned around again, and I noticed the right pocket of his jeans bore a ring from a tobacco tin. For another minute or two we said nothing. Then he moved past me toward the door to the garage.

Under my breath I said, "Nice talking to you." I thought I

saw his lip twitch, but the door shut behind him before I could tell if he was smiling.

While the coffeemaker gurgled, I dampened a paper towel and swiped at my swollen eyes. Streaks of mascara came off on the wet paper. Great. I probably looked like a raccoon, and my mouth felt dry and cottony. Since I'd fled the Hollisters' without warning, I didn't even have a toothbrush.

Selecting a mug from the cabinet next to the stove, I filled it to the brim and inhaled the aroma of dark roast. The coffee would be too hot to drink for a little while, so I padded back to the studio. Regina was standing by the window. I sat on the futon where I'd slept. "I met your contractor," I said. "He's on the quiet side."

She waved her free hand in the air. "Oh, yes. You let me talk about the chickens for so long last night, I forgot to mention he'd be here this morning."

"Sorry I let you talk so much."

"Anyway, you're wrong about Caleb being quiet. With the right person, he's quite the conversationalist."

"Caleb? Caleb Stone?" No wonder he looked familiar.

"You went to school with one of the Stone boys, didn't you?"

"Yes," I said. "I knew Ezra." Ezra Stone and I were freshmen when his older brother, Caleb, graduated. Caleb Stone had joined the army and was deployed after 9/11. Beyond that I'd heard nothing about either of the brothers in a decade. Was Caleb now living back in town? I didn't know whether to applaud this kind of loyalty or feel sorry for him for never moving on.

"Caleb's in the house next door," Regina said. "He bought the place last summer after Arthur Nelson passed. You know it was a week before the smell of Arthur's corpse caught the attention of the mailman and—"

"Yes," I said. "You told me."

"Arthur always was a nasty old thing."

"Still. No one should have to die like that. Alone."

Regina sniffed. "There are worse things than being alone, you know."

"None I can imagine."

As a young girl, I'd been frightened of Mr. Nelson but also deeply fascinated. With little but Regina's warnings about our neighbor to go on, I concocted my own stories. I imagined Mr. Nelson luring helpless women and children into his home to be his makeshift family. And only a kiss of true love would save him. I was a sucker for fairy-tale endings. I sketched pictures of the dungeon and wrote poems about a monster transformed by love. When I was especially lonely, I pretended Mr. Nelson was my father.

"I wonder if Caleb has any kids," I said.

"Some people aren't cut out to be parents." Regina said this without a trace of irony. I fought a momentary urge to blurt out everything I'd discovered about Jake and Josie, but Regina kept her gaze fixed out the window. She wasn't thinking about me at all. "That Caleb sure does have a nice set of tools on him," she said. She turned toward me and raised an eyebrow. "He's a sexy one, isn't he?" she asked, but I wasn't in the mood for her leering.

"Is he married?"

Her lips puckered, like a mouth around a lemon. "For his sake, I sure hope not." Suddenly I heard Regina's voice, an echo from the past: *Unlike you, I refuse to be owned, Lia. To be a wife, you have to sell yourself. You'll regret marrying Jacob. Mark my words.* It was a good thing I hadn't told her about Josie after all. At best Regina would say *I told you so.* At worst she'd have questions I couldn't answer.

I'd spent the entire drive up to Santa Cruz asking myself how Josie had crashed into Jake's life. Was she the result of a one-night stand? Some long-term love affair? Did Jake care about his daughter's mother? It was then that I'd pulled off the road, rolled down the window, and screamed *Stop!* Speculating was pointless and harmful. Maren would find out the true story for me.

Maren. I'd completely forgotten about her.

"Lia?" Regina leaned forward, peering into my face. "What's the matter?"

"Nothing. I just need to make a call."

"Go ahead."

"I'd like to be alone. Please."

"Fine." As Regina sailed past me, I smelled incense and coconut shampoo. Her hair was a cascade of auburn-streaked silver falling down her back. "I'll be in the kitchen," she said. "With my sexy neighbor."

Ugh. Poor Caleb.

Maren was out of breath when she answered my call. "Sorry," she panted. "I ran upstairs so I could talk without Nora listening." When I heard Nora's name, my stomach clenched. I'd promised to be there for her egg hunt, but I'd fled without saying goodbye.

"Is she OK?" I asked, even though I wanted to skip straight to talking about Jake.

"Nora's fine. We're all a little tired. Yesterday was insane."

The fingernails of my free hand dug into my kneecap. Four tiny half-moons. "Insane. Yeah."

"Anyway, how are you?" asked Maren. "More importantly, *where* are you? You didn't answer your phone, so I drove by your house. Your car wasn't there. We've been so worried."

"We?"

"Danny and I."

"Right."

"So." Maren paused. "Did Jake get in touch with you?"

"No." I didn't bother telling her I'd blocked him.

"He seemed pretty shaken up after you took off."

"Forgive me if I don't feel sorry for him."

"Lia." Another pause. "I hope you know Danny and I had no clue he was bringing someone."

"*Someone?* You mean his *daughter.*" My throat closed on the word. "Jake has a daughter," I repeated. It still tasted wrong in my mouth.

"All things considered," Maren said, "you sound better than I expected."

"Ha!" I pictured those smears of mascara on the paper towel, my swollen eyes, and gnarled hair. "You're lucky you can't see me." A giggle, sharp and hysterical, rose up from inside me.

"Are you laughing?"

"I don't know what I am." I swallowed. "None of this has

sunk in yet. It's like I'm outside a glass door looking in on someone else's life. A bystander to some train wreck happening to another Lia."

Maren groaned. "Oh, sweetie."

"Is it weird that I keep thinking this is a nightmare? I even pinched myself trying to wake up from the bad dream."

"It's not weird," she said. "But you're not dreaming. Jake really has a daughter."

"I didn't get to see her," I said, more to myself than Maren. "So it doesn't feel real."

"Well, she's a mini-Jake. Except a girl. Long lashes. Black hair. Same crooked smile."

"Oh." I flashed back to the parents at open house, each face a ghost of what their children would become someday. "Charlotte," I muttered.

"What?"

"Jake's sister. Josie must look like her."

"You're right. She does," Maren said. "I didn't realize until you said it."

"I wonder if Charlotte knows about Josie."

"Who the hell cares?" Maren snorted. "This isn't about her."

"Still. If Josie looks like her aunt, she must be beautiful."

"She is. They both are, dammit." Maren sighed. "I'm so sorry, Lia."

"That Jake's daughter is beautiful?"

"That he has a daughter in the first place."

"It's not your fault."

"I feel terrible, anyway. Danny and I both do. About all of it."

I almost asked Maren what she meant by *all of it*. Were she and Danny keeping something from me? Had they been before? The thought made me dizzy, but I couldn't worry about that now. I had to focus on Jake and me. I pressed a palm to my forehead. "Did Jake stay long?"

"No. When you left, Dan laid into him pretty hard—like what the hell he was thinking, how could he just show up with a kid and no warning—stuff like that. I'm glad the girls were upstairs. They couldn't hear, I'm pretty sure. Anyway, Jake said he didn't know how else to tell us. And he *really* didn't know what to tell you. Apparently, *that* was his biggest problem. He was hoping we'd help him break the news to you. Gently. Like I'd ever do that!" Maren's voice cracked. I almost felt sorry for her.

"So what's the whole story, then?" I asked. "You can tell me. No matter how bad it is."

"I wish I knew." Maren made a sound then, a *tsk* of disgust. "After Danny called him on his crap—which he totally deserved, by the way—Jake excused himself and went up to Nora's room. We figured he was just checking on the girls, but he came back down holding Josie's hand. And he apologized. Told us he'd forgotten they had somewhere else to be. Then they were gone. Nora was so sad."

"Oh." I sucked in a breath.

"Not about Jake leaving," Maren added quickly. "Nora just didn't want Josie to go."

"It's fine. I get it. Nora likes her." My cheeks flamed at my pettiness, me being jealous of a child. None of this was Josie's fault. She was a victim in her own way. I didn't want to hate the girl. And yet.

"It was actually kind of sweet, how nice Josie was to Nora," Maren said. "Considering their age difference." And there it was, the question I'd been afraid of. So much depended on the answer. I didn't know what to hope for when I asked.

"How old is Josie, anyway?"

Maren paused. "Ten, maybe. Eleven. I didn't find out exactly."

"OK."

"But that's good news, right? It means this all happened a long time ago." Maren waited for me to respond, but I said nothing. "It means Jake wasn't necessarily involved with someone else while you two were married."

No. Not necessarily. Still, my heart pounded hard. If Jake already had a daughter when we met, how had he kept her from me? And why? He was the one who didn't want kids, and I let him convince me. Not that he gave me much choice.

"Are you still there?" Maren asked.

"Yes," I said. "I'm just—" There came a knock at the door, and Regina stepped inside. She held a spatula up, and for a moment, I wondered if she was actually making me breakfast.

"Sorry to interrupt," she said. "It's Jake. He wants to talk to you."

My phone slipped from my hands. "What?"

"Jake wants to talk to you."

"No, no. I heard you the first time."

"He seems to think you blocked his calls."

"That's because I did."

Regina frowned. "What's going on?"

"Just tell him I don't think I can... what I mean to say is... I won't..." My voice trailed off, and I looked down at my phone. Why had Jake called Regina's house looking for me? The man was finally free from me, free of us. He could move on to his new life. So if he was reaching out to me here, now, maybe he'd reconsidered. Could Jake be having second thoughts?

Oh God, Lia. Breathe.

This was what I'd been hoping for, after all. Since the night Jake left, I'd held onto the belief that after he'd had time to think, he'd realize his mistake. I'd been desperate for him to change his mind, prepared to do anything if he'd come back to me.

Until yesterday.

Until Josie.

How could I ever trust Jake again after that kind of betrayal? I couldn't. That was the answer. No matter how much I wanted our old life back, Jake didn't deserve me. He didn't deserve us.

"Lia?" Regina peered at me. The spatula hung at her side.

"No."

"What do you mean, no?"

I squared my shoulders. "Tell Jake I'm busy, and if he calls back, let the answering machine pick up."

Regina shook her head. "I can't do that."

"Please," I said.

"But Jake's not on the phone. He's in the living room."

Eight

I found him slumped on the mustard-yellow couch, looking more exhausted than the upholstery. A potted ficus drooped in one corner. The coffee table between us was a clutter of used napkins and wine glasses. I stood across from him with Regina's blanket wrapped around my shoulders. Still. When Jake made eye contact, I shivered.

"Are you gonna sit?" he asked. I bent my head, but I didn't respond. "I knew you'd be here," he told me. *What did he think I'd say to that? Congratulations for knowing me so well when I don't know you at all?* "I would've called here first," he continued, "but I figured you'd tell me not to come."

"I would've told you not to come."

He shifted then, both palms flat on his thighs. "I need to apologize," he said. "For everything. For the way I fucked up this whole situation."

This whole situation, I thought. *What a strange way to describe the total destruction of our lives.*

"Jake!" Regina emerged from the hallway, stopping short as if surprised to see us there. She'd changed into overalls and braided her hair, corralling the end with a red bandanna. "Can I get you a cup of coffee?" *From the pot I brewed,* I thought. "I've discovered the most wonderful beans," she told him. "They're the best I've ever tasted, and I've been to Colombia."

Jake kept his gaze fixed on me. "No thanks, Regina. I'm all set."

"Have it your way," she said. "But my boy, you don't know what you're missing." She strolled to the glass slider that led to the backyard. "I'll be in the garden if anyone needs me." She left the door open behind her.

Alone with me again, Jake cleared his throat. "I didn't know you'd be at Danny and Maren's. That's not the way I wanted you to find out. Any of you. Any of it. I made an already awful situation even worse."

"Yes," I said. "You did."

"I had no idea how to tell you, and I'm sure it sounds crazy, but I was hoping Maren and Danny might have advice. Some way we could all move forward."

"Move forward," I repeated. "Right."

"Like I said." Jake shook his head. "Crazy."

"No, I don't think you're crazy." A hiccup of anger escaped me. "I think you didn't trust me."

"Trust you?"

"You were afraid I wouldn't follow your script. When I found out about… your news."

"No," he said. "That's not it."

"Oh, come on." I raised my voice a notch. "You can't stand to lose control, even over little things. And this is a big thing, Jake. The biggest." He was quiet then, and I knew that was the closest I'd get to an admission. "So, where is she now?" I asked. "Your daughter, I mean. What's her name again? *Jo?*"

"Actually, I'm supposed to call her Josie," he said. "Only her mom's allowed to call her Jo, but I still forget sometimes when I—"

I turned my head away.

"Jesus." Jake stumbled over his words. "I'm so sorry. I'm a goddamned idiot." I looked back at him, and he ran a hand through his hair. "Anyway, she's with her mom."

"Oh." My shoulders sank. Hearing this hurt almost more than I could bear.

"I swear to God I didn't know," he said. "About Josie. Not until a couple months ago. Less than two."

I blinked. "So you've been lying to me for weeks?"

"I was waiting for the right time to tell you," he said. "But there was never a right time. And after everything you gave up for me—for us—I figured you'd probably kick me out. I even packed a couple bags in case."

"Is this the part where you don't need to be in control?"

"No. I was just working out the best way to explain things. The thought of hurting you was killing me. And then that night at *Mangiamo*, you looked so damn happy."

"I was happy." Tears stung my eyes, and I bit the inside of my cheek.

"That's when something in me snapped," he said. "No more postponing the inevitable. Yeah, my timing was crap, but I couldn't take it anymore." He lowered his voice. "I thought leaving was the only way."

"Only way to what?"

"I don't know. Make a clean break? I figured I owed that much to you. Owed you your freedom or some shit like that. Like I said. I didn't think. I wasn't planning to go that night. It just... happened."

I waited a beat to be sure he was finished. "I believe you," I said.

He nodded. "Thanks."

"Don't thank me. It was awful. It still is. Awful."

"I know," he said.

"No, I don't think you do." I pulled the blanket more tightly around me. "So, if that's all you came here to say—"

"It doesn't have to be." He leaned forward, and my heartbeat quickened. What exactly was he angling for? A hug? To be comforted? Some assurance that, despite everything he'd done, I'd be OK? Well, I wasn't OK. I felt like I'd never be OK again. Jake had a daughter. And whether or not he'd just discovered her, the girl still existed. Now and always. So did her mother. And her mother wasn't me.

"How did it happen, anyway?" I asked.

Jake cocked his head, and I decided not to clarify the question. Let him figure out what I meant. Maybe he'd say something I didn't realize I wanted to hear. "The details don't matter," he said. "And they won't help."

"That's for me to decide," I snapped. "I'm the one who wasn't enough for you."

"No." His jaw shifted. "Nothing was missing," he said. "I wasn't looking for a daughter. But once I saw her, it was obvious she was mine."

Mine, I thought. Or maybe I said it out loud. Either way, Jake still hadn't addressed who, what, why, or when this had happened. But he kept going before I could ask more.

"After spending five minutes with her," he said, "I just knew."

"Knew what?"

"That I had to be there for her."

"*Her?*"

"Josie."

"But not for me?"

He balled his hands into fists. "I couldn't ask you to take that on," he said. "My kid. Being a parent. We'd already decided it was too much, remember?"

"How could I forget?"

"We didn't want kids."

"*You* didn't want them."

"And you agreed with me."

"Yes." My pulse was racing. Jake had been right. This conversation was doing more than good.

"Then I met Josie," he said, "and I changed my mind."

"Maybe I would've changed my mind too," I said. "But you didn't give me the chance. You chose for me." I tilted my head, waited until he met my gaze. "Again."

"Jesus, Lia." Jake exhaled, a thin gust of resignation. He didn't like to think about that time in our lives, the piece of our past we'd already buried. "I'm so damn sorry."

"So you've said."

Jake tugged at the collar of his shirt. "I didn't want to put you on the sidelines while I tried to be a part of my kid's life," he said. "And I couldn't ask her to make room for you, either. That's not her job. I've got lots of lost time to make up, and only a few weekend days a month free."

"I'm well aware of your busy schedule."

"Listen. I'm doing the best I can here." His words came measured and slow, and I wanted to slap him, or at the very least tell him not to speak to me like a child.

"Just be honest, Jake, for both our sakes. It's not about me or Josie. Everything you do, everything you've ever done, is to make things easier on you. You hate when things get a little bit hard or, God forbid, messy."

"And you don't?" His eyes flashed. "Now who's the liar?"

I inhaled sharply. A gasp of truth. "I suppose you're right," I said, hoping my voice sounded steadier than I felt. "I hate messy too. Which is why you need to leave."

"Lia."

"Go."

Jake shook his head. "Not until I know you'll be OK."

Just like I thought. Always the good guy. "Get out. Now."

"You deserve better than me," he said.

I let the blanket slip to the floor. "Right again."

Nine

Regina was in the garden on her knees weeding a patch of what I thought were radishes. Maybe turnips. Tipping over an empty bucket, I sat beside her and hugged my knees.

"The rabbits have been feasting again," she said without looking up.

"I thought you always gardened at night."

"Never say *always*, Lia." She eased a worm from the ground and held it up, dirt-caked and writhing. "It's the *sometimes* that gives life its spice." For a moment I was quiet, weighing what to tell her, wondering what she'd already guessed. The smell of fertilizer, faint and fertile, drifted over us.

"Jake left," I said.

"I figured."

"I mean he left for good. He left *me*." Regina shrugged, and the worm writhed in her fingers, fumbling for its home. "He has a kid, Mom."

She dropped the worm and lifted her head. I wondered what surprised Regina more: that Jake was a father or that I'd called her "Mom." "So there's someone else," she said.

"There's a daughter."

"Where there's a daughter, there's a mother."

I licked my lips and tasted salt. "Not necessarily," I said. Josie's existence was torture enough without my examining that part of the story. Thinking about another woman felt dangerous. Like staring at the sun. "Don't forget, I never had a father."

Regina snorted. "That's different," she said. "You were special. We were special. We didn't need a man."

"So you've told me. Many times. But I know nothing else about *the man*."

"What's there to know?"

"Did he want me? Did he know I existed? Did you ever love each other?"

"You never asked."

"I did. Many times. But you weren't listening. Or you didn't want to hear." Regina smiled at me then. Above her a single cloud hovered in the sky.

"Help me up," she said. I reached out to her, and she grunted to a stand, wiping her bare hands on her overalls. Regina liked to say she needed no protection from nature, that real gardeners wouldn't let gloves come between their skin and the dirt. I watched the worm jerk its way back under the earth, and a part of me wanted to bury myself there too.

"Her name is Josie," I said. "Maren says she's pretty."

"Hmm."

"I feel like maybe I've gone insane." I tried to laugh, but the sound disappeared into the trees. I looked back at Regina's house, then down at my dress. It was wrinkled now and dusty.

"So. Jake's gone then," she said.

"Yes."

"You sent him packing, did you?"

"So to speak."

"Good," she said. "That needed doing. Now I need you to do something for me."

৽৽৽

An hour later, I was roaming the aisles at Lowe's in Regina's sweatpants and a tie-dyed T-shirt. Caleb Stone trailed a few yards behind. Each time I glanced over my shoulder, his gaze darted away. When we reached the kitchen appliances, the thud of his boots stopped. I turned around to discover him hunched over a copper sink, studying its tags.

How much is there to find out about a sink besides the price?

I shifted my weight from one hip to the other. Besides the sweats and T-shirt, I'd borrowed Regina's spare Reeboks, which were two sizes too big. "Hey. Did you find a good one?" I asked.

Without glancing up, Caleb touched the sink, ran a finger along the copper edge. He moved on, and I noted the ring from a tobacco can on the pocket of his jeans again. "Copenhagen or Skoal?" I asked, raising my voice to help the conversation. During our drive into town, Caleb hadn't spoken a single word.

"Neither," he said. When he reached the corner and turned into the next aisle, my phone chimed. Three texts from Maren in rapid succession.

Where are you?
What happened with Jake?
I'm dying here.

Without replying, I set the phone to vibrate. Maren was concerned about me, and I loved her for it. But what I needed was a distraction, not reminders that my life was collapsing.

Sinks, I thought. *Focus on sinks now. You can ignore Maren for a while longer.*

Caleb poked his head around the corner and motioned for me to join him. "What is it?" I asked, but he disappeared again. I followed him into the next aisle where he was checking out a long, white farm sink.

I peered into the basin. "Is this the one she wants?"

He shrugged. "She's *your* mother."

"Regina Lark gave birth to me," I said. "That doesn't mean I understand her." Instead of responding, Caleb wrote down the order number of the sink on a slip of paper. Then he headed down the aisle toward a row of checkout lines at the front of the store.

"Wait!" I called after him. "Does this mean we're buying that one?"

"Nope," he said. "You are."

I am?

"Did Regina tell you that?" He kept walking, and I skipped along behind him clutching Regina's sweats so they wouldn't fall down. "I can't pay for the sink. I didn't bring my purse!" At this, Caleb planted his feet, and I crashed into the back of him. He looked down, and I blurted out, "I'm sorry."

"It's all right," he said. He ran a hand over his dark scalp and continued toward the checkout line. While we waited our turn, the scent of sweat and fresh-cut wood hung between us. No tobacco that I could smell. Caleb might've caught me sniffing him, but he didn't back away. "I'm sorry," I told him again. "About the money."

He nodded.

"Like I said, I don't understand Regina. At all. I mean, sure, we lived in the same house for years, but we have nothing in common. And besides, she was hardly around. Ever. Did you know the place isn't even hers? I mean, it is now—hers and my uncle's, he lives in San Francisco—but when I was a kid, the house belonged to my grandparents." I paused, and Caleb said nothing, so I continued to fill the silence. "They took us in when we had nowhere else to go. Regina kept saying it was temporary, but we just stayed. Then my grandpa had a heart attack. After that, my grandmother started losing it. Then we lost her for real." I swallowed. "She'd been suffering, so it was a blessing. At least that's what everyone told me."

As the story poured from me, I couldn't believe I was sharing all this with Caleb. But I couldn't help myself. It was like something in me had jarred loose. Something I had to get out. Fortunately, the cashier with pink hair and matching pink lips motioned us forward, an excuse for me to stop talking. While she rang Caleb up, I felt completely useless. I stood behind him shuffling my feet. The cashier handed Caleb the sales slip and grinned at him like he was the best thing she'd seen all year.

"Sorry," I told him for the third time. "Keep the receipt."

He said, "I will."

❧

The sink was brought to us in an enormous cardboard box by a worker dressed in blue who helped load it onto a cart. The cart's wheels skittered across the parking lot the whole way to Caleb's truck. While he unloaded the sink into the flatbed, I kicked at the asphalt. Still useless. He secured the box with rope and slammed the tailgate shut. He turned to face me, and I blinked up at him. The sun was bright, and I was beginning to sweat.

"I have a favor to ask," I said.

"Another one?"

I put a palm up to block the glare. "Could you run me by Target? It'll just take a minute. Maybe ten. I need a few things if I'm going to stay here for spring break."

"But you don't have your wallet," he said.

"Right."

Caleb nodded. "I'll keep the receipt."

He waited for me in the Target parking lot while I used his cash to buy deodorant, a package of cotton bikini underwear, and a new toothbrush from a discount bin. Then he took me to the McDonald's drive-thru where we ordered two chocolate shakes, a couple of Big Macs, and some large French fries.

"Regina hates fast food," I told Caleb, shoving a fistful of fries in my mouth. While I chewed, he drove across the street to the student parking lot of Ulysses S. Grant High. It was our old alma mater, and the place was deserted. I figured it must've been their spring break too. Caleb parked and pulled a Big Mac from the bag, spreading the wrapper on his lap.

"Thanks again," I said. "For the food. For everything."

He took a bite. Then another.

"You must be starving," I said. My phone vibrated, and I checked the text.

What happened with Jake?!

"It's just my friend Maren," I told Caleb, although he hadn't asked. "Anyway, what've you and Ezra been up to these days? I don't think—"

"Let's just eat," he said.

"OK." I dug back into the fries. Chewed. Swallowed. Thought. Again, Maren texted.

Call me! Now!

I sighed, texted her back. *I'll be home soon. Talk then.*

Her reply was immediate. *THIS CANT WAIT!*

Caleb stared out over the dashboard while I made a big show of turning off my phone and sticking it in the cup holder. "So," I tried again. "Did Ezra ever—"

"Nope."

"All right. I'll be quiet," I said. "But it's going to be a long week."

Caleb

Yeah, I recognized Lia Lark that first morning in Regina's kitchen. I saw her standing there—sorta wrecked—and I could tell she had no idea who I was. But today, sitting with her in the parking lot at Grant High, that shot me right back to this one afternoon, maybe eighteen years ago, when she and Ez got busted sneaking off campus. Well. Ez got busted. Again. I don't know how Lia got caught up in it.

Ma and Pop were at the deli that day of course because they never got a day off 'til they died, and I was back home, staying with them between tours. So guess who had to go bail my little brother's sorry ass out of the principal's office when the school called? Yeah. I did it for Ma. I figured I'd play up the whole military thing with whatever secretary was there and get the punk kid off the hook.

And while I was waiting, this girl comes down the hall looking like someone just kicked her dog. She was a few years younger than me, but old enough to notice. Not that I'd do anything about it. I mean, she was in high school for Christ's sake. So I kept my eyes low while she walked by and watched her all the way out the door.

Later that night I asked Ez about her. Why he'd been with a girl like that in the first place. "I wasn't with her," he told me. "She was just trying to get home to pick up some project or some shit she forgot at home. And she got caught with me. Yours truly being the career criminal and all."

"Yeah," I said. "That makes sense. She didn't seem like your usual type."

"What the hell does that mean?"

"She was walking upright, not dragging knuckles. Too clean. Pretty."

Ez clicked off the TV and stared me down. "Listen, Caleb. Stay the hell away from Lia Lark."

"Whatever," I said. "She's a baby. I'm not interested."

"Seriously," he said. "Just don't."

Now, let me tell you something: Back then, nothing pissed me off more than being told what to do. Or what not to do. Especially by Ez. His eyes sparked, like he wanted to beat my ass, but he didn't have the guts. And yeah, I wanted to punch him out too. I didn't. But I was tempted.

"What's your problem, asshole?" I said. "You want her for yourself or something?"

"No." He got up, about to storm out of the room. Then he stopped. "Hell no. It's just, Lia's trouble."

"*That girl?* No way."

Ez gave me a look like I was stupid.

"Bullshit," I said. "What kind of trouble? She psycho or something?"

"Nah." Ez shook his head. "She's too nice."

"*Too nice?*"

"Yeah," he said. "So keep your distance, is what I'm saying. A guy like you could break her, man."

So all I could think today with Lia is I wish Ezra could see the two of us.

We're both pretty goddamned broken. For real.

Ten

For the rest of spring break, Caleb remodeled Regina's kitchen during the day, while Regina spent nights weeding the garden or "intuiting" her new chicken coop. As for me, I took frequent naps and read old paperbacks in her art studio. My phone remained off the entire time, in the glove box of my car where I'd stashed it after that parking lot lunch we had in Caleb's truck.

This week was my escape, after all, from the land of people who ate meals at actual tables and slept on mattresses rather than futons. Texts and voicemails would've ruined it, just reminding me of what I'd left behind. Still. When I slipped on the last pair of new underwear from the six-pack, I knew it was time to face reality. Back home I had papers to grade. Lessons to prepare. My new single life to begin.

I left early the next morning, which put me back at the bungalow before noon. After a hot shower, I lay on the queen-sized bed and studied the popcorn ceiling. Jake and I used to lie here on weekend mornings, searching for designs in the swirls. The duck in the corner was always his favorite. Across the room was mine, The Big Dipper. I thought it brought the stars indoors. Staring at the same spots now, I waited for the familiar shapes to pop out at me, but I couldn't see the old patterns I loved. Kind of like my life. Nothing was recognizable.

I checked the time. 12:30. Beside the clock, on the

nightstand, my wedding picture mocked me. *So much for vows,* I thought. At the first sign of conflict, Jake had bolted toward a new commitment. Maybe someday I'd be able to step outside my loss and admire his decision to be a dad. As for my own father, I knew almost nothing about him, besides the fairy tales told to me when I was young.

Once upon a time, Regina Culpepper lived in a beautiful garden community. She was happy there, working the land side by side with her earthy neighbors. One fine day she returned to her parents' doorstep with a baby girl and a new last name. Regina Lark hadn't found a husband; she'd simply found The Real Her. Then she'd come home to give her child a better life. Ophelia Lark. The reason for my mother's great sacrifice. The end.

Unsatisfied by the vague resolution to this story, I'd tried questioning my grandmother about my father, about Regina's sacrifice. "Don't let my daughter fool you." She'd put a bony hand on my knee. "Regina wasn't thinking about you, Lia. She came back here because she was broke and scared and alone. She didn't know how to be a mother, and frankly, she didn't want to learn." My grandmother shook her head then, her eyes a kind of apology. "Loving someone is easy," she said. "Living for them is hard."

To my seven-year-old self, this made no sense, armed as I was with children's books and Disney movies. From them I'd learned happy families came in different shapes and sizes, sure; but in none of the books or movies were the mothers and fathers weak. Stepmothers were cruel. Fathers might be dead. But living parents were strong, and their children were worthy.

What was wrong with me?

I turned and checked the clock again. 12:45.

Maren would be here soon.

When I'd finally turned on my phone last night, I had dozens of missed calls and texts. Most of them were Maren's, but a couple had come from Pauline. She still knew nothing about Jake. Neither did anyone from book club. Veronica Stinson had left me a voicemail to remind me our next meeting was at Tina's. Not that I would go this month. Or ever again.

Without listening to any of Maren's messages, I called her.

When she answered, I blurted out, "Please don't be mad!" before she could start in on anything else. "I know I blew you off, but I wasn't ready to talk about Jake. Honestly, I didn't even want to think about him. It was too soon. I needed time. But I've caught my breath—at least a little bit. Plus, I ran out of underwear. So I'm coming home tomorrow. I'll be back by noon. Can we talk then?"

Maren was quiet for a moment, and I wondered if she actually *was* mad at me. This whole week I'd been assuming she'd cut me slack for the radio silence. I was about to start begging her forgiveness when she said, "Fine. I'll bring sandwiches."

"Will you bring Nora?"

"Nah, I'll hire a sitter." Maren sighed. "I hate spring break. The preschool's been closed, so this has been the longest week ever."

"I'm sure it's been really rough for you."

If Maren caught my sarcasm, she didn't let on. "I mean, don't get me wrong," she said, "I love being a mom, but kids are the absolute worst, right? I swear, if I have to play one more game of Candy Land I'll—" Maren cut herself off then. She'd probably heard it too. *Kids are the absolute worst, right?* "Oh crap. Lia," she said.

"It's OK. I completely understand."

I told her this, but of course I didn't understand. Not completely. I had no idea what it was like to be dying for a break from someone I also loved so much. Jake's absences had been frequent enough that I never got sick of him. And now, before I'd had a chance to ever wish that he would leave, he was gone. So although I didn't say it out loud, I was glad Maren wasn't bringing Nora today. The last thing I needed was a reminder of what I didn't have. What she and Jake always would.

A daughter.

I climbed out of bed and stumbled to the computer. In my inbox was a new email from Declan McKinley.

Dear Ms. Townsend,

I can't thank you enough for this project you gave Luke. He said you want us to keep the assignment "just between us," and I get it. You don't need all your students banging down the doors for extra credit. But privately, I wanted to tell you that here at the McKinley house, you're kind of a rock star. Thanks to you, Luke can get his grade up while doing something he loves.

After you met with him, he came home more excited than I've seen him in at least two years. I can't thank you enough—not only for what you've done for him, but for what that did for me.

I've been so worried about him. (Maybe the fact that I keep emailing you already gave that away?) Now, with your help, I think Luke and I may have finally turned a corner. And between you and me, I think you're going to love what he's working on. (Then again, I'm hardly unbiased.) He's trying to make it perfect and trying to catch up on all his other school work too. You've inspired him, that's for sure. Luke said this project is for next year's class, so I hope you're OK with him taking a while to get it done. Also, if it's OK with you, I'd like to be there when he shows it to you. Mostly because I'm proud of him, but also because he's been using my very expensive video equipment. I'm a dad, but I'm also practical. Either way, let me know.

Thanks again. For everything.

Declan McKinley

I read the email three times. This man's love for his child—this parental love—was something I'd never felt. He was a father, like Jake. But unlike Declan McKinley, Jake was new to the game. Jake had lost years with Josie. So if he wanted to live for her now, I wouldn't cut in, or take that focus away from him or from her, no matter how much losing him hurt. I closed my eyes, focused on my breathing. In. Out. I could move on. Keep going. I had to.

Dear Declan,

First things first: If I'm going to call you Declan, you need to start calling me Lia. Secondly, OF COURSE you can watch Luke present his project whenever it's ready. I'm sure he'll appreciate the support. Third, since this was an off-the-record project, I didn't give Luke a deadline, so we can plan to meet when he's done. For the record, Fridays are usually the best for me. I don't schedule any clubs or meetings for those days. If Fridays aren't good for you just let me know, and I'll try to make myself free.

Thanks,
Lia

I was still proofreading the message when Maren showed up with sandwiches and a bag of Ruffles. "*Hola, chica!*" she sang, barging through the front door. "*Y buenos dias mi amiga muy bonita!*" When I looked up from the email, Maren was grinning at me. She seemed far too happy for the circumstances, and I knew this meant she was nervous. "*Como estas?*" she asked.

"Umm," I said. "Fine?" Her smile went crooked, and my stomach churned. What did Maren have to tell me? I wasn't sure I could handle any more bad news, so I decided to keep the conversation as light as possible. "We're speaking Spanish now?"

"*Si!*" said Maren. Then she waved a hand in front of her face as if swatting the word away. "Danny thinks we should start teaching Nora a second language, and I'm trying. I really am. But damn, high school was a long time ago. I'm out of practice."

"Well. Good luck with that."

"I think you mean *bueno suerto*. Or something."

"Close enough," I said.

After one last glance at my email, I decided to hit send. Then I moved to the couch while Maren arranged lunch for us on the coffee table. Paper plates. Napkins. Two large turkey sandwiches and a large roast beef.

"Three sandwiches?" I asked.

"I wasn't sure if you'd be in the mood for turkey or roast beef. We can split whatever's left." She looked at me sideways. "You could use the calories."

I shrugged. "Guess I haven't had much of an appetite since… well. Since before."

"Sure, sure." Maren nodded toward my computer, like she was trying to change the subject. "What did I interrupt? Was it important? You seemed pretty focused when I got here."

"No, it's nothing. Just dealing with a parent of one of my students."

"Ahhh." She studied my face, lifted an eyebrow. "Is he cute?"

"What are you talking about?"

"Is. He. Cute?" Maren grinned again. *God. What was she doing?*

"How did you even know he *was* a he?"

"I didn't. But you're blushing."

"Whatever." I ignored the heat in my cheeks and picked up half a turkey sandwich.

"Too soon for me to tease?" she asked. "I'm an asshole. Please ignore me."

"I'm fine."

"Are you? Really?

"Maybe not yet. But I will be. Eventually. Fake it 'til you make it, right?"

"Nice cliché."

"Well, that's what I'm doing anyway. Clichés exist for a reason."

"Hmm." She picked up a wedge of the roast beef and bit into it. A shred of lettuce dangled down her chin. I lifted my turkey sandwich, then set it back down again.

"Here's the thing," I said. "Life goes on. Jake may have left me, but I won't let that kill me."

Maren groaned, sucked the lettuce into her mouth. "Don't say it'll make you stronger. That's one cliché too many. I might vomit."

"Ha!" I picked up my sandwich again but couldn't bring myself to take a bite. "I won't say it because I don't feel stronger." I paused. How real could I get without falling apart right now? "I feel… different," I told her. "Like when you peel the rind off an orange. It's still an orange, but it's… different."

"You're an orange, now?"

"A peeled one, yes."

"OK…"

"What I mean is, I'm raw. Exposed. And all I want to do is find my skin again and crawl back under it, but instead, I'm more visible than ever."

"Wow." Maren shook her head. "You are an English teacher, aren't you?"

I took a bite. "Language arts *and* social studies," I said with my mouth full.

Maren smirked. "Well, you don't teach etiquette, that's for sure."

Over the next half-hour we finished all three sandwiches and the entire bag of potato chips. Maren filled me in on Danny's promotion at Northrop Grumman—which we both agreed was overdue—and I told her I'd decided not to apply for summer school. Tutoring would be a better option this year. Yes, it was less predictable, but I wanted the flexibility. And at a hundred dollars per hour, I stood to make more money tutoring than teaching.

As I was licking the last of the potato chip crumbs from my palm, Maren said, "I'm ready now."

"Ready for what?"

"To talk," she said. "For real."

"Oh." I swallowed hard. "Don't worry," I said. "There's nothing you can tell me that's worse than what's already happened."

"Maybe," she said.

"Jake has a daughter." I wiped my hands on a napkin. "That's as bad as it gets."

"But—"

"He wants to be a full-time father now, and as far as I'm concerned, he should do that. I know what it's like not to have a dad, Mare. I refuse to come between him and Josie. I can't. I won't. End of story."

"But what if his leaving isn't entirely about Josie?"

I cleared my throat. "It is though."

"I know that's what Jake told you." Maren took my hand. "But I think Josie's mother might be a… source of interest too."

And there it was again, the unavoidable subject I'd been laboring to avoid. Josie's existence was bad enough. I didn't want to think about the relationship behind it. "Jake wouldn't lie to me," I said.

Maren lifted an eyebrow. "Has he ever mentioned someone named Addie?"

My heart skipped a beat, and I pulled my hand free. Yes, I'd heard of Addie. A portrait of her with Jake still hung above the Townsend's staircase. Pink lips. Dark curls. Swan neck. A graceful hand at Jake's elbow. Alexandra Barrow. The one who came before me. "She's an ex," I said, hoping my voice didn't tremble too much. She was *the* ex. Why hadn't I even considered her? Because that would've been too hard. It would've meant the end, for sure. "How do you know about Addie?" I asked.

"Danny was on the phone with Jake. I only got one side of their conversation, but still." Maren paused.

I looked down at my lap.

"I tried to tell you about it when you were at Regina's, but—"

"I remember." I shut my eyes to block the dizziness. For the past week, I'd tried to convince myself Jake had left me to be a good father. At least a decision like that could be noble, in a way. But dumping me for Addie was a different story. *Jake chose her over me.* I opened my eyes. "What else did you hear? Did Danny say anything to you after?"

"That's the other thing we need to talk about." Maren balled up her napkin, stuck it in the empty Ruffles bag. "Danny's worried—we both are—that things could get ugly if we take sides. Between you and Jake, I mean. So we decided I could tell you about Addie, because I found out about her by accident, and then I couldn't un-hear her name. But going forward, things could get sticky, and we all need some ground rules."

I shook my head. Confused. Maren was rambling now.

"Ground rules?"

"Like, Danny and I won't tell Jake anything you say to us, and vice versa. Or whatever. No lying, but no sharing, either. We'll just keep things to ourselves."

I stiffened. "I didn't ask you to spy for me."

"I know that!" Maren started talking even faster now, and her eyes were shining. "You never would. Jake wouldn't either. Which is why Danny and I agreed."

"Agreed what?"

"That we want to support you and Jake. Both. But separately." She leaned closer to me. "Because you're separate now."

"Oh." The word was barely a whisper. So I repeated it. "Oh."

"Danny and I just want to be fair." Maren touched my knee. "To each other. To you."

"And to Jake." I nodded, but I couldn't feel my face.

"I hate that he hurt you," she said. "So much."

I tried swallowing again, but the gulp caught in my throat. "You're Jake's friend too. You and Danny."

"Yes," she said. "We are."

Maren took her hand off my knee, and we both began to cry.

Eleven

The first time Jake drove me to his family's home, my fingers twitched, and my palms grew damp. The stately colonials in the Townsends' neighborhood stood in stark contrast to Regina's sagging rancher. Delicate hydrangeas flanked their walkway. The wraparound porch boasted Adirondack chairs. As Jake ushered me through the front doors—painted red because *Mom likes color!*—my legs trembled, and all I could do was hope that no one else would notice.

In the grand foyer, Charles Townsend greeted his son with a hearty slap on the back. Ivy, Jake's mother, led us into the great room where we sat across from each other on high-backed sofas. The Townsends wore khaki slacks and pastel golf shirts. Both had neat helmets of salt-and-pepper hair. When they spoke, they paused to finish each other's sentences. They served each other lemonade from a crystal pitcher.

After Charles filled us in on the latest at Townsend, Wycoff & Stein, Ivy explained her most recent fundraisers, one for the local soup kitchen and the other for the Daughters of the American Revolution. *Two wonderful programs!* When Jake dropped his big news—he'd made captain, *the youngest at the airline!*—Charles put a hand on his wife's elbow.

"Well. Isn't that something."

Ivy nodded. "Yes. It's wonderful!"

Lunch was *a simple affair* of homemade minestrone and

Caesar salad. Ivy apologized that Rochelle, their housekeeper, had left the rolls in the warming drawer *a smidge too long*. While we ate, I fielded inquiries about my career. *Were the students at a public school respectful? Why did we give so many standardized tests? Had I joined the teacher's union?* To that question, my *yes* was followed by tiny frowns. But the rest of the time, Charles and Ivy listened politely. Smiled often. I couldn't help wondering what Jake might've shared with them about Regina—or my childhood, our past—since he himself balked when he'd first heard.

"Hold up!" His eyes had bugged a little. "You're telling me you were born on a commune?"

"No, not exactly. No. Yes." I stammered and blushed, wishing I hadn't said anything at all. "More like a co-op."

"With free love and composts and gardening? Shit like that?"

"There was also a small library and a museum. They had a theater group that did Shakespeare. Regina starred in *Hamlet*. That's why she named me Ophelia."

"Ophelia? Jesus." Jake shook his head, taking it in. "Isn't Ophelia the one who goes nuts?"

"She kills herself."

"Jesus," he repeated.

"When I started school, my grandma said Ophelia was too big a name for kindergarten. She called me Lia, and since she was more of a mother to me than Regina, Lia stuck."

Jake chuckled. "Regina's a big name too."

"Regina Culpepper. She always hated it."

"Culpepper."

"Mmm hmm."

"I thought you said your mother never got married."

"She didn't."

"So where the hell did Lark come from?"

"That remains… unclear."

More chuckling from Jake. "You mean she just made up a new last name? For both of you?"

"I guess so. Maybe. I don't know for sure. Those are the names on my birth certificate. Mother and daughter. Regina Lark. Ophelia Lark."

"And you never asked her how? Why?"

"Of course I did," I said. "But Regina's a master of changing the subject. She'd end up telling me she was petitioning to have her astrological sign switched from Aries to Libra. Or that when she died, she wanted me to sprinkle her ashes on the moon. Eventually I gave up."

At this, Jake flat-out laughed. "That's the strangest thing I've ever heard."

"Maybe you should spend more time around Regina."

I'd laughed too, in on the joke, but my discomfort was tinged by defensiveness. The fact that this story was the strangest Jake had ever heard revealed as much about him as it did about me. And when I finally met the Townsends—despite their politeness, or maybe because of it—I'd felt terminally out of place. Jake's family came from warming drawers and alphabetized spice racks. I came from a pantry of dented cans.

That afternoon, Jake gave me a tour of the rest of the Townsend estate, their expansive grounds which included an avocado orchard and a "small" tennis court. I opted not to tell Jake that, in my mind, there was no such thing as a *small* tennis court. When we got to the swimming pool, he suggested a swim. I told him I'd forgotten my suit.

"We could play tennis," I said. "I'm not very good, but—"

"I hate tennis. Let's go inside."

Jake took me upstairs to see his childhood bedroom and the room of his sister, Charlotte. Pulling me down on her bed, he kissed me until I giggled. "Now do you forgive me for forgetting my bathing suit?"

"This time." He grinned. "This time."

On our way downstairs, I paused in front of the portrait of Jake and a young woman on the wall. "Who's this?"

"Just Addie. We used to be together. No big deal."

"Then why is your picture still up?"

"Probably because the frame was custom. And expensive. You know my mom."

No I don't.

Later, on our way home, I'd pressed until Jake shared a few superficial facts about Addie. Her father was a professor in Oregon, her mother lived in L.A. She was some kind of author. "I never even met them," he said. "The Barrows are divorced."

Apparently, Jake and Addie met during his second year of law school. That was before he'd dropped out to become a pilot. "Needless to say, my parents disapproved."

"Did Addie? Is that why it ended?"

"Addie and I wanted different things, had different life goals. We went our separate ways. No big deal."

"You said that already."

He frowned. "It was years ago."

"So the breakup was mutual?"

"Basically," he said.

For the rest of the drive, my insides roiled. With jealousy. Insecurity. The thought that Addie was a better match for the Townsend family made me physically sick. Still, I'd wanted Jake so much, I convinced myself the past with his ex was over. Jake's future was with me. But Addie Barrow had reentered his life in the most permanent way possible. They shared a child, a flesh and blood connection. She'd been there all along. The only good news now was that my days of living in denial were over. Jake wasn't coming back to me. And with Addie Barrow in the picture, I couldn't compete.

Even if I wanted to.

Twelve

My life took on a puritanical cycle: early to bed; early to rise, like Ben Franklin if Ben Franklin were a middle school teacher. My days were equal parts cursing my wedding pictures and dancing in the living room to "I Will Survive." Maren and I still met up at Peet's. We'd still talk about everything (but Jake). She'd tell me I looked pretty. I'd tell her I was trying.

In the middle of May, Uncle Quentin called. He was coming to L.A. to interview interns and wanted to meet for breakfast. At fifty-five, Quentin was almost eight years younger than Regina. Like his sister, Quentin had never married. Unlike Regina, he had no children.

That I know of, he was fond of joking. When I was ten, I'd found that funny.

Back then Quentin was as foreign to me—and as glamorous—as a movie star. Everything about him seemed fascinating. His suits. His money clip. His black framed glasses. (None of them had tape across the nose.) He'd worked hard and gone to college. Started his own company that made *investments*. Regina claimed he was boring. *A numbers guy. Ugh.* But I was never bored by Uncle Quentin. After my grandmother passed, and Regina started disappearing for days at a time, I used to daydream my uncle would take me to live with him and whichever beautiful woman he was dating. Surely they could make room for me once they discovered I was alone.

Again.

But my uncle never saved me, at least not permanently. He'd stop by to stock the refrigerator and pay off Regina's bills. Twice a year, he hired a cleaning service. I'd spy on him opening envelopes while a stranger scrubbed our kitchen. When he left he'd hug me, and I would breathe in his cologne, pretending the scent stayed in my lungs like superpower air.

"If you need anything," he would whisper, "you have my number."

I never called.

Instead, I invented a game called *Princess Rescue*. I played it each time the food ran low or I got scared Regina wasn't coming back.

I became an expert.

Here was how it went: I'd rip a page from one of Regina's half-blank journals and make a grid, assigning to each square the name of a different boy, city, number. Or job, car, pet. The fourth column never changed: Mansion. Apartment. Shack. House. (This was my lonely version of *MASH*, the paper-folding game other tween girls played.) But I made my results special. Whichever man, home, career, or number of kids I got, I'd write a story about how we got to our happy ending. Each one began with the same words: *Once upon a time, there was a princess named Lia who was trapped in the forest by a witch named Regina until the handsome prince named _____ showed up.* What happened next was always different. I hid the fairy tales under my mattress.

After a day or two, Regina would return, fuming about another opportunity gone awry. This idiot couldn't see her vision. That dumbass was intimidated by her brilliance. But always, beneath the anger, thrummed a familiar theme:

Regina Lark was not capable of failure. She was an inspiration.

Later, over whatever haphazard dinner I'd pieced together—soup, oatmeal, spaghetti, if we were lucky—Regina would tell me this: "Don't settle for ordinary, Lia. I raised you for better than that." I never found the words to tell her ordinary was what I dreamed of.

❧

On Sunday morning, I arrived at Uncle Bill's Pancake House early. The wait there was usually long, and I wanted to request a spot out on the front patio. Quentin loved that the place I'd suggested was named for someone's uncle. As for me, I was craving a Mitch's Scramble. I figured if my appetite was making a comeback, the rest of me would follow.

I waited for him inside, watching families with their chili cheese omelets and banana nut pancakes. My mouth watered, the clink of forks on plates like the bells for Pavlov's dogs. *I will survive*, I hummed to myself. *As long as I know how to love.*

Someone tapped my shoulder, and I spun around expecting to see my uncle. Instead, I found a stranger. His bright eyes reminded me of someone. So did the thatch of sandy hair. Was it a Prince Harry thing? He'd been in the news a lot lately. Maybe that was —

"Ms. Townsend," the man said, sticking out his hand. "I didn't get a chance to introduce myself, but I'm Declan McKinley. Luke's father." He ducked his head. "You probably don't remember."

That was it. The guy from Open House, minus the suit, plus workout clothes. His cleft chin was still the same though. And his eyes were definitely green.

"Mr. McKinley," I said. "Of course I remember you, but I was kind of distracted that night. The whole line-of-parents thing can be overwhelming."

"You did just fine." His hand was warm, and mine felt cold when he let go.

"So where's Luke?" I asked.

"He's home putting the finishing touches on his extra-credit project. The kid's pretty talented. Then again, I might be biased." Declan smiled, and I saw again the slight crookedness to his bottom teeth. The pride on his face made my stomach twist. Was this how Jake felt about Josie? How he'd learn to feel?

Shaking off the thought, I said, "Let me know when Luke's ready to unveil the finished product."

"I was hoping this Friday might work," Declan said. "Fridays are good for you, right? I can bring the equipment so Luke doesn't have to lug it around school."

"Sounds good." I shifted my weight from one foot to the other. "Anyway, I'm just here waiting for my uncle." A flush blossomed on my neck.

Declan smiled again. "I'll leave you to it, then. I have to pick up our take-out order." As he moved around me, I smelled soap, clean and fresh. "By the way," he said, "I highly recommend the Mitch's Scramble."

⁌⁍

Breakfast with Uncle Quentin turned out to be an extravaganza of awkwardness. Thanks to Regina, he'd heard about Jake and me, and he'd come to discuss the separation. While he scarfed hash browns doused in ketchup, I told him about Josie. Addie. The night Jake left for good. I moved my eggs around the plate. So much for my appetite. At least I'd managed to get a table outside.

"Tell me again what Jake's exact words were," he said.

"He told me *you can keep everything.*"

"But did he mean *everything* as in the furniture and potted plants? Or the real stuff. The house. Car. Bank accounts."

I set my fork down. Hearing my life reduced to a list of assets, both big and small, was cutting. I felt an actual sharp pain in my chest. *Maybe if I had a heart attack, Jake would come back. But no, Lia. You don't want him, remember?*

"Forgive me for being blunt," my uncle said, "but we need to move on this. The sooner the better."

"Move on what?"

"Your future. For me to help you, I need to know exactly where you stand."

"Thanks, but—"

"Jake's family is wealthy. You aren't. Could he have hidden money from you? Does he have property or investments you might not know about?"

I looked down at my lap. "I guess if I don't know about them, then I don't know, right?"

"Of course." He patted my hand, and his gentleness made my nose sting. "There are ways to find these things out," he said. "Just leave it to me."

I lifted my head. "That sounds kind of ominous. I don't want Jake's knees smashed with a bat."

Uncle Quentin's mouth quirked. "I'm not talking about any kind of Tonya Harding action. But I do know a few people who can investigate accounts without anyone finding out."

"Perks of the trade, huh?"

"Keep that between you and me," he said. "And don't worry. There probably aren't any big secrets."

My face grew hot. I needed to change the subject. "Speaking of job perks, when are you retiring?"

He looked at me from over the top of his glasses and laughed. "Just how ancient do you think I am? Wait. Don't answer that. Let's just say I expect to be working for at least another decade."

"Supporting Simone?"

He stopped laughing.

"How long have you two been together now?" I asked. "Five whole minutes?"

"More like three years." He leaned back, and we were both quiet for a moment. Then he said, "Sure, Simone's a lot younger than me and a hell of a lot prettier. But she brings plenty to the table besides that. And she loves me."

"I'm sorry." I cleared my throat. "I'm an asshole."

"You're hurt," he said, "and looking for it in everyone else. Expecting it, even."

My eyes started to water. "Anyway, who am I to judge? I trusted Jake!" I forced out a quick laugh to keep from crying.

Uncle Quentin smiled. "Hell. I just got lucky."

"I'd say you both did."

"If you insist."

I tilted my head. "So what does Simone do, exactly? I'm embarrassed to admit I have no idea."

"She's a marriage and family therapist," he said. "Sorry about the irony."

I laughed again, this time with actual feeling. "That's not exactly ironic, and it's certainly not your fault. She probably tried to tell me more than once but couldn't get a word in edgewise around Regina."

"My sister does like to talk," Quentin said. "She's the real wordsmith in the family. I'm just the guy with the spreadsheets."

"So she's mentioned. More than once."

He stared at his almost-empty plate, picked at a potato. "It must've been hard for you. Especially after Grammy passed. I should've come around more. I just—"

"Believe me. When it comes to Regina, you don't have to explain any *justs*." We nodded at each other then, two people who understood.

"So I hate to go back to the money issue..." His voice trailed off, and I closed my eyes. The unfinished sentence floated above us. I wanted to enjoy the rest of our time together, not talk assets. When I opened my eyes, he'd pushed his plate away. On his chin was a streak of ketchup. I focused on that instead of his face, which was too full of concern for me to bear.

Don't cry, Lia. Not over a plate of scrambled eggs. Any more tears and you might drown.

"Jake took his clothes," I said, getting back to facts. Strictly business, not emotion. "And of course he's got his Subaru. But we'd paid that off last year. My Honda too," I said. "That leaves the bungalow. Jake's giving me the bungalow."

My uncle leaned forward again. "I don't suppose you have that in writing?"

"Jake's a man of his word."

Quentin chuckled. "Forgive me for being skeptical."

"I know it sounds crazy, but I trust him."

"Fine. What about his parents? Didn't they give you the money for the down payment?" I reached out and wiped my uncle's chin. I was stalling.

And he was right.

After our engagement, the Townsends wrote us a check in the total amount they'd spent on Charlotte's weddings and both her divorces. Jake tried to refuse, but his parents insisted. They said it would help them in the future to keep everything even between their children now. So we made an offer on our bungalow, the one Jake told me I could keep. But now that their son was no longer living there, would Ivy and Charles want me to repay them?

"Let's assume," my uncle said, "they don't ask you to sell the place or buy them out. Can you afford the mortgage on your own?"

"I've been wondering that myself," I said. "And I wish I had a better answer than *I don't know.* I'm planning to tutor this summer. And I have my teacher's retirement account."

"No." Quentin shook his head again. "Don't touch that."

"But I might—"

"Lia. Promise me you won't."

A waitress stopped by to fill our water glasses and drop a check on the table. My uncle reached for his wallet.

"Thanks for the breakfast," I said. "And the advice."

"My pleasure, sweetheart. And please remember. If you run into trouble, I can help. My friend Brent is a divorce attorney and—"

"No. That won't be necessary."

"You're thinking mediation, then?" My uncle's expression turned grim. "Simone works with couples all the time who start out amicably and eventually turn to lawyers. Don't get me wrong, mediation's great, in theory. But sometimes people get greedy, look for legal loopholes. Don't let Jake get the better of you."

I dropped my head. "He won't."

"Your optimism is inspiring," Quentin said. "But dissolving a marriage brings out the worst in the best of people."

"It's just that… Jake and I…" My heart pounded, and I froze. *Should I tell him? We'd never told anyone.*

"You and Jake what?"

"It's kind of a long story," I said.

He touched my hand. "Life's kind of a long story."

A seagull hopped past us on its stilt feet, and I whispered the truth into my lap.

"Pardon me?" my uncle said.

"Jake and I. We aren't actually married."

⤜✥⤛

We were at the beach when we decided. Below us
sprawled ropes of seaweed. The salt air licked my skin. It was a
cloudless night, each star a pinprick in the drape of black. I
told Jake that when I was a girl, I'd decided the Milky Way was
a cosmic joke some scientist fabricated to keep his job. Like,
he *knew* we humans were just creatures in some enormous
galactic circus. So what if the stars weren't stars at all, but
instead tiny holes in this huge, celestial tent? Maybe strange
giants on the other side were peeking at me. What if they were
friendly?

Jake listened as I talked about my childhood, these made-
up stories from a lonely girl. He didn't laugh at me. Not once.
He squeezed my hand with sand-gritty fingers. When it was his
turn to speak, he said I'd never have to be alone again. And
with the ocean as our witness, he made declarations. He made
sense.

"Why mess with a good thing?" he said. "A piece of paper
is just a piece of paper." Over a crash of wave he added,
"What matters is we're together."

There was also the fact that our combined salaries could
propel us into a higher tax bracket. A legal marriage might cost
us more each year if we had to file together. Not to mention,
in future job interviews, the hiring committees would prefer if
Jake were a bachelor.

Single pilots made better candidates.

Less baggage, he'd said. *No pun intended.*

Most importantly, he concluded, a commitment of the
heart was more indelible than our signatures on a document. I
told him there was no such thing as *more indelible.* Something
either was indelible or it wasn't. He grinned, called me his
beautiful genius. Then he gathered me in his arms. I'd be his.
He'd be mine. And legal documents would play no part in it.

You're absolutely right. I repeated. *We love each other.* That was
the thing to remember. Even now I didn't want to believe he'd
had doubts about us then. That already he'd been preparing
his eventual escape.

We shared our plan with no one. Not Maren, whose
protests would chip tiny nicks into my happiness. Not the
Townsends who were *simply thrilled* to invite their friends to

Jacob's wedding. Not Regina, who would've written an ode to our wonderful nonconformity. No, I was sewing my own patch of rebellion by not telling her news she'd like.

"Jake's just sticking it to his parents," Regina told me, "marrying someone like you. He's showing Ivy and Charles they can't make all his big decisions for him."

"That's ridiculous," I told her.

"Doesn't mean it isn't right."

I acted insulted, but still. Hadn't I been secretly thrilled to choose a partner so different from Regina? Jake was proof I was nothing like her, proof she'd never control me again.

"You can't possibly think the Townsends want you for a daughter-in-law," she persisted. "Mr. and Mrs. Fancy Pants with their golf course memberships? They need someone with a pedigree. A merging of empires. You'll never be one of them."

If the Townsends wished Jake had selected someone of finer breeding, they never let on to us. Ivy and Charles took pains to embrace me. Charlotte Townsend too. Sure, that portrait of Addie Barrow and Jake remained upon their wall. But it was just a beautiful picture. And Ivy liked beauty. That was all.

One Sunday afternoon after our engagement, while we were in the dining room eating pot roast, Ivy broached the subject. "No pressure," she said, "but if you two kids think you might want a reception at the club, we'll need to reserve the ballroom at least a year in advance."

Charlotte smirked. "Third time's the charm, right? I failed twice. Maybe Jake's marriage will take." When Jake suggested we might *go a different way*, Ivy pursed her lips.

"I'm sure whatever you decide will be lovely." Then she patted my hand. I tried to imagine what her face would look like if her son told her the truth: that we had no intention of getting married, at their country club or anywhere else. There'd be a wedding, yes, for appearances, but nothing more. This was our secret.

Jake found a non-denominational officiant who was willing to go through the motions and pretend our vows were real. Our ceremony would be merely performance with no legal implications. The officiant wore a white suit that day and her gray hair in a bun. We wrote her a check and nodded our assent.

Our bond was more indelible.

After the ceremony, not much shifted in my daily life. I was still Lia Lark on my paychecks. In the classroom—and everywhere else—I called myself Ms. Townsend. I felt married in my heart, and that was the important thing. Besides. I already knew a person could present herself to the world using whatever last name she pleased. My mother had set that precedent, and Jake had learned this too.

When he laid out The Plan on the beach, I saw zero cause for rebuttal. His parents would host the reception at Shutters on my birthday, April 1st. Instead of a honeymoon, we'd return to our bungalow and get on with our lives. Nothing had to change. No one would be the wiser.

No one.

Not even me.

Thirteen

Lia,

Happy Friday! As a thanks for everything you've done for Luke and me, I'm bringing lunch today. Don't even think about refusing. It's the very least I can do. Just let me know if you have any allergies or food you're not a fan of. (Example: I hate tomatoes.) Otherwise, I'll pick up a variety of things from Wahoo's. (Unless you hate Wahoo's.)

Declan

Declan,

I love Wahoo's, so I wouldn't dream of turning down your offer. I'm allergic to poison oak and cats, but I don't think either is on their menu. At least I hope not! When you get here, you'll have to pick up a visitor's pass from the attendance office (it's in the building to the left of the parking lot—the one with the oak tree in front of it). Lunch is from 12:05 to 12:50, so I'll see you around noon.

Lia

I went to the closet and changed out of my jeans and into a blouse and skirt. I wasn't dressing up, exactly. But if a parent was coming to my class today, I wanted to *look* professional. I hadn't *felt* that way in weeks. At school, I visited the faculty workroom to collect my mail before classes started. Pauline was in there already making photocopies. When she saw me, she motioned me over to the machine.

"Guess what." She leaned in close. Her black curls brushed my shoulder. "Wait, no. Don't guess. I'll just tell you." She glanced around the room. "Eddie and I." She grinned. "We did it."

"Did what?"

"Seriously, Lia?" Pauline arched a brow and waited for me to understand.

"Oh," I said. "Oh! I guess my brain's a little slow this morning."

"Then I'll catch you and your slow brain up on the details at lunch."

"Ooh. I can't today." I winced, pretending to be disappointed. But Declan and Luke were bringing me Wahoo's, and I was looking forward to eating with someone other than Maren.

"How about happy hour, then? We can split a pitcher of margaritas while I fill you in on the budding love story of Eddie Lundgren and Pauline Herrera."

Love story. Right.

I still hadn't told any of my work friends what had happened between Jake and me. Honestly, I didn't want to be the source of faculty gossip, or worse—pity. And besides, this was my business to share. When I was ready. Which I wasn't. Which was also why I didn't think I could sit there at happy hour listening to Pauline talk about sex and love and Eddie without telling her about my situation. It felt wrong. Like lying by omission. But before I could turn down the invitation, Pauline answered for me.

"Do *not* say no, Lia. Unless you want to break my heart. It's Friday. Being spontaneous for once won't kill you! I pinkie promise."

"I—"

"It's just happy hour. You could be home in time to cook dinner. Or Jake can meet us if he's around this weekend."

"He's not."

"Even better," Pauline said. "Girls night! Come on, Lia!"

"I'll think about it," I said.

Pauline grinned again. "Well, that's a start."

෴

I was in my classroom at the beginning of lunch when Declan McKinley appeared at the door. "Safe to come in?" he asked.

"Welcome to middle school!" My voice sounded loud and weird. But Declan smiled and stepped inside anyway. He was wearing a fitted gray suit, and he held a large leather case, probably full of video equipment. I had no idea what Declan McKinley did for work, but his wardrobe said something important. Businesslike. Still, his scruff of hair—the color of sand—was on the playful side.

Luke shuffled in behind Declan, carrying a Wahoo's bag. He set the food on my desk and took off his hat. His hair was a matted-down version of his dad's.

"Thanks for making this happen," Declan said.

"It's my pleasure. Really." My tongue felt thick, and my palms were sweating. Why did I find it easier to address a room full of students than one adult? "If you two are hungry, we could eat first," I said. "Or watch the video. Whatever you want."

Declan glanced at Luke, then back at me. "We only brought food for you."

"Oh, right! Fine. Yes." I hoped neither of them could see the blush on my cheeks.

"It's just that we've already taken up so much of your time," he said. "I figured you'd want to get the show over with and enjoy lunch in peace."

"Of course," I said. "Good." Lunch alone again. A lump of disappointment clogged my throat.

"Where should I set up?" Declan asked. I pointed at the media cabinet in the back.

"Sorry, but it's all pretty ancient."

"Oh, I get it," he said. "Budget cuts." He smiled, and our conversation from Open House came back to me—his laugh when he joked that I must be ready for spring break. Luke's mom was a teacher too. The McKinleys were a family.

You knew that, Lia. What were you thinking?

Nothing. I was thinking nothing.

"So, Luke." I cleared my throat. "Here's the old rubric." I handed him a blank grade sheet from the Mesopotamia dioramas. "We'll need to come up with a new one for this project telling everyone how long the video should be. How many songs to use. Stuff like that. I'll give you some time to think about it, then we can figure out the guidelines together. Sound good?"

Luke nodded, but his expression was serious.

"I want this to be challenging but still fun," I said.

Luke smiled then. "It was fun."

"I'm glad," I said, again a little too loudly and weird.

And that's when Pauline popped her head in my door. Her gaze cut to Declan, then back to me. "Didn't mean to interrupt," she said.

"You're not at all," I told her quickly. "What's up?"

"Grunions. Five o'clock," she said. "I invited Sari and Helen too, so now you have to come. We've gotta show the young ones how it's done. The future of happy hour hangs in the balance."

Making an excuse would've been easy, but I was tired of being alone. "Guess I can't let happy hour down," I said.

Pauline pumped a fist. "See you at five."

∽∾

I survived Luke's video presentation without embarrassing myself too much. He had outdone himself, and I was glad I'd had *a positive impact on his attitude toward school in general,* so Declan told me. Before they left, he shook my hand. He thanked me again. And then once more. The pride on Declan's face—that parental love—made my stomach twist. But at least I had Wahoo's to fill up the emptiness after the McKinleys were gone.

By the time I got to happy hour, I'd talked myself into trying to be happy. I'd be with friends, after all, without Jake around to whisper to me *maybe you've had enough*. And if I had to suffer through listening to Pauline gush about Eddie, so be it. I'd been in love before. I'd had my chance. Now Pauline was having hers.

She'd beaten me to Grunions and scored a pub table in the back. The lighting was dim—perfect—and the air smelled of beer—less perfect. A neon sign for Sam Adams hung on the wall. It was an ad for their ale but also a mirror. I avoided looking at my reflection.

Look happy, Lia. Be happy.

A group of guys in red jerseys were watching the Angels game. The two tables they'd pushed together were already crowded with empty pitchers. A barback hurried over with a wet rag to wipe down our table, and a cocktail waitress in a high ponytail and tight black shorts delivered four salt-rimmed glasses along with a pitcher of margaritas.

"I took the liberty of ordering for us," Pauline said, pouring out two glasses. "Hope you don't mind." After a few healthy gulps, she went straight to work filling me in on her and Eddie.

"So we were at the Tuesday night board meeting," she said.

I made a face. "Blech."

"Right? It was torture. And that's why Eddie suggested we grab a drink after. As a reward, you know?" She licked stray grains of salt from her lips. "We had a few beers, and then I told him I didn't think I could drive home. So…"

"So…" I repeated. I knew where the story was headed, but I figured the less I said, the better. I wanted Pauline to keep talking about herself. Then I wouldn't have to talk about me.

"So, Eddie came back to my place." Her voice trailed off again, and I figured she wanted me to comment. Instead I squeezed a lime into my margarita and took a sip. "I opened a bottle of wine," she said.

I nodded, took another sip.

"And then one thing led to the next thing…" Pauline fixed me with a stare, and I knew I had to say something.

"Sounds like you two had a good time."

"Twice," Pauline crowed. "We had a good time twice! Let me tell you, Lia, I know Eddie Lundgren may not look like it on the surface—I mean, the guy wears navy blue Dockers and all—but he's a champion in bed. A goddamn champ!" She slapped the table, and I couldn't help smiling. She looked so happy, and happy was good.

"Wow, Pauline. I don't know what to say."

"Right? And sure, maybe it's too soon and all, but I think—" Her head snapped up. "Oh, hey! Great! The girls are here!"

I looked across the bar and saw Helen Ishikawa and Sari Sarkissian weaving through the bar on their way over to us. They were first-year teachers in the math department. They both had long dark hair and longer legs. As they passed the guys in Angels jerseys, I heard a couple of low whistles. The biggest one—a bear of a man with bushy mutton chops— actually clapped.

Pauline laughed and poured two fresh drinks. "Which one of you single ladies gets to take that guy home tonight?" She was talking to Sari and Helen, but I squirmed a little. I was single, they just didn't know it yet.

Sari lifted her margarita. "I nominate you, Pauline."

"Seconded," said Helen.

"But I might not be single anymore," Pauline told them. "And if it's OK with Lia, I'll start from the beginning."

⚜

An hour later, Grunions was officially packed, the air around us thick and warm. My head was spinning. I needed food desperately. A glass of water too. I looked around for our waitress and saw her moving toward us with another full pitcher of margaritas.

"For you ladies," she announced, "from the *gentlemen* in red." She nodded at the Angels fans who were now waving at us. Pauline called out a thank you and topped off my glass. The man with mutton chops high-fived the rest of his group and lumbered off his stool. Then he took a few unsteady steps in our direction, pausing to haul up the waistband of his jeans.

"Heads up, girls," I said, but my words were lost in the noise of the room. The mutton-chop man kept swerving toward us, and I watched in frozen horror as he tripped and fell headlong into our table. There was a horrible crash of glass as our drinks and pitchers smashed to the ground. Every patron in the bar turned to stare at us.

"My apologies," the man slurred. He smelled of beer and cheap cigars. He grabbed my arm and collapsed, pulling me down on top of him. While his friends cheered and howled, I struggled to free myself. But I couldn't move.

From above me came a familiar voice. "Need a hand?"

I looked up, and there was Declan McKinley. His tie was loosened, the suit jacket gone.

"Yes," I said. "I do."

In the dark room, his eyes were bright.

Fourteen

He kept a hand at the small of my back while he led me across the bar. Behind us, Pauline was cursing. Sari and Helen couldn't stop laughing. The rest of the patrons were staring, all eyes on me. I felt the grief I'd been pushing down—for days, weeks, the past month and a half—begin to swell. Could everyone else tell? Did they see through my pretending?

At the door to the ladies' room, Declan said, "I'll wait for you out here."

"You don't have to."

He smiled. "I want to." He was being so kind. But he was also so married. An invisible seam inside me split. I could almost hear the pops of thread.

"It's no good," I muttered.

"Are you all right?" he asked. "Lia?"

I shook my head and fled.

Out in the parking lot, the fresh air didn't help as much as I'd hoped, and at this point, I wasn't sure anything would. I'd completely lost it in front of Declan, and I couldn't tell him why. Mostly because I wasn't sure, myself.

At my car, I bent over to catch my breath and told myself to get a grip. Where did I think I was going, anyway? I was in no shape to drive. Besides, my keys were in my purse on a stool under that damn Sam Adams sign. I leaned against the trunk, my stomach sinking when I realized there was no one I could call for a ride.

Fridays were Maren and Danny's date night, and Jake was obviously not an option. There was always Uber, but then I remembered my phone was in my damn purse along with the keys to my stupid car.

A bubble of hysteria rose in me, and I actually giggled. Softly first, then louder. Worried I looked drunk—or worse, insane—I glanced around the parking lot. Declan was headed toward me. I wiped my hands down the skirt I'd changed into that morning. Had a part of me been trying to impress him? A married man? How pathetic. My skirt felt damp where margarita had spilled on me. I hoped I didn't smell of tequila.

Declan stopped a few feet away from me, like he was scared to get too close. *You can do this, Lia. Be normal.*

But really. What could I say to him?

Hello, Declan. I'm a wreck of a woman whose husband left her, but the joke's on me because we were never actually married! Hilarious, right? And get this: For our fake five-year-anniversary—which also happens to be my birthday—I thought Jake was going to give me a ring; I thought maybe he'd propose again. I thought that this time, we'd do things right. But instead, he ended them. Jake ended all the things.

Declan took a step toward me. "Did he hurt you?"

He. Which he? Ha! Of course Declan meant the man with the mutton chops, but I giggled again. Maybe I *was* drunk. Or insane. "No," I told him. "I'm not hurt."

"Then what happened in there? Why'd you take off?"

I blew out a breath. "It was just too much."

"Too much what?"

"Too much *everything.*"

Declan nodded. "Happens to the best of us."

"Does it?"

Someone called my name then. "Lia!" I turned my head and saw Helen hurrying over to me holding up my bag. "You forgot your purse," she said, "but don't go yet. The waitress is bringing us a new pitcher. We're going to order some food, and then we'll Uber home later." She turned to Declan. "I'm Helen, by the way." She stuck out her hand.

"Declan."

"Well, hello there, Mr. Declan. Nice to meet you." Helen's grin was so wide I could almost see her tonsils. "You should totally hang out with us, right, Lia? Tell Declan you're coming back inside, and he should totally hang out with us."

"As tempting as that sounds," he said, "I think Lia's ready to go."

"But Lia's been drinking," Helen said. "She can't drive!"

"I'll make sure she gets home safe," he said.

"You don't have to do that," I told him.

"I want to."

Helen tilted her head, shifted her focus from Declan to me. "OK. So. I should tell the girls you're good, then?"

"I'm good." I lifted my purse. "Thanks for this."

"What are friends for?" Helen flashed one more smile at Declan before heading back inside.

"You think your friends will be all right?" Declan asked.

"Pauline's resourceful."

He laughed. "And kind of loud."

"If you want to go back in there with them—"

"I don't."

"OK." I shrugged, although I wasn't sure why. Maybe I wanted Declan to think I didn't care about his opinion. I wished I didn't care.

"I should probably get you home then," he said.

"That's really not necessary." My tongue was a tangle, and I heard the slur on each S. I hated feeling flustered. So I dug my phone from my purse and pretended to scroll through the contacts. Once Declan was gone and I could concentrate again, I'd order an Uber.

"I promised your friend I'd get you home safe."

"Thanks," I said, "but I'm sure you have somewhere to be." I glanced at the band on his ring finger.

"Ah." He raised his hand. "This."

"Yes. That." I swallowed hard, telling myself I was in no position to judge Declan McKinley. I'd taken pretend marriage vows without a license. I called myself Townsend with no legal claim. Worst of all, I was standing outside a bar with the married father of one of my students.

"I wear this for Luke's sake," he said. "And because I haven't been ready to take it off. But my—" A couple exited the bar and began walking our way, laughing loudly, heads pressed together. Declan and I waited until the couple passed us. Then he cleared his throat. "My wife died two years ago," he said. "Her name was Shannon."

Suddenly his words from Open House came back to me:

My wife was a teacher.

She *was*. Past tense.

"Oh, Declan. God. I'm so sorry."

"Yeah," he said. "I am too."

I wanted to tell him that I understood. That I'd lost someone too. But I stopped myself. Comparing my pain to his was ridiculous. Declan's wife was gone forever, while Jake was just not with me anymore. I was unlovable. And leave-able. Jake had a choice, and I hadn't been worth the fight.

"So." Declan's eyes met mine. "Will you at least let me stay with you until your ride comes?"

A flush spread down my neck. "Actually, I don't have one."

"In that case, let me drive you home." He smiled. "I was here for work, so I haven't been drinking. I'm an architect. Did you know that? Not that it matters. Anyway, I was meeting with a client, answering some last-minute questions before the contract stage."

"At Grunions?"

"What can I say?" He laughed. "They have great French fries." Now Declan was the one who sounded flustered, and I couldn't help wondering whether he'd arranged this meeting before or after he heard Pauline say we'd be here.

"They do have good fries," I said.

"My point is, I stuck with Perrier."

"Wish I could say the same." I looked down at my damp skirt. "Tequila and an empty stomach aren't a good combination for me."

"A bad combo for anyone, I bet."

"OK," I said.

"OK?"

"I'll take that ride."

"Well, all right." Declan pointed at an Audi in the next row. "That's me. The gray one that needs a wash." As we walked together toward his car, Declan pressed a button on his key fob. The horn beeped twice, and the headlights flashed. He moved to the passenger side first and held the door open for me. The scent of leather and spice made me catch my breath.

"After you, Lia Townsend."

I gathered my skirt and slid inside.

Fifteen

I gave Declan general directions to the bungalow, but he took a detour and drove us to an outdoor mall featuring dozens of brightly lit storefronts. The tree trunks along the walkways were strung with white lights, and people strolled in pairs or packs, pausing to look into shop windows.

"Spoiler alert," I said. "This isn't my house."

"Wait." His eyes went wide. "Are you sure?"

I let myself laugh, felt myself let go. "What're you doing, anyway?"

"I'm making an executive decision. If that's all right with you."

"Hmmm," I said, and the hum felt good across my lips. "Isn't asking permission the exact opposite of an executive decision?"

"Maybe," he said. "But that's how I do things." He smiled at me and ducked his head. I was beginning to like that move. Here was a man who wanted to know my wishes, who cared about what I needed. And he was nodding toward an ice cream shop one store up from where he'd parked.

"Manhattan Beach Creamery?"

"I was hoping you'd be up for it," he said. "I'm a sucker for dessert, and I figure a couple scoops might do you good."

"You're right," I said, "I'm pretty much starving."

"Then wait right there, Ms. Townsend." Declan hopped out of the car and came around the front of it to open my door. I reached out a hand and let him help me from the passenger seat. "I know it's old-fashioned, but I blame my dad," he said. "Feel free to call me uncool."

"For opening my door? I think it's sweet. And I'll get you back next time."

"Next time?" He laughed. "Lucky me."

My cheeks flamed. "Maybe I'm getting ahead of myself."

"Not even a little bit." We began walking side by side toward the Creamery. "Shannon used to warn me that modern women might be offended by chivalry."

"I'm not," I said. "Offended, I mean."

"Are you modern?"

"That remains to be seen."

Declan smiled. "I like a little mystery."

When we got to the shop, I held the door for him. Once inside, we perused our options, then ordered our ice cream in cups instead of cones. I insisted on paying our tab in exchange for the ride home. Declan seemed fine with this arrangement, and I liked this about him. He was generous but also flexible. His father had done well.

We found an empty table outside the shop where we made quick work of our scoops. With each frozen bite, I felt myself thawing. Declan McKinley made me warm. We discussed Luke and the awkwardness of the middle school years. I asked him about Shannon, so he told me she'd taught elementary. Third grade. They'd been high school sweethearts and were married for more than a decade. "Is it weird for me to talk about her with you?"

"Not at all," I said. "I'm the one who asked." When I scraped the bottom of my cup, Declan pointed at the empty bowl.

"Better?"

I nodded. "Much." I licked the spoon and set it in my cup.

"Ice cream solves most problems," he said. "Hey. Can I see your phone?"

"Why?"

"Please," he said. I pulled my phone from my purse, unlocked the screen, and handed it to him. "I'm putting my number in your contacts," he said. "In case you have another emergency with drunk Angels fans and spilled beer."

I laughed. "Thanks, but I was drinking margaritas."

"I'm available for tequila emergencies too." He gave my phone back to me and for a moment we were both quiet.

"So," I said.

Declan smiled at me. "I guess I'll get you home now."

ৎৡৣৢৡ৶

When we reached my street, Declan took it at a crawl, the houses blurred by a thick marine layer. Here, there were no sidewalks. Truncated driveways gave way to road and the streetlights projected their glow at rare intervals. On these blocks nearest the ocean, the houses huddled together. Each beach lot cost a fortune. When Jake and I bought the bungalow, it had been in foreclosure. That was the only way we could afford to live here, even with his parents' money as a down payment. Although Jake loved the challenge of a fixer-upper, I was reluctant to sink our money into something so risky. Plus living near the ocean scared me. I hadn't told Jake I couldn't swim yet.

If the real estate market tanks, I argued, *we'll lose everything.*

Not each other, Jake said. He spoke with the confidence of a man who'd never worried about finances. We stood on the porch hand in hand, and his promises washed over me.

Think of the equity we'll inherit, he said. And I'd surrendered to the waves.

I wiped at the window now, clearing a circle of fog from my breath. "It's up ahead." I pointed. "The white one with the wood shake roof."

"Nice place," Declan said. He pulled up and cut the engine. I turned to thank him for the ride, but he was staring past me toward the house.

"You expecting a visitor?"

"I don't think so," I said, but I followed his gaze to the dark porch. Someone was seated in my rocking chair.

Jake?

I'd told him that when I was little, I used to sit for hours on Regina's stoop hoping someone—anyone—would drive by. We had no chair, and my bones would ache waiting for her on the concrete step. To me a chair was the difference between a house and a home: a comfortable place to wait for the ones you love. The rocking chair had been a gift from him to me the day we moved in.

"I have no idea who that is," I said, hoping my voice wouldn't crack. "Maybe my friend Maren, checking on me? It was her date night, and—"

"Stay here," Declan said. "I'll check it out." But I opened the door and hopped out of the car first.

"Hello?" I called. The figure stood and moved into the light from a streetlamp. Not Jake's size but still tall, her height increased by high-heeled boots and excellent posture. "Charlotte? Is that you?"

"Lia!" she said, coming toward me. She wore a fitted blouse tucked into trousers, and her black hair was sliced into a bob. "Don't worry. I've only been waiting for hours."

"Everything OK?" Declan asked.

Charlotte peered over my shoulder, appearing as surprised to see me with a strange man as I was to find her on my porch. "And who might this be?"

Declan approached, put his hand out. "Declan McKinley," he said. "Ms. Townsend is my son's teacher." Charlotte regarded him for a beat, then shook his hand without responding.

"Declan was just giving me a ride," I said. "We happened to end up at the same restaurant tonight and—"

"Hi there, Declan," Charlotte interrupted, as if already bored by my explanation. "I'm Charlotte. Lia's sister-in-law." She looked back over her shoulder at the bungalow. "Speaking of which, where is that husband of yours?"

Husband.

There came an intake of breath behind me. Declan had heard Charlotte's words. In that moment, I felt like I might be the most terrible person in the world, and I could only imagine Declan thought the same. Not more than ten minutes ago, he'd been telling me about Shannon, while I'd revealed nothing about my own situation. I'd let him believe I was available. *Because I am available.* At least from a legal standpoint.

So, why hadn't I told him about Jake?

"From the look on your face," Charlotte said, "I'm guessing my idiot brother forgot I was coming. I know, it's not my usual time to visit, but Tim's mom kept moaning about seeing her grandkid more, so Tim offered to bring Madge to Philly to spend her birthday with TJ. And obviously there's no way I'm sharing the city with my ex *and* his mom, so Jake said I should come here. That was a month ago. He didn't tell you?"

No. He didn't. And also Charlotte *obviously* didn't know about Jake and me yet. He must've invited her here, before.

Before.

The two syllables carved me up. Charlotte was one more person Jake had left for me to tell. About him. About us. About a girl named Josie who didn't like to be called Jo by anyone but her mother. Charlotte had a niece, but I couldn't share this with her now. Not while Declan was standing behind me.

Was he still standing behind me?

I spun around, and Declan took a step backward. He must've heard everything, but there's no way he could know what it all meant. And there was no good explanation. "Thanks for everything," I said. I bit my lip, and it still tasted like ice cream.

Declan ducked his head. "Night, Lia." As he walked away, my shoulders sank. I wanted to stop him, but what could I say? The man had opened up to me and shared about his life. In return, I'd offered him nothing. "Nice to meet you, Charlotte," he called out from his car.

Charlotte.

If she hadn't been here tonight, would Declan have tried to kiss me at the door? I imagined fumbling with the lock while he waited, then turning and lifting my face to his. I would've let him rest the tips of his fingers under my chin.

Charlotte sighed. "So, are we going to stand around forever?"

"No, no. Of course not." I moved to unlock the door.

"You guys really should keep a spare key under the mat," she said.

"We have one hidden in a ceramic frog next to the fountain." I kept my back to her and hoped she didn't see me flinch over the word *we*. "You know Jake. There's no way he'd do something as obvious as keep a key under—"

"Speaking of my OCD brother," Charlotte interrupted, "he's a total lunatic about checking his schedule." She paused. "The man's a planner. Beyond. There's no way he just forgot about me coming."

I pushed the front door open, my stomach in ropes. The small living room appeared cavernous. "Hard to believe, right?"

"Impossible," she said.

I stepped inside and motioned for Charlotte to follow. She stared at me, her eyes two pools of black, just like Jake's. I flashed on him carrying me over the threshold, back when our future had felt limitless. She took a step forward and touched my shoulder. "You want to turn on some lights and tell me what's going on?"

"I think I'd like to keep them off."

"Sounds serious."

"It is."

Charlotte dropped her bag, crossed the dark room, and sat on the couch. "Sit. Spill." She patted the cushion beside her. "Whatever this is," she said, "it can't be worse than all my shit."

"It is."

"OK." Charlotte reached out to me. "Then think of this as your chance to make me feel better about myself."

So I took her hand and held on until I'd told her almost everything.

Sixteen

Charlotte Townsend-Harris and I met at a backyard barbecue six months before my wedding. "My daughter's the one dressed in white," Ivy told me. "After Labor Day. Quite the rebel." Charlotte tilted her chin in our direction.

"She looks like Jake," I said.

"You think so?" Ivy wrinkled her nose. "Charlotte, dear. Come meet Lia!"

As Charlotte crossed the pool deck, her skirt billowed like a sail. When she reached us, she hugged Jake and said, "Your bride-to-be's gorgeous. Congratulations." Then she turned to me. "Is it bad luck to be congratulated by someone who's been divorced twice?"

I stammered, "I don't know."

Charlotte took my hand. "Don't worry," she said. "It's probably not contagious."

Over steak and veggie skewers, I learned more about Charlotte's story. She had a five-year-old son with her second husband, Tim Harris. Her first marriage—a Vegas elopement with a man named Bo Dickson—had lasted only as long as it took Ivy and Charles to file the annulment.

"That Bo was handsome enough," Ivy told me, "but dumb."

"As a rock," Jake added.

"At least Tim's brilliant," Charlotte said. "But damn. He's cold as a fish."

"Are fish cold?" I asked.

"I guess so." Charlotte smirked. "Thank God TJ's nothing like his father."

Ivy sighed. "I love my grandson but—"

"But what, Mom?"

"If it weren't for TJ we could all wash our hands of Tim Harris now, couldn't we?"

Jake leaned over and whispered to me, "Another reason not to have kids."

From the beginning of our relationship, he'd been clear: Kids were a deal-breaker. Jake didn't hate children, he just loved his freedom, the wide-openness of our future. Also, he refused to be like his own parents who he swore had tried to shape him and Charlotte into Ivy and Charles clones. He believed procreating was narcissistic. Plus, the world was overpopulated. Why would anyone willingly deplete the earth's already vanishing resources? As Jake's list of reasons grew, so did his confidence in his position. And I, in love and breathless, had agreed with him.

Well. Mostly.

The afternoon I met Charlotte, I convinced myself her two failed marriages had influenced Jake's attitude about parenthood and marriage. Ivy and Charles didn't help matters, either. They appeared more like a couple in a wax museum than people who'd ever been in love.

They had Jake and Charlotte.

Charlotte had TJ.

Jake and I would be different.

We would have each other.

We were painstakingly careful.

Until the day I was prescribed antibiotics, and my doctor warned me they made the pill less effective. In my sick, cloudy state, I told Jake this over the phone. And when I was well again, and he'd returned from his latest trip, Jake brought home a box of Trojans.

Better safe than sorry.

The sex that night was urgent—it had been almost two weeks. I can still picture Jake's frantic face afterward when he saw the broken condom.

"It's fine," I said. "Don't worry!" I leapt out of bed and started doing jumping jacks.

"Don't be stupid," Jake said.

I was being stupid.

"What are the odds?" I called from the bathroom, while cleaning myself up. "There's no way."

That's what I said to him, but the truth was I already felt different. Three weeks later, a second line appeared in the window of the home pregnancy test. My heartbeat quickened as the thread of pink emerged—slowly, then all at once—like a swimmer when the waves retreat.

We're having a baby.

I could barely breathe. I waited two days to tell Jake.

"It must be fate," I said. "Or God. The Universe. Mother Nature. Some force of goodness wants a new Townsend in the world. This is a sign we're supposed to be parents, right?" When the cramps came and emptied me out, Jake bounced my own rationale back at me.

"You see?" he said. "It's a sign. This wasn't meant to be." He rocked me gently while I sobbed into his shoulder.

"I just thought maybe—"

"Shhh," he whispered. "Shhh."

My gynecologist told me the loss was so early, most women wouldn't have even known they were pregnant. But I'd felt something like permanence inside me. A small taste of eternity. At the end of the same month, Jake scheduled a vasectomy.

"I did it for you," he said. "So you never have to go through that kind of pain again."

But he hadn't told me until it was over.

On the day of the procedure, he'd filled out a stack of paperwork, splashing his signature on page after page. He accepted terms of liability, agreed to mediation *in case of complications.*

Yes, he understood the repercussions.

Yes, he'd been informed of the office's privacy policy.

Yes, he had received instructions for his aftercare.

No one requested my permission. I offered up no signatures.

When the doctor asked if he was married, Jake answered honestly.

"No. I'm not."

Seventeen

"Wake up, Sleepyhead." A cool hand touched my shoulder. I dragged a pillow over my head, but Charlotte was insistent. A rustle of drapes, a scrape of window.

"It's the weekend," I muttered. "I get to stay in bed."

"Come on, Lia." Charlotte tugged the pillow free.

"Go away." I blinked up at her. "Please."

"Not a chance. Maren and I have big plans for today. Things to do before I leave. Important things. Things you won't want to miss."

Charlotte and Maren in collusion? I must be worse off than I thought.

"What do you two have up your sleeves?" I groaned.

"Wouldn't you like to know?"

I sat up and spat a tangle of hair from my mouth. "Yes. That's why I asked."

"All information will be delivered on a need-to-know basis," Charlotte said. "Just trust me."

Other vague instructions followed.

Casual dress. Nothing fussy. Aim for comfortable. Maybe a little cute.

I showered and let my hair air dry, slicked on mascara and a little lip gloss. From the closet I chose white pants, a teal tank top, leather sandals. When I grabbed my denim jacket, Jake's voice played in my head: "You're not just cold-blooded, Lia; you've got ice cubes in your veins."

I never argued with that. I'd always hated being chilly, and even when it was hot out, people ran their air conditioning. So I over-layered. Better safe than sorry. Still, I wondered now if Jake meant something else. Was I too frigid? Stand-offish? It's not like I'd done a bang-up job of warming up to Declan. It was one thing to be out of practice. But what if I'd never been *in*?

Charlotte was waiting for me in the living room dressed in black from head to toe.

"Are you sure this is a good idea?" I asked her. "I might not be the best company."

"This is my chance to treat you to a day of fun," she said.

"Fine," I said. "I'll try."

"You hungry?"

My stomach growled. "Surprisingly, yes. I am."

"Perfect. Because brunch is Step Two of our secret plan."

"What's Step One?"

"Repeat after me," she said. "FUCK YOU, JAKE!"

"Charlotte!"

"What? He deserves it."

"He's your brother."

"Exactly. And as Jake's older sister, I hereby give you permission to kick the man's ass. Verbally, of course." She grinned at me. I shook my head. "I know this isn't a joke to you," she said. "It's not to me, either. And that's why I'm dedicating today to pulling you out of your slump."

"Slump?" The word scratched my throat.

"OK," she said. "Pit of Despair. Well of Depression. What do *you* want to call whatever it is Jake tossed you into?"

"Hey." I lifted my chin. "Jake didn't toss me anywhere. I'm still on my feet."

"Atta girl." Charlotte snaked her arm through mine. "Today's going to be great."

୭ঙ৶

As we walked up Manhattan Beach Boulevard, the air smelled of seaweed and salt. I took a deep breath and sighed. "Feeling better yet?" asked Charlotte.

"Absolutely not."

"Then Step Two is just what you need." She came to a stop at the entrance to Simmzy's where Maren called out, waving us over to a table on the patio. In front of her were three Bloody Marys stuffed with bacon, olives, and celery. As Charlotte and I took our seats under an oversized red umbrella, Maren pushed our drinks toward us. She had her hair in a messy bun and wore a pink tunic over green leggings.

"You look cute today," Charlotte told her.

"Ugh. I'm a giant strawberry. But after half a Bloody Mary, I decided not to care. I got two more so you don't have to care, either."

I picked up my drink and swished it with the celery stalk. "Vodka before noon, huh?"

"Very thirst-quenching," Charlotte said. "Excellent call, Maren."

Maren handed us each a menu. "I already ordered a plate of shrimp cakes for an appetizer," she said. "Hope that's all right."

"Are you kidding?" Charlotte slid a pair of Prada reading glasses from her purse. "You're officially my hero, and I'm officially starving."

We were still studying the menu when a server with a nose ring and a tattoo of a cobra on his neck delivered our shrimp cakes. With a flourish, he produced a bottle of Tabasco from his apron and placed it near the napkin dispenser.

"You all ready to order, or do you need more time?"

Charlotte lifted an eyebrow. Was she flirting with him? "Maybe a few more minutes," she said. "But could we add an order of shoestring fries to start? With garlic aioli, please?"

The server grinned at her. "You got it, miss." As he hurried toward the kitchen, Maren gawked.

"Did that kid just call you 'miss'?"

"I love it," Charlotte said. "And the nose ring."

"He's a little young, don't you think?" Maren asked.

"Nothing wrong with young."

"Let's address the more immediate issue," I said. "When are you two going to tell me what you've got planned for today?"

"You'll have to ask Charlotte." Maren smoothed a loose strand of hair back into her bun. "All I did was recommend Simmzy's. She handled everything else." I wondered if Charlotte caught the note of frustration in Maren's voice.

"Breakfast is the most important meal of the day," Charlotte said. "And this place is perfect." She glanced around the patio. "Outdoor seating. Beachy. Casual."

Maren fiddled with her necklace, a silver chain with a heart-shaped locket. Danny gave it to her for Christmas with a picture of Nora and him inside. "It's just brunch," Maren said. "I didn't invent the wheel or anything."

"Never underestimate the power of good food." Charlotte popped half a shrimp cake into her mouth.

"I probably shouldn't look a gift compliment in the mouth." Maren blew out a breath. "Considering I spend my days sweeping Cheerios and folding laundry."

Charlotte swallowed, dabbed her mouth with a napkin. "And that's bad because…"

"It's just… I used to be a damn good interior designer, you know?" Maren frowned. "And sometimes I worry I lost my edge. I did lose my edge, dammit."

"You'll get it back," Charlotte said. "When you're ready." She scraped a shrimp cake onto a plate for me, then forked one onto Maren's plate.

"Maybe," Maren said. She flashed a pointed look at Charlotte. "But you're a mom."

"I am."

"And you're still chic and professional and fabulous."

"Hey." Charlotte shrugged. "You stayed married. That's more than I could manage." She cut her gaze to me. "Shit. Sorry."

"Don't be," I said. The last thing I wanted was more eggshells for us to walk on.

"Anyway, what happened isn't your fault, Lia." Charlotte sucked an olive from her swizzle stick. "Jake's an asshole."

"And crazy," Maren said. She leaned over the table, lowered her voice. "Did Lia tell you he's got a daughter?"

"Yeah." Charlotte nodded. "She told me."

Maren sat back. "I met her, you know. Jake's daughter.

Did Lia tell you that?"

"Please," I said, before Maren's competitive streak ramped up. "If I'm going to move on, we can't keep talking about Jake. He's the past. I need to find out who I am now, you know? Who I'm going to be."

"You're so right," Charlotte said. "A toast!" She lifted her drink. "To finding Lia."

"To finding Lia," echoed Maren.

"Yes," I said. "To me."

৩৵৫

By the time the waiter came back with our fries, we'd decided it was a little late for brunch food, so we ordered sandwiches, side salads, and another round of Bloody Marys. While we ate, Maren and Charlotte kept the tone light, and I loved them for trying so hard. We talked about books and movie recommendations, speculated on the latest Hollywood plastic surgeries. The three of us were doing fine—laughing even—when Maren asked Charlotte about TJ.

"Oh God," Charlotte groaned. "When he's with Tim for a week, it's like my foot's gone. No, more like my entire leg."

"I get it," Maren said. "Sometimes, I'm so desperate for a break from Nora I want to scream. But then when I'm away from her for more than an hour, I start scrolling through pictures on my phone. Actually missing her!"

"What the hell is wrong with us?" Charlotte asked.

"Nothing's wrong with you," I said. "You're mothers. It's normal to feel that way." I forced a laugh. "I mean, I assume it's normal. I'm not a parent."

Maren tilted her head. "Lia—"

"I still can't believe Jake is though," I said. "A parent."

"Right?" Charlotte's expression darkened. "He hasn't returned any of my calls or texts. And I'm guessing the message I left made things worse."

"What did you say?" I asked.

"I called him an idiot. Told him he and Addie should be ashamed of themselves."

Maren sucked up the last bit of her Bloody Mary. Loudly.

"I'll bet that Addie's a real bitch." She glanced at Charlotte. "Is Addie a bitch?"

At this Charlotte cringed. "She used to be pretty nice, actually."

"Well, not anymore," said Maren. "Now she's a bitch!"

"No," I said. "This isn't Addie's fault. Jake made his own choices."

"But—"

"He found out he had a kid, he felt caught between Josie and me, and instead of trying to work things out, he left."

Charlotte shook her head. "Like I said. Idiot. All men are. Except for our waiter. He's OK."

"And Danny," I said.

"Ha!" Maren giggled. "Danny's definitely an idiot."

"You two agree to disagree," Charlotte said. "In the meantime, let's get the check. I want to see that cobra tattoo again. And besides, it's time for Step Three."

ぬぬ

After Charlotte and Maren split the tab, we walked to *A Cut Above* where Charlotte had booked me a three o'clock appointment with a stylist named Nancy. Nancy's purple bangs were pinned with a yellow barrette, and she was dressed in army fatigues. As she led us all to her station, I saw myself reflected in mirror after mirror. Pink cheeks. A dusting of freckles. Caramel hair I'd never highlighted. Jake liked my hair long and natural, and I'd done my best to please him.

"All right, Miss Lia," Nancy said. Her voice sounded like she was singing. "What do you want to do today?" I checked my reflection again and snorted. So many mirrors, and I didn't recognize myself in any of them.

Charlotte whispered loudly. "She's had some vodka."

"It's just that question," I said. "*What do I want.* It's hilarious." I covered my mouth.

Nancy nodded. "Go ahead and laugh, honey." She produced a book with hundreds of hairstyle samples, and Maren and Charlotte pulled up chairs so the four of us could flip through the pages. My head was swimming—so many choices—then I saw it.

What I wanted.

"You'll be beautiful no matter what," Maren said. "But are you sure?"

I considered Maren's question. What was I sure of these days? The answer was *pretty much nothing.* I'd never thought to ask before. The day we met, I'd allowed Jake to take the reins. In fact, I *wanted* him to. He cared more about things, had stronger feelings and opinions. Why wouldn't I defer? The lonely girl inside me wanted nothing more than to please Jake. I'd been so afraid to lose him. *Then I lost him anyway.*

I looked at Maren. "Being sure is overrated."

"That's my girl." She smiled.

Charlotte said, "You can do this, Lia."

I was doing it.

I would.

༺⚭༻

Step Four turned out to be shopping. I played along, even caught myself having fun. In Anthropologie, the three of us collected armfuls of clothes and headed into separate dressing rooms. I slipped on an emerald sundress and a pair of strappy sandals. Then I peered at myself in the three-way mirror.

Auburn. My hair was auburn now, streaked red and warm and rich. Long layers framed my face and draped along my shoulders. Had my eyes ever looked this blue? I forced a smile. I'd done it. Everything could change. I touched my nose to the glass.

Hocus Pocus. It's the New Lia!

"How are you doing in there?" a sales consultant asked. I gazed at the dress, the green silk cool against my skin.

"Fine," I said. "I'm fine."

"Need anything different?" *Different.* I needed different, all right. Head to toe. Heart to brain. I needed a whole-person transplant.

"I'm good, thanks," I told her. I stuck my tongue out at the New Lia.

I looked like Regina.

Why hadn't I seen it before?

My hands flew to my face smoothing out my frown, erasing the scene. Lips flat, eyes flat. Somewhere inside was the real me. My phone dinged twice in my purse, the signal for a new email. I sat on the dressing room bench to check my inbox. And there it was. The name in bold:

Declan McKinley.

My stomach twisted.

Lia,

I'm sorry for emailing you, but I thought a face-to-face meeting wouldn't be right. I'm not mad. You owe me no explanations. I was surprised. That's all. Luke had no idea you were married, and you don't wear a ring, so I made an assumption. But our night ended before I got a chance to thank you, one last time. Luke really likes you. You brought him out of his shell and made him feel like someone (besides me) actually cared. And not just because they felt sorry for him. You did that for me, too, and for both these things, I'm grateful.

When Shannon got sick, I promised not to leave anything unsaid. Ever again. So, I don't regret meeting you. You're a good woman, and I wish you nothing but happiness.

Be well, Lia.
Declan

I turned off my phone.
That was that.

Eighteen

I heard Charlotte's cab idling at the curb, but I stayed in bed until she was gone. Hugging her goodbye felt impossible. A part of me thought I'd never see her again. It had always been Jake that Charlotte called when she was going to be in town. Jake arranged her visits, then informed me after the fact. So yes, Charlotte was disappointed in her brother, in what she called *the Josie debacle*. She claimed her loyalties lay with me now. But Jake was family. Blood. It was that simple. And complicated. With all the Townsends, I assumed.

Over the past month, I'd considered reaching out to Ivy more than once, but each time, I reminded myself she hadn't contacted me. Jake would've told his mother he'd left. Or maybe Charlotte had filled her in. Either way, I was sure Ivy knew. She'd made her choice. I made mine too.

We all had to move on.

Unable to sleep more, I padded into the kitchen wearing the terrycloth robe Jake had given me for Christmas. Charlotte must've made coffee before she left. Half a pot was still steaming in the carafe. I poured myself a cup, then sat at the table mulling over Declan's email.

You're a good woman, and I wish you nothing but happiness.

It had taken all my self-control not to email him back in the dressing room. And I might have done it, if I'd had fewer Bloody Marys and more of an idea of what to say. About Jake. Our non-marriage. Josie. I should've told Declan everything the night he'd opened up to me about Shannon. But I didn't then, and I couldn't now. Maybe it was too hard to admit I'd been so easy for Jake to discard. Maybe I didn't want Declan to think I was a fool. Or weird. Or something. Either way, I'd thrown out bait and left the man dangling on a line. I deserved better than Jake. But Declan McKinley definitely deserved better than me.

Moving to the bedroom, I slipped on jeans and a hooded sweatshirt. I had to get out of here. While I walked to the beach, the wind lashed my hair, auburn strands stuck to my neck. The air tasted salty, and the ocean grew louder. Crossing the path between two properties, I emerged onto my favorite stretch of shore. The place was still deserted, so I spread a blanket on the sand. Knees hugged to my chest. Chin down. I counted to fifty in my head.

Don't think, Lia. Just look at the waves.

I wanted to love the ocean, but its depths terrified me. At the edge of the tide, I could be a visitor. Beyond it, I didn't belong. The sea was murky darkness. A swish of shark fin. Twisted weeds. Razor-sharp coral. There I'd be surrounded by danger and sink into a world too foreign to comprehend.

Unlike me, Jake ruled the water. A diver. Swimmer. Fish. He was at home in the Pacific and in the Townsend's private pool. He couldn't wait to take me to their fancy country club, probably to show off. While he swam laps, I reclined on a lounge chair, pretending to read. He asked me to join him, but I made an excuse. I can't remember which one. *The water's too cold. I just washed my hair. Chlorine will ruin my bathing suit.* It was months before I told Jake the truth: I'd never learned to swim.

Over the years, he'd offered to teach me, but I refused him every time. Once, he accused me of not trusting him. I grew defensive, but he was right. A part of me was afraid Jake expected more than I could deliver. Would he take me into the water and not be there when I failed to float? Eventually, he stopped asking, and for the record I was relieved. Life became easier with fewer reminders of the ways I disappointed Jake. I could focus on how I *did* fit into his life. I shifted, molded, bent myself until I wasn't Lia anymore. I became the person I thought Jake wanted me to be. I never stopped to wonder if my acquiescence might be more damaging than good. For me. For him. Not until that night at *Mangiamo* when he pulled his hand away and left without an explanation.

What kind of man did that?

Why hadn't he told me about Josie then? Was he afraid I'd try to talk him out of raising his daughter? Or that I might petition to be a part of something he wanted to keep for himself? Maybe he was worried I'd make a scene. That I'd throw my champagne in his face. Rage and scream. Well. Maybe I would have.

Maybe I should've been raging all along.

At Regina's house, the day after I found out about Josie, Jake claimed he didn't leave me because of Josie. Not entirely. He said he knew I wasn't happy, that I'd been pretending all along. And if he was right, if none of it had been real, that was a death in itself, wasn't it? I didn't just lose Jake. I'd lost the past I thought was good between us and the future I expected we'd share. Those were years I wouldn't have going forward. Years I couldn't get back.

Gone.

Above me a seagull squawked, then landed ten feet from where I sat. He looked at me, head bobbing as I stuck my thumb in the sand. I drew a heart, then added an arrow, a crack down the middle, thick and jagged. With my palm, I smoothed over the grooves and began to write.

Lia Lark.

I said it out loud. Twice. Then, like a snow angel—except with sand—I fanned my legs over the letters of my name.

An hour later, when the sun finally peeked through the clouds, I peeled off my sweatshirt and dug through the pocket for my phone. I read Declan McKinley's email again even though I'd already memorized it. Then, hitting the reply arrow, I started a new message.

I'm not married.
It's a long story.
I'm at the beach down the street from my house.
Come find me. Please.
Love, Lia

The seagull hopped closer to me, flapped its wings twice, then launched itself into the sky. Alone again, I deleted my email to Declan one word at a time.

Nineteen

Lia? It's Regina. Sorry I didn't call back sooner, but time gets away from me these days. Anyway, how are you holding up? Staying strong? You're a Lark, you know. So if that prodigal husband of yours tries to come home, tell him he's not welcome. You've wasted years of your life shackled to that man. He might've stolen your light, but you can rekindle it. We Lark women always do. Anyway, I called for a reason, but for the life of me, I can't remember it. Ring me back when you're free, and hopefully by then something will come to me. I'll be gone for a few hours buying chicken feed, and then I've promised Beverly—you know Beverly Swanson don't you? From down the street?—Well, I promised to paint her portrait as a surprise for her husband's seventieth. I think she's planning a nude. Can you imagine? On second thought, try not to. She hasn't held up as well as I have. Anyway, I should be back by dinnertime unless that Caleb Stone has me off running another errand for him. Honestly, Lia. Sometimes I don't know how I do it. But at least he's sexy.

Delete.

LIA! Where are you? I haven't heard back from you all week. Danny and I miss you. Nora misses you too. We all miss you. Like, a lot. So call me. Or text. Or whatever. Where the hell are you?

Delete.

Happy Friday, Lia. Just checking in to be sure you're good and to tell you TJ says HI and THANK YOU for the birthday card and the check. He's got ten friends sleeping over tonight. Dear God, what was I thinking? Ten ten-year-olds. You can't imagine the noise and the smell. I'm hiding in the basement now. Be glad you're not here with me. You're probably out on the town tonight, so no pressure to call back. Have fun for both of us, will you? Love you! Bye.

Delete.

Lia? It's Veronica. Are you ever coming back to book club? We missed you in April and May, so you absolutely have to come in June. I'm bringing my new neighbor, Bets Farinelli. She just moved here from Conejo Springs. Isn't that where you did your student teaching? Small world! Anyway, her son's starting at your school in the fall, and I promised you'd give Bets the scoop on the place, so don't make me a liar! Jillian's hosting, and we're reading The Awakening. *It's by Kate Chopin, and I think you'll love it. Kiss kiss. Ciao.*

Delete.

Hi, Lia. Charlotte told me you included my name on the card for TJ, and I wanted to let you know I didn't forget. His birthday, I mean. But I didn't send him anything, either. So thank you. Guess I'll have to get better at that stuff. Soon. Anyway, I hope you're doing OK. It's almost summer, so you must be looking forward to that. It's weird to not know your plans. Let me know if you need anything. Otherwise, well... Take care.

I listened to Jake's message three times, analyzed the voice, the pauses, his breath.

Delete.

Twenty

The invitation lurked like a landmine, buried under the utility bills, a Trader Joe's flyer, and advertisements from local real estate agents. It was past midnight, but I suddenly felt awake, sorting mail at my desk next to our kitchen.

The kitchen.

My kitchen.

An elegant *T* adorned the back of the envelope, and on the front, my name appeared in calligraphy. Ivy Townsend had outdone herself, addressing the invitations by hand. She'd always prided herself on her commitment to what she called *real correspondence.* She still sent handwritten Christmas cards and used email sparingly. Every year, invitations to their Fourth of July party arrived six weeks before the event.

The party would be, as it always was, an explosion of red, white, and blue. Hired caterers and bands. Guests playing croquet in closed-toe sandals. When the pool filled with splashing kids, a teenaged lifeguard would circle the deck, fielding instructions from a watchful Ivy. Across the property, Charles would oversee construction of the backyard fireworks display. (These were illegal, but Charles played golf with the local fire chief who, each year, looked the other way.)

Alongside the invitation, a small square peeped out from the envelope. Another handwritten note from Ivy. Pulling the note free, I got a paper cut and sucked the tip of my finger while I read.

Dear Lia,

I would very much like to see you.

There's something we must discuss in person.

Charles and I both hope you can make it.

Mom

Regina would roll her eyes at Ivy referring to herself as *Mom.* She felt the practice was old-fashioned and pedestrian. What people did *in less-than-modern times,* like getting married or taking your husband's name. Regina didn't approve. I dropped the note on the desk and picked up my phone. Maren mumbled when she answered.

"What time is it?"

"Are you asleep?"

"Yes, Lia. I always talk on the phone in my sleep."

"Sorry," I said. "But the Townsends invited me to their Fourth of July party."

"Really? Wow."

"You sound surprised."

"Because I am."

"Well, I was their daughter-in-law for five years."

"*Was* being the operative word." There came a long pause, then Maren said, "Seriously though. Why do you think they invited you?"

"I don't know. Maybe they finally want to apologize for their son's *most-appalling behavior.*" I said this in an exaggerated rich-person voice, like Mrs. Howell on *Gilligan's Island.* When I was a little girl and Regina would disappear overnight, I'd watch old black and white reruns of that show. I figured if those shipwrecked misfits could survive being on a deserted island for years, I could survive a day or two alone on Marview Lane.

"I hate to even say it out loud," Maren began again, "but what if the Townsends want their money back? Like for the bungalow? I mean I know it was just the down payment. And they don't exactly need it, but…"

At this, my insides clenched. The thought had occurred to me too. But I said, "I'd like to think that if they wanted money, they would've asked me to sell the place by now."

"Maybe. Maybe not. You're not actually going to go to the party, are you?"

"I'm still debating. But do you think you could find out if Jake will be there and tell me? He doesn't need to know I asked. I don't want him to change his plans because of me."

Maren was silent for a moment. "We talked about this, Lia. Please don't put me in the middle. I can't. I promised Danny."

I took a breath and reminded myself to respect Maren's loyalty. She wasn't telling Jake anything about me either. This was the deal. We had agreed. "You're right," I said. "But I'm not asking you to divulge any huge secrets."

"Just whether or not Jake will be at the party?"

"Yes," I said. "And Addie. Oh, and Josie."

Maren sighed.

"Please, Mare."

"OK," she said. "I'll try."

The next day dragged on forever while I waited for Maren to call me back. I paced the classroom between my four morning periods and watched the clock during my lunch break. As anxious as I was to hear from Maren, I wasn't sure which answer I was hoping for. If Jake was going to the Townsends' party, I could RSVP *no*. But if Maren found out he wouldn't be there, what then?

Should I go?

Despite Ivy Townsend's handwritten request, I wasn't obligated to spend any time with Jake's family now. Or ever again. He and I never had kids, so our future wouldn't feature any joint birthday parties or graduation ceremonies. No sporting events or concerts. I'd never have to sit next to Ivy and Charles in the front row of an auditorium while their grandchild performed the lead in a school musical.

In a way, this made me luckier than my friends who were stuck negotiating holidays with unsupportive in-laws. But there was a dark side to my good fortune, a question I kept suppressing: Would Jake have left me in the first place to raise Josie if I hadn't miscarried? If we had a baby, would he have stayed? My heart hammered at the thought.

I crossed the classroom to sit at my desk. Next to the computer I kept a picture of me holding baby Nora that Danny took the morning she was born. Only now did I realize I'd never brought a picture of Jake and me to school. *No wonder Luke McKinley didn't know I was married.* I studied the picture, taking in my grin and Nora's bow lips. A tiny fist stuck out from her blanket like she was waving to the camera.

I set down the picture when the door to my classroom creaked open. There, standing in the entryway, hat in hand, was Luke McKinley. Lately I'd caught myself sneaking quick peeks at him out of the corner of my eye. I couldn't help wondering what he was thinking, what he may or may not know. Had Declan mentioned anything about me? About us? The question was absurd. I was Luke's teacher. Why would Declan bring me up to his son? More importantly, why did I care?

"Hey, Luke," I said. "What's up?"

He shifted his weight and ducked his head, a smaller version of his dad. "I heard you aren't teaching summer school."

I hesitated before answering. "No. Not this year."

"I'm just checking because…" His voice trailed off. I wanted to put an arm around him and tell him whatever it was he had to say would be fine.

"Because what?" I prompted.

"My dad's saying I might need a tutor, like I might forget what I learned and backslide in eighth grade. I told him no way, but he says maybe I don't get to decide."

"All right."

"So, I thought if he makes me… if I have to have a tutor… I want it to be you."

"Oh." My throat felt tight.

"It's just that I don't like most teachers. And I don't think they like me. Ever since my mom…" He took a beat. "It's like no one knows what to say to me, so I'm a problem for them before I even do anything, you know?"

"I think I do."

"But you don't look at me like that."

"I didn't know. About your mom."

"You do now." He ducked his head again, and my face felt warm. I wanted to help Luke, to make one thing a little easier in his life. But would Declan want me around his son this summer? I didn't think so.

"What did your dad say about me tutoring you?"

"I didn't ask him yet," he said. "I wanted to find out if you could do it first. If you can't, I'm not getting tutored, no matter what my dad thinks."

I tilted my head, weighed my options. What could I say to make this right? I didn't want to get Luke's hopes up or cause problems between him and his father. But I did want an excuse to see Declan again. "I'd be happy to tutor you," I said. "If that's what you want. And if your dad agrees."

"Oh, he will. He likes you." Luke smiled at me.

I hope you're right.

My phone rang then. Maren, finally! I watched Luke leave—he was still smiling as the door shut—and answered Maren's call.

"Hey!" I felt suddenly breathless.

"Jake's not going to the party," she said without fanfare. "Neither's Addie. Or Josie."

"Thanks so much for finding out," I told her. "I know you didn't want to."

"For the record, Danny and I don't think you should go either."

I stiffened a little. I didn't want to get into this now with her. "Duly noted," I said.

"You'll just be making yourself vulnerable to Ivy and Charles. You don't even know what they want from you. What their motives are."

"Which could be a reason for me to show up."

"Oh." Maren took a beat then. Her voice softened. "You've already decided to go?"

"First I need to get through the rest of this week and the rest of the school year." I forced a laugh. "Then I'll work on the rest of my life."

⊱◈⊰

The next day, one week before finals, Luke approached my desk at the beginning of class. He slid a piece of paper across it without looking at me. "What's this?" I asked.

"The rubric you wanted me to do. You forgot about it, but I didn't. So, yeah. There it is." When he took a step back and still made no eye contact, I assumed the worst. Luke must've talked to Declan about me being his tutor, and I guessed it hadn't gone Luke's way. *Dammit.*

"Thank you," I said. *I'm sorry*, I thought. I scanned the rubric, impressed. The new grading sheet he'd created for the Mesopotamia project looked upgraded and thorough. "You did this yourself?"

"My dad helped." Luke kept staring at his shoe. My heart ached for him, for anything I'd done that might've hurt him.

What had Declan told him when he asked if I could be his tutor?

"It's perfect," I said.

Luke cleared his throat. "No big deal."

"But it is." Another sliver of guilt stabbed my insides. Luke had trusted me. He'd let himself like me. And I'd let him hope. *A dangerous thing.* "You should be really proud of yourself," I said. I kept my lips tight so they wouldn't shake.

"Whatever," he said. "At least my dad's not making me get a tutor."

Luke turned and walked away.

Twenty-One

The first weekend after school let out, Maren and I rescued an antique desk and filing cabinet from a garage sale. I spent a few days sanding them down, then stained both pieces a rich mahogany. The only thing my new and improved spare bedroom still needed was a coat or two of fresh paint. So I'd spread a tarp across the floor. In the corner sat brand new roller brushes, cans of primer, and semi-gloss paint in robin's egg blue. Tomorrow morning I'd wake up ready to slather yet another layer of Lia over years of *Mrs. Jake Townsend*.

When we'd first moved into the bungalow, Jake had argued against a home office. *You have a whole classroom to use*, he'd reminded me. And as a pilot he didn't need office space. So even though his sister was our only visitor—and she visited just once or twice a year—Jake thought our second bedroom should be for guests.

Charlotte hates staying with Mom and Dad.

From then on, my extensive book collection had gathered dust in our living room, and my computer lived in the nook beside our kitchen. But with Jake gone, I could finally have an office. A room of my own with a door to shut. Or to leave open.

Whatever I wanted.

I was securing painter's tape around the baseboards when Maren called out to me from the front of the house. "Lia! Where are you? Get your butt out here!"

"Patience, grasshopper," I said, as I joined her in the living room. Maren was standing beside the old guest room mattress and box springs that were propped against the bay window. Hefty bags stuffed with clothes crowded the other side of the entryway. I'd arranged for everything to be picked up by a truck collecting donations for the local women's shelter.

"Looks like somebody's been busy," Maren said.

"That's one word for it."

"Is all this for Safe Haven?"

"Yup."

"That's so great!"

"Well." I took in the clutter around me. "It's a start."

It was also the first Wednesday of June, and Maren was here to take me to book club. She'd rejoined six months after Nora was born, during a time when her sheer exhaustion—not to mention her desire for an evening free of diapers—helped me convince her to try another meeting. One month led to the next, and Maren had kept on trying. She still grumbled about the book choices and gave Veronica a wide berth, but she also loved an excuse to leave the house, and Danny loved his one-on-ones each month with Nora.

Since Maren and I had skipped the past two months, she'd suggested we "get back on the book horse." Her gaze traveled from my messy ponytail down to my bare feet now. "This is what you're wearing?"

"I'm having second thoughts," I said. "Would you hate me if I flaked tonight?"

"Yes," she said. "I would."

"But—"

"Please! I promised Veronica, and she scares me more than you do."

Maren's eyes pleaded with me, and I could tell this wasn't about Veronica. Maren was worried about me. "Fine," I said. "I'll go change. But I probably won't enjoy myself."

"Book club's not about enjoyment," Maren laughed. "It's about following through with a commitment."

While driving us to Jillian's house, Maren kept up her continual pep talk. She even suggested I use tonight to tell everyone about my marriage.

My marriage. Right.

"You don't want news leaking out. This group loves a thread of gossip. If you bring it up, you'll be in control." Once we stepped inside the house, however, the only one in control was Veronica Stinson.

First, she forced us to put our phones in our purses and leave our bags by the front door *so our discussion wouldn't be interrupted.* Then she dragged me into the kitchen to introduce me to her new neighbor.

"Lia, this is Bets Farinelli," she gushed, handing me a glass of wine. "Bets, this is Lia Townsend, the one I've been telling you about. Lia works at MBMS. You two have so much in common." She grinned at us. "So, chat!" Without another word, Veronica dashed off to intercept Tina Garcia and her purse at the front door.

"Welcome to book club," I said.

"Thanks." Bets smiled and twisted the napkin in her hand. "Is it always like this?"

"Pretty much," I told her. "Wine helps." I lifted my glass and attempted a laugh, but Bets looked like Bambi caught in headlights. That's when I realized Veronica was right.

Bets and I did have something in common.

Veronica clapped her hands to get everyone's attention and instructed all of us to take our seats. Maren motioned me over to the couch just as Veronica produced a dog-eared copy of *The Awakening.* Its pages were riddled with color-coded post-it notes. "Green represents the main character's strength," she said. "Yellow is her pain.

"Speaking of pain," I whispered to Maren, "I kind of want to drown myself like poor old Edna Pontellier."

Maren frowned. "Who are you calling old? Edna's younger than you are."

"Maybe," I said. "But I do see the appeal of walking fully-clothed into the waves. They'd feel so cool and lovely. And then *this* would all be over."

"Stop," Maren giggled.

"No, seriously. For the first time in my life, I'm glad I never learned to swim."

"I'm not giving you mouth-to-mouth," said Maren. "I'm only here because of you."

While the rest of the group sipped our wine, Veronica read us her favorite passages. During a brief pause, Tina Garcia suggested Edna's suicide might've been cowardly. Veronica peered at Tina from over her reading glasses.

"Let's analyze the book chronologically, not jump to the end, shall we?"

Tina said, "I just thought—"

"Do you have a specific passage marked?"

Tina's shoulders sank. "I ran out of post-its."

"So!" Jillian, the hostess, jumped in with her own question. "What bottle should I open next? Another white or are we ready for red?" I glanced at my own full glass of Sauvignon Blanc. *What had I been thinking coming here?*

"Maybe this is a good time for a break," Tina said, casting grateful eyes toward Jillian. Everyone else agreed, and Maren squeezed my knee.

"Don't drown yourself," she told me before rising from the couch. "I'll get us some snacks."

"But—"

She put a hand up. "You work on that wine." Left alone, I glanced over at Bets Farinelli and offered her a sympathetic smile. She was getting thrown into the deep end at her first meeting, but I was in no position to save her. So I pretended to leaf through my book until Maren returned carrying two plates of peel-and-eat shrimp with dollops of cocktail sauce.

"Seafood," she said, handing me a plate. "Get it?"

"Got it." My smile was more like gritted teeth.

"Are you mad at me for making you come?"

"No," I said. "I'm not." At least I didn't want to be.

"Is it Jake, then?" she asked. "Please tell me it isn't Jake." Veronica appeared, leaning over Maren's shoulder.

"What about Jake?" Veronica asked. I took a breath and groped for patience. Veronica cared about me. She did. But her intentions sometimes got lost in the execution. "Is everything all right?" she asked, and I almost said *yes, everything's fine,* but then—before I could think twice—I decided I might as well be honest. After all, tonight we were discussing a story that, in its own way, celebrated independence. *No time like the present, Lia.* My new truth wasn't going away.

I cleared my throat and got everyone's attention so I couldn't change my mind. "The thing is, Jake and I split up," I blurted out. Only after the fact did I notice I hadn't said *We're getting a divorce.* It was a small, unintentional detail, and anyway Jake and I weren't legally married. Maybe *splitting up* was the most accurate way to describe us.

"Oh, Lia. No!" Veronica set down her book and squeezed into the space between Maren and me. She gathered me into a hug, and when I finally pulled away, the rest of book club was staring at us.

"It happened more than two months ago," I explained. "So I've had some time to get used to it."

Veronica shook her head. "You never get fully used to it."

"What happened?" Tina asked. "Was it mutual?"

Maren interjected on my behalf. "It is now." I nodded half-heartedly, and my face flushed.

Veronica gasped. "So Jake left you?" When I didn't answer, she offered a weak smile. "Figures. Men are assholes."

"Yes, but some women are too," I said. Then I found myself repeating the same benign language I'd used when I'd told Pauline and Helen and Sari. *We're amicable. It's for the best. Some things aren't meant to be.* And my favorite optimistic gem: *I'm ready for my Act Two!*

Veronica took my hand. "Did Jake—I mean—there's no easy way to ask this, but is there someone else?"

I shrugged. *Josie. She was someone.*

"That means yes," Veronica said almost triumphantly, as if solving some great mystery.

"It means it doesn't matter," Maren told her.

"Maybe not," Veronica said, clucking. "I'm sorry, Lia. It's none of my business. I'm being dumb and nosy. Can you forgive me?"

I smiled at her, but my eyes grew wet. Veronica wasn't the first person to be curious, and she wouldn't be the last. "Onward and upward," I told her. "Really. I'll be fine."

Across the room, a phone went off inside someone's

purse. The sound was muffled, but I recognized the ringtone. I'd heard it a million times before. Danny was calling Maren. I took my hand back from Veronica while Maren hopped up to check her phone. Tina Garcia sat in Maren's spot. "Are you teaching summer school this year?" Tina asked. I started to tell her about my plans for the bungalow instead.

"Shhh," Maren said. "I can't hear my voicemail." We all quieted while she listened. Maren's expression clouded, then her hands started to shake. She looked at me and dropped her phone. "It's Nora. She's in the hospital."

Twenty-Two

On the way to the hospital, Maren played Danny's message on speaker phone. His voice sounded eerily calm. *Nora fell. We're in an ambulance on the way to Harbor. It's bad, but I don't think her neck's broken.*

"Nora will be all right," I told her. "She has to be all right." Maren sat beside me, stony-faced and silent. I was rushing her to the hospital where—less than four years ago—Nora had been born.

Each detail of that night was still etched in my heart like grooves on a vinyl record. Those short frantic ripples of Nora's first cries. The coppery smell as the doctor stitched up Maren. Danny waving me into the delivery room while Jake stayed in the hallway, hands stuffed in his pockets. When I leaned down to hug Maren, her gaze flickered between me and her baby. Nora's legs appeared bent, the folds covered in a sticky film. Maren begged me to find out if something was wrong.

What are they not telling me? What's happening with my baby?

A nurse recording Apgar scores said, "This little girl's just fine." Then she swaddled baby Nora and handed her to Danny. I stood beside him marveling at her squishy nose and baby-doll lashes. Two miniature ears, like seashells, were pressed against her head. "Look at her, Lia," Danny gushed. "My daughter's magic, isn't she?" When he handed her to me, I touched her skull, the thin skin pulsing there. Yes. She was a miracle. I was holding a miracle. But I wasn't her mother.

I passed Nora to Maren who unwrapped the blanket and ran her fingers down her daughter's scooped-in legs. For an hour, I watched her stroke those soft bones, willing them to straighten. It was a week before she believed the curve of her limbs was not unusual. Nora was simply mirroring her cramped position in the womb.

What a relief, Jake and I agreed when the legs fixed on their own. Days later, when I visited Maren, I was surprised to find her sobbing.

She confessed to how terrified she'd been that Nora might be deformed. Maren's fear had run so deep, she'd refused to trust the doctors in the hours after delivery. Instead of bonding with her baby, Maren had been heartsick and miserable. A week later, she was still torturing herself. "I'm the worst mother ever," she cried. "I'm evil, Lia. Evil."

"No, Mare. No, you're not."

"How stupid and superficial! I don't deserve a perfect baby! God, Lia. Why did I give a shit about crooked legs?" At the time, I didn't answer her. The question was rhetorical, and anyway, I had no idea how I would've felt in her position. There was a reason pregnant women insisted, "We just want a healthy baby." But was it unforgivably shallow for a mother to want her child to be smart and strong and lovely?

I shook off the memory as I pulled into the lot and dropped Maren at Harbor's emergency room. When Maren sprinted through the automatic doors, my hands trembled.

What if Nora's paralyzed? Could she die from such a fall?

I parked Maren's car in an adjacent lot and headed straight to the main lobby. There, a gray-haired volunteer gave me directions to Nora's room, and I hurried down a long, sterile hallway walled with sliding glass doors. Inside each room was a curtain drawn for privacy. As I passed, I wondered about the patients in those beds. Were they scared? Alone? Did they have people here who loved them? I turned the corner to the pediatric wing and froze. Jake was standing there, slouched against the wall.

He looked up at me, his mouth a thin line. "Hi, Lia."

I lifted my chin. "What are you doing here?"

"I was with Danny," he said. "Tonight. I swear we never took our eyes off her."

"What happened?"

"Nora fell out of the tree house."

"Oh. Oh God, Jake. No!"

Jake and Danny had built the tree house together, a project for Nora's third birthday. It was Jake's idea, and Maren had protested, loudly, claiming her daughter was still too young. "She won't be living out there," Danny told her. "We're not building her a dorm room. Just a place for tea parties and supervised climbing. You got something against climbing?"

OK, Maren said, relenting. *But no tea parties. Lia and I hate tea.*

Jake approached me slowly, as if I were a rattlesnake poised to strike. When he reached my side, I dropped my head and let him wrap his arms around me.

"How's Nora?" I said into his chest.

"The nurses won't tell me anything, but I overheard someone say they're moving her to Cedars."

My stomach seized, and I pulled away from him. "Moving her? Why?"

"I don't know."

"She has to be all right, Jake."

"Yes," he said. "She does."

"How's Danny?"

"I haven't seen him. Not since he left in the ambulance." Jake swallowed. "Maren wouldn't even look at me when she got here. She flew in there, and the door shut. Someone pulled the curtain. I have no idea what's happening." He reached a hand out to me, then dropped it. "I'm glad you're here."

"What do we do now?"

Jake shook his head. "We can wait here, but if she's being moved…"

"I'm going to Cedars."

"We'll both go," he said. It was then that I remembered Maren had picked me up for book club. Her car was in the hospital parking lot. Not mine.

"Shit."

"What?"

"We drove here in Maren's car. Mine's at home." *Our home. My home.*

"I'll give you a ride."

"No," I told him. "Thanks."

"Now's not the time to be stubborn, Lia."

"Ha!" I glared at him. When had it ever been the right time to assert myself with Jake?

"You can be mad at me," he said. "I won't try to talk you out of it. But let me drive you. Please."

"Fine," I said, hoping I sounded strong. "But just take me home. I'll drive myself to Cedars."

"If that's what you want," he said. "Should we go now?"

I nodded. "Remind me to grab a couple of sweatshirts from home." I took a beat. "I mean from the bungalow."

"I knew what you meant." Jake's voice was gentle, and my eyes welled. I blinked back tears, then decided to let him see.

Tears don't mean you're weak, Lia. They mean you're strong enough to love.

୭ৎ

I was silent on the ride home, mulling over worst-case scenarios. As scared as I was for Nora, I couldn't imagine how Maren felt. Had Regina ever been this worried about me? I seriously doubted it. In a moment of insanity, I wished my own neck were broken so I could maybe find out.

When we reached the bungalow, Jake stood behind me while I fiddled with the lock. I invited him in, and he followed me into the living room. I heard him exhale, but I didn't turn around. I didn't want to watch him scanning this space that once was his. Our mattress. The trash bags. My books stacked on the floor. I wouldn't let myself wonder what he was thinking. But he told me anyway.

"We should wait until tomorrow to go to Cedars," he said. "We'll be in the way tonight."

"What are you talking about?"

"Nora's transfer could take a while, and you know Danny. He'll start acting like our host, asking if we've eaten or slept.

Hating that we're stuck waiting around."

"I need to be there for Maren."

"She shouldn't have to worry about us. We'll hear from them when they're ready. Think about what's best for her. And for Nora and Danny."

"Oh, I see. So now you're thinking about others."

Jake winced. "What's that supposed to mean?"

"It means you didn't think about me much." I squared my shoulders. "And now that we're on the subject, tell me. How is Addie?"

"Yeah. About that." Jake ran a hand through his hair. "Maren said she told you Addie's Josie's mother." At this, my nose began to sting. Maren had talked about me with Jake? Why did this shock me? I shouldn't have been surprised.

"I guess somebody had to tell me," I said.

"Would things have been better if you'd heard from me?"

"It couldn't have been worse."

Jake nodded. At least we agreed on something. He stepped over a pile of Hefty bags and took a seat on the couch. "I haven't been with her, you know. Addie. Not in that way." His palms cupped his knees. "Not since you."

"I don't care."

He looked at me. "Yes, you do."

"It doesn't matter. You're together now."

"No," he said. "We're not." When I frowned he added, "Addie's moving to Portland at the end of the month."

"Ha!" I snorted. "Oregon?"

Jake nodded, lowered his gaze. "She wants to be near her dad. To work on things. Their relationship's been... strained."

"Oh." I paused then, and my cheeks burned. "So what about Josie?"

"She's going to Oregon too." His voice was quiet. Even vulnerable. To avoid sounding hopeful, I turned to sarcasm.

"Gee. I'm really sorry to hear that. I was hoping things would work out for you three."

Jake flinched. Almost imperceptibly, but I saw it. "It's what's best for them," he said. "Addie's a writer, so she can work anywhere. In Portland, she'll get to spend more time with her dad, and Josie can get to know her grandfather."

"What about Josie spending more time with *her* dad?" I asked. "That was the whole point, wasn't it? You left me to be with them? And now they're leaving you." My mouth twisted. "I wonder if that qualifies as irony."

"I knew they were going, Lia," he said. "Before."

"Before?" I choked on the word.

"Yes."

Jake had known Addie and Josie were moving, but he left me anyway. I could barely breathe, but I forced myself to speak. I had to know. "I assume you'll be joining them then," I said. "One big happy family in the Pacific Northwest?"

"Maybe," he said. "Maybe not. Either way, you won't have to be miserable anymore."

I took a step backward. "*I* was miserable?" I said. "You did this for *me*?" I laughed then, a hollow rasp.

Jake set his jaw. "Admit it, Lia. You weren't happy. You haven't been for a long time."

"I was happy, and you're rationalizing bad behavior. You can lie to yourself all you want, but you can't lie to me."

His eyes flashed, ready for battle. "You want to talk about honesty? You were *never* honest." I glared at him, but he nodded like we finally understood each other. "You were so determined to make things work with us, you became a different person. A stranger. I couldn't even recognize you, Lia. Tell me I'm wrong." A grim smile sliced his face. "It won't be true, but you can say it anyway."

"You're wrong."

"OK, I'm wrong," he said. "And now I'm leaving."

"Wait," I said.

"What?" Jake stood, met my gaze. "What?"

Without thinking, I advanced, crushing my mouth against his to shut him up. Stunned and still, Jake kept his arms at his sides, but then his lips began to part. I raised my chin, and his tongue moved to my throat, tracing a long, slow path along my neck. When he moved to embrace me, I took a step backward, and we began fumbling with our clothes. I tossed my blouse, heard his belt crack against the hardwood floor. The old guest room mattress loomed above us as we knelt together there. Naked and shivering, we clung to each other.

He pressed against me gasping for breath. My nails tore his back. He bit my lip. I tasted blood.

Good, I thought. *Good.*

Between us now was everything we'd ever known about each other, both familiar and strange. Our eyes locked as I shuddered in his arms. For a while we lay there like that, quiet. Then I looked away.

"All right," I said. "All right." Then I rolled off him.

"Jesus," he whispered. "What was that?"

"That was the end, Jake. And it's over. Now get out of my house."

Twenty-Three

When I was Nora's age, give or take a few months, Regina almost killed me. She never could pinpoint the date, but she thinks it probably happened in the spring. In any case, by the time she figured out that her herbal remedies weren't curing my "little bellyache," I was half dead from a burst appendix. Thank goodness for my grandmother, who finally took me to the hospital.

I spent more than a week there, but I was too young then to remember much about it now. I vaguely recall a nurse named Annabelle with a sugary voice and gentle hands. When I accidentally called her *Mama,* she smiled, and I wasn't even embarrassed. I told her I liked pudding, and after I could eat solid food again, she brought me one tapioca and one chocolate each night before bedtime.

My most vivid memory of my time in the hospital was the smell: a blend of citrusy soap and blood. Something else acrid and sharp. My own rotten breath, probably, since I don't recall anyone brushing my teeth. That smell kept me away from hospitals for a long time afterward, even when my grandmother was dying.

Back then, Regina told me my visiting wouldn't help. In fact, she insisted my grandmother would hate for me to see her like that. So fragile. A shell of who she'd been. I was too young to grasp the concept of *closure,* so I didn't beg to go. It wasn't until years later that I regretted not saying goodbye.

After that, on each of my grandmother's birthdays, I wished for one more chance to hold her hand. I thought about what I would've whispered in her ear had I been there at the end. What if my presence could've been a comfort to her? I vowed then never again to let my own fears keep me from the bedside of someone I loved.

Nora's birth was my first time back in a hospital after the week I'd spent there as a child. Unlike the ER and post-op rooms I'd been in, the maternity wing was its own joyful planet. In the Women's Pavilion, the walls were painted with grinning storks, each carrying bundles in their beaks to deliver to expectant families. Behind thick glass windows sat rows of bassinettes filled with newborns wrapped in pink and blue striped blankets. I watched for hours as nurses plucked them up one by one to be rocked. Fed. Loved. The entire space felt miraculous, calling out to me as if the air itself were singing.

Later that night, back at the bungalow, I couldn't sleep for all my racing thoughts, so I crept to my computer nook— quietly, so I wouldn't wake Jake—and googled nursing schools. Becoming a labor and delivery nurse would cost money, sure; but we had a little bit of money in the bank. After all, we'd been saving for a ring and a honeymoon. And I was willing to give that up for this new dream. As for the emotional toll nursing school would take, I'd already surrendered myself to teaching for the better part of a decade. I was ready to be moved by something new.

Whenever Jake talked about flying, the thrill of being a pilot radiated from him. I wanted a similar spark, some fresh goal to inspire me too. I assumed, or at least hoped, he'd understand this. I mean, he'd traded in law school for flight school. I felt equal parts excited and nervous to tell him.

In the morning when Jake awoke, I gushed to him about my plan. My heart hammered. I was desperate for his support. He nodded while I spoke, waited until I was done to weigh in, share his thoughts. That's when he told me I was free to take whatever path I chose. But when I pressed for his opinion, Jake had a list of cons.

Of course he did.

For one thing, teaching offered stability, and I wasn't

exactly one for recklessness. Plus, I had a credential already, and I was excellent at my job. Not to mention, everyone's enthusiasm waned for any given career. What if I grew tired of nursing? Would I want to change jobs again? Then there was the fact that my future nursing shifts could conflict with his flight schedule. I might be assigned nights and weekends when he was home. Did I want to risk precious time with him to rock a stranger's baby? The answer was no. Naturally. Making Jake happy was my most-important priority. And so, my bubble burst before I'd ever tried to fill it.

After I'd told Jake to leave the bungalow—get the fuck out, to be more accurate—we didn't speak again. He dressed in silence and left barefoot, carrying his shoes. As his car pulled away, I yanked on my pants and tank top without bothering to find the blouse I'd been wearing over it. I'd tossed it somewhere and was in too big a hurry to look. But I did remember to collect two sweatshirts from my closet. One for me. One for Maren. God, she must've been so scared. I was desperate to get to her, so I grabbed my car keys and rushed out into the night.

If Jake wanted to wait until after he'd heard from Danny to go to Cedars, that was all well and good for him. But I planned to be there before Maren arrived. Or, at the very least, soon after. Maybe she'd sense my presence in the waiting room or feel my support subconsciously. And even if she didn't, I'd know I'd been there. For her. For Nora. For Danny.

For me.

I didn't need Jake's approval or anyone else's for that matter. From now on, I'd show my love in my own way. And if I was ever miserable again, I'd have no one to blame but myself.

I arrived at Cedars hoping to beat the Hollisters there, but a woman at the reception desk said visitors weren't welcome until 8 a.m. When I inquired about Nora, she frowned and explained their privacy policy. She couldn't give information to non-family members.

Are you a family member?

No.

I thanked her for her help and returned to my car to get a little sleep. Visiting hours would arrive soon enough, and I'd be here. Ready. Maybe I'd been hasty to come here without being asked first, but I didn't regret my decision. "Jake was wrong," I said to no one but myself. Then I reclined my seat and tucked the spare sweatshirt I'd brought for Maren under my head.

Once again, the dream began on the beach.

I sat on a high dune, warm and safe beneath the blue sky, until the wind began to blow. Gently at first. Then the gusts became more urgent. As the sand slipped out from under me, grain by grain like an hourglass, I scrambled to my feet, but I couldn't stop the slide. Suddenly the sand disappeared, and I was bobbing, weightless on the waves. I opened my mouth to scream, but the squawk of a seagull came out instead. My wet clothes would drag me below the surface soon. I already felt too heavy. So I lay back, surrendering to the ocean, drifting. Drifting. The sun drenched me, and I grew hotter. So hot. Too hot. All at once, I realized I was naked, and my fingers began peeling my skin off in one long, thin piece. It didn't hurt, but I rolled over, face down on the water. Someone was calling to me from the shore. *Stop. Stop.* The voice was distant. Why wasn't I sinking? When had I learned to swim? The water was cool now. I'd be fine. But the strange voice called out again and again. Stop. Stop. A rhythmic pulse that I resented.

Let me float.

Stop. Stop.

I opened my eyes, and my phone was buzzing in the cup holder. I answered Maren's call, my stomach in knots. "Hey! What's going on? How's Nora?"

"She's stable for now." Maren sounded small and far away. "There's a lot of swelling, but her spine wasn't severed."

"Oh, Mare. What a relief! I was thinking of all the worst possible—"

"I know," she said. "Me too."

"I'm so sorry." I wiped at my eyes. "You must be a wreck."

"I can't be," she said. "Danny's completely fallen apart. He won't stop crying, and he keeps apologizing. He's useless right now, and one of us has to keep it together. For Nora."

"Jake told me she fell out of the tree house."

Maren paused before replying, and I wondered if she blamed Jake at all for what happened. "You saw him?"

"Jake? Yeah. Last night."

"So you know he was with Danny. At our house."

"Yes," I said. "I know."

"Did you know that's why I offered to pick you up for book club? I didn't want you to come by and see Jake at our place. But you might as well hear it from me now, since I'm sure he didn't have the balls to tell you."

"What are you talking about?"

"Jake's been staying with us."

I sucked in a breath.

"I didn't tell you because it's only temporary, and I knew you'd be upset. But I can't worry about your feelings right now. Not after Nora." Maren's voice sounded flat and dull. "I'm done walking on eggshells, Lia. With both you and Jake."

I closed my eyes, trying to wrap my brain around what I was hearing. How long had Jake been living with the Hollisters? Was he there the night I asked Maren to find out about the Townsends' Fourth of July party? And what about Addie moving to Portland? Did Maren know about that too? Sure, we'd agreed not to talk about Jake, but if he'd been staying there... Oh God. What did they all say to Nora?

We don't want to hurt Auntie Lia's feelings, so we can't tell her about Uncle Jake.

Jake.

All at once I recalled how my mouth felt pressed against his last night. He'd been cold at first, then eager. Jake wanted me, and I'd wanted him too. But when I told him to get out, he must've gone to Maren's after leaving our place. *My place.*

Shit.

I shouldn't care where Jake went. He wasn't my concern

anymore. But Maren was, and I had to assume now that she and Danny had been talking about me to Jake. Talking about Addie. Josie. Oregon. All of it. And why not? He was living with them. I wasn't.

My throat tightened, a noose around my neck.

"Lia? Say something."

I swallowed. If Maren was looking for some kind of fight to redirect her fear, well, she wouldn't get it from me. Not now. "Nora's what matters," I said. "I've been so worried about her."

"Of course you have." Maren's words were softer now, and slow. She sounded more exhausted than I'd ever heard her. "I would've called sooner," she said, "but my phone died. I had to borrow a charger from one of the nurses in the PICU."

"I have a charger," I said. "I'll bring it up. Can Nora have visitors yet?"

"There's a two-person limit, but the nurses seem to like us. I think visiting hours start at eight. That's in, like, fifteen minutes? I can ask them to let you in."

"Are you sure?"

There was a pause, and I imagined Maren nodding. At least I hoped she was. "I've never been so scared, Lia. I need to see your face."

"Done," I said. "But besides my face, what else can I bring you?"

"Coffee. Dan and I've been awake all night, but neither one of us wants to leave Nora."

"Oh, Mare." My eyes filled with tears. "I'll bring you two giant vats of coffee. And none of that hospital crap, OK? There's got to be a decent coffee shop near Cedars I can hit up in the next fifteen minutes."

"Probably," Maren said. There was a pause. "But we're at Harbor."

"What are you talking about? Jake said—"

"There was talk of a transfer, but Nora's doctor decided—Wait. You went to Cedars? How long have you been there?"

"Well..."

"Crap."

"No, no! It's fine. No big deal. Not at all. Promise." I started up my car. "Just focus on Nora. I'll be there as soon as I can. With coffee. And I've got a sweatshirt for you too."

"Lia, I don't know what I'd do without you." *I don't know either*, I thought. But we could talk about that later.

Now was not the time.

ᔒᔕ

My car was parked outside the Coffee Bean on Harbor Boulevard when the battery died. I'd been in such a hurry to get in and order, I left the keys in the ignition. At least the car hadn't been stolen. But when I came out with a bag of chocolate chip muffins and a cardboard carrier of to-go cups, the engine clicked at me. *Tick tick tick.* I pounded the dashboard.

Goddammit!

I couldn't call Pauline. She was teaching summer school. Uber was fast, but then my car would be stuck here, a problem on the back end. I flat-out refused to ask Jake for help. He'd learn soon enough that Nora wasn't at Cedars, and I didn't want to see his face when he realized he'd been right not to rush there. My new Triple-A card was still sitting in a pile of mail on the kitchen counter. What the hell was I supposed to do? I scrolled through the contacts on my phone and—without thinking—placed the call.

"I'm so, so sorry to bother you," I blurted out, my words rattling like machine-gun fire. "But I'm stuck on Harbor Boulevard at the Coffee Bean, and my car won't start, and I have to get to the hospital, and I swear I wouldn't ask, but it's an emergency."

"I just dropped Luke at the Y. I'll be there as soon as I can. Take a breath."

"Thank you," I breathed. "Thank you so much."

I closed my eyes and leaned back in my seat to wait for Declan McKinley.

Declan

Being a widower is very sad and also very odd. You're a mess and desirable at the same time. People want to fix the parts of you that broke while kind of hoping you stay wounded. You're a project for them, something to work on. But once you're strong again, the appeal's gone. At least that's what it felt like to me.

When Shannon died, I figured that was it. She'd been the love of my life. Irreplaceable. But everyone kept saying I'd find somebody new. Someday. *You're only 35. You owe it to yourself. And to Luke. It's what she would want. Take your time, but when you're ready, I have a nice woman for you.*

I told them Shannon was nice.

It took about a year for well-intentioned friends to start sending me numbers. *Someone you might like to meet.* A few suggested dating websites. Jimmy Krakauer even tried to make me a profile. On Match, I think. Maybe Tinder. I wasn't interested.

Thanks but no thanks.

Luke was all I cared about, the only thing that mattered. He looked just like his mother, which was a blessing and a curse. To see the person you love, the one you thought you'd grow old with, reflected in the face of your kid? It felt like a miracle when Shannon was alive. It tore me up when she was buried.

But the last thing Luke needed was his dad falling to

pieces. The poor kid was only ten and down a parent already. So I threw myself into fatherhood, took care of all the things my wife used to. Pediatrician appointments. The dentist. Soccer practice. Open House.

That's where I met Lia Townsend.

Lia was different. She treated Luke like a person, not like a job. And since her class was two years after we lost Shannon, she never got that obligatory email from the counselor:

Watch out for Luke. His mom just died. He might be fragile.

Damn, Luke hated those emails. He said he could feel the teachers watching from across the room, waiting for him to crack. So he didn't crack, even when he needed to. Then Ms. Townsend came along. She didn't know I was a single parent. She didn't know Luke had no mother. She cared about him anyway. She seemed to care about us. It felt like it, at least.

Lia looked at me in a way no one had in years. I didn't see pity in her face, just a smile that said, *Hey, you might be interesting.* What an ass, right? I wanted to be interesting to a woman for some reason other than my dead wife. Maybe. Finally.

The thing is, I liked Lia Townsend. A whole hell of a lot. I even started thinking about the future again. A future with her.

And then I found out she was married.

Twenty-Four

On our first drive up the coast together, Jake and I got a flat. And while I sat on the guardrail doing nothing, he replaced the tire himself. I was already half in love with him and found his competence super sexy. Competence was something I wanted even more than sex back then. I needed someone who could handle his own business and maybe help out with mine. When I told Jake he looked sexy, he laughed, but I was serious. I was also so nervous about bringing him to Regina's I could barely muster a smile.

At that point, Jake had heard stories about her, but I wasn't sure he was ready for the real thing. I pictured Regina's toilet handle rigged with a coat hanger. The rusty old sink in her kitchen. Linoleum floors patched with particle board and glue. After my grandparents passed, Regina would start a repair, then move on without finishing the task. Although she claimed to be gifted in many ways, she lacked follow-through. With everything, really.

Including raising her daughter.

I was in middle school when, thanks to a string of uncomfortable slumber parties, I learned other families didn't live in a constant state of disrepair. After that, I stopped inviting people over. I was afraid Regina would be ripping up the carpet with big plans to paint the concrete. Or that she'd be covered in clay and claim her pottery was a gift for the president of the United States. Because worse than the wire hanger was the unpredictability of Regina's behavior toward others. She either fawned over someone or talked incessantly about herself. Both options made me embarrassed. No, mortified.

In some ways, the days Regina took to her bed were a relief. That routine was predictable, at least. I'd bring her oatmeal in the morning. Soup after the sun set. At night she'd cry for hours, while I sat there rubbing her shoulders. In those moments, Regina needed me, and that felt good. Purposeful. When she'd wake up manic and whirling again, all I wanted was to escape.

Now, as Declan McKinley prepared to jump-start my car, I couldn't help thinking *Here you go again, Lia. The helpless princess being rescued by a prince.* But what else could I do? I had to get to Maren. To Nora. Declan was just—

"Almost done," he said, glancing over his shoulder. He'd caught me staring at him for sure.

"You're not going to shock yourself, are you?" I asked.

"Nah. This is easy stuff." He turned back, attached his jumper cables to some part of my car I couldn't identify. "Let's try starting her up," he said, heading toward his car. After revving his engine, Declan waved his arm, and I turned the ignition. *Click click click.* I pressed the gas, and my car roared to life.

"Yes!" I shouted above the rumble. Declan hopped out of his car and detached the cables stretched between our hoods. Then he came around to my window. "Thanks so much," I said.

"No problem." He took a beat. "You changed your hair."

My hand flew up to what must've been a tangle of auburn. I'd slept in the car after all, after having sex with Jake. My cheeks flamed thinking about it. "Just the color," I said. Did he like it? I stopped myself from wondering. This wasn't about me or my damn hair.

His gaze cut to the box of to-go cups in my passenger seat. "You sounded pretty upset when you called me," he said. "I'm assuming the emergency isn't about coffee?"

"It's my best friend's daughter," I told him, fielding a stab of guilt at having forgotten about Nora even for a minute.

"There was an accident. She's in the hospital. The coffee is for her parents."

"Ah." Declan nodded.

"She's not even four years old. Nora, I mean. I'm her godmother. Well, not actually. Just an honorary one, if that makes sense. It probably doesn't make sense. A lot about me doesn't." Declan nodded again, and I wanted so badly to explain the whole truth to him, for his own sake as well as mine. But I needed to get to the hospital, and anyway, I didn't know how to broach the subject. *So, hey. About that husband you think I have…*

"I'm just glad I could help," he said.

"Guess that's a theme with you."

He smiled then. Just a small one. "Well, you helped us too." I noticed he said *us*. Not me. Not Luke. Us. But then a shadow crossed his face. "Look, Lia. I'm sorry about that last email. I shouldn't have said anything about Luke or Shannon or—"

"No!" I interrupted. I couldn't let him leave thinking he'd done something wrong. "It's my fault, and there's something I need to tell you. About the night you met Charlotte."

"She didn't think anything was going on with us, did she?"

"Of course not. But she wouldn't have minded."

"She's your husband's sister, isn't she?"

"Yes and no. She's Jake's sister, but he's not my husband. Not anymore. I mean, he never was."

Declan shook his head. "Now, I'm really confused. I'm also late for work."

"It sounds complicated, I know, but I can explain."

"Please." His hands flew up, like he was being arrested. "Don't let me add to the complications. I've had enough of those in the past couple years. Luke and I are fine now. I hope you'll be too."

"But—"

"The school year's over, Lia."

"Yes."

"And I gotta go." He started walking toward his car, and I felt my insides begin to unspool.

"Wait!" I blurted out. "I can still tutor him." When Declan

looked back over his shoulder, I said, "This summer, I mean. If you decide he needs it."

"I don't think it's a good idea."

"If you change your mind..." I let the sentence trail off. Instead of responding to the half-offer, Declan pointed at my hood.

"Leave the engine running for at least a half hour," he said. "Or it'll die on you again. And you should probably get your battery checked. From the sound of it, this one's on its last legs."

He climbed into his car then, and the message was loud and clear: Declan McKinley was not signing up to be Lia Townsend's new prince charming. *Fine,* I thought. *I need to figure things out on my own anyway.* But as he drove away, I felt lonelier than I had in a very long time.

৩৵৻

I stayed by Nora's bedside with Danny and Maren the rest of the day while Jake went to the Hollisters' to disassemble the tree house. Just before three o'clock he called me, and I stepped outside Nora's room to talk. My cheeks burned at the sight of his name on the screen.

Hadn't he done enough? What did Jake want from me now?

He was quick to apologize for bothering me, but apparently Danny and Maren weren't answering their phones, and he was desperate for an update. Nora was his goddaughter, too, and he felt guilty about the tree house. So I filled him in on everything, answering his questions the best I could. But when Jake's pauses lengthened, I sensed he had something else on his mind.

"You're sure she's going to be fine," he repeated.

"Yes."

"And they won't have to move her to Cedars."

"No." I waited for him to tell me he'd been right, but he didn't. Instead he said, "I couldn't sleep."

I leaned back against the wall. "It was a long night."

"Should we talk about it?"

"No." There was nothing left to say. We'd both been

vulnerable and scared last night, and we'd wanted things to be normal. Sex used to bring us together. Afterward I'd lie in Jake's arms feeling safe. Secure. Loved. But anger and fear sparked what happened last night, not love. That was no reconnection.

It was an amputation.

"Anyway," I said, "I should get back to Maren." Without waiting for Jake to respond, I ended the call and silenced my phone.

From the doorway, I watched Maren stroke Nora's damp head and found myself wondering, for just a moment, about Jake's feelings for Josie. Did he inherit paternal instincts the minute he found out he was a father, or were these emotions developed over time?

I had a friend from college, Melissa Shallenberger, who never warmed to motherhood. Everyone promised her she'd be a fantastic mom. And when Mel admitted to being nervous, people scoffed. Everyone at the baby shower told her, "Just wait. It's a love like no other!"

We believed it. So did Mel. But when I saw her after her son was born, she didn't rave about her baby. No, she barely looked at him. Her face was gaunt, eyes emptied of light. One day, Mel just took off, left her husband to raise the baby on his own. There'd been plenty of speculation, then, much judgment and clicking of tongues. What a shame, people said. How could she be so selfish? But I felt sorry for Melissa.

How horrifying to discover the maternal feelings you'd been promised never materialized. In our final conversation, Mel admitted being a mother wasn't anything like she'd expected. Not wonderful or even terrible. There was no black and white. Her life was just... gray. Maybe some people were immune to the parenting virus and wouldn't ever settle into the role, no matter how much they wanted to. This would explain a lot about Regina. She never wanted to be a mother in the first place.

When I told Maren that Jake was getting rid of the tree house, she kept her eyes fixed on Nora and said, "He never should've bought it for her."

From his chair across the room, Danny spoke up. "I

helped build the damn tree house too," he said. "Jake loves Nora as much as anyone."

"Not as much as I do," Maren said.

༖

When Nora was finally released, the doctor told Maren and Danny to keep her activity to a minimum. "For at least a day or two." He also warned that in the future, they should be mindful of concussion. Her head was fragile now. More susceptible to damage. Suddenly, Nora seemed extra breakable. Watching Maren flutter over her, I was certain she'd secure the girl in bubble wrap if she could.

As we left the hospital, the Hollisters pulled up next to me at the light. Danny honked, and I tried to smile. But a pit opened in my stomach. The three of them were returning home, and I knew Jake would be there too. As long as I'd known him, Jake never worried about intruding. I was the one who used to point out when Danny yawned or when Maren checked the clock. *We should go*, I'd whisper. *It's time*. Jake would look at me like I was crazy.

Without me hinting around, would Jake even realize the Hollisters needed space? I almost called him but decided not to. From now on Danny and Maren could hash out their own dynamics with Jake.

Then, after Nora was better, Maren and I could work on ours.

When I got home, my neighbor, Harold Green, was washing his Volkswagen out front. For the task, he'd donned a red bathing suit and slicked his gray hair into a ponytail. When he saw me, he raised a soapy sponge, and I acknowledged him with a nod.

No, I thought. *Not now. Please, Harold. I can't.*

A bachelor, in his late sixties, Harold enjoyed discussing the weather. Upcoming elections. Gas prices. He was a friendly guy, and I liked him. Usually. But Jake's car had been gone for weeks, then it reappeared again out of nowhere last night. I figured Harold would've noticed. There was little he didn't see.

"I like to keep an eye out," Harold told us the day we moved next door. "It's what good neighbors do," he said. "Don't worry. You two can count on me." He had a telescope in his bedroom, and Jake and I used to joke he had it trained on ours. The two houses were so close you could touch them at the same time by spreading your arms.

Harold strolled toward my car now, shielding his eyes against the sunset. "Howdy," he said when I opened the door. "Everything OK?"

I nodded.

"You look tired."

I nodded again.

"School out for summer?"

"I'm heading inside," I said, not wanting to nod a third time. Then I smiled. Harold's kindness was almost more than I could bear. He took a step forward, lines grooved across his forehead.

"If you need anything," he said. A lump swelled in my throat.

"Thank you, Harold." I turned then and trudged to the front door.

For a long time, when I thought back to that moment standing there with Harold in front of my house, I remembered the goose bumps on my arms. I'd accidentally left my sweatshirt in Nora's hospital room and was wearing only a tank top. An ocean breeze had kicked up.

That's it, I thought. *I'm just chilly.*

But later, I decided a part of me must've sensed what was coming, and my body was already preparing for the change. It became almost funny to me, really—not laughing funny, more like ironic—that after all those dreams of drowning, I was dry the day I watched my life burn up.

Twenty-Five

The smell was nothing like I expected. Even after I'd showered twice and put on fresh clothes, it lived in my hair, had crawled under my skin. There was a new layer inside me I couldn't shake. And this stench—caustic and chemical—was even worse than the sound of the fire, although that stuck with me too. Loud pops in my ears, sharp and crackling, like lashes from a whip. They kept coming no matter how hard I tried to stop them.

And I did try to stop them.

I swear.

Later, outside the smoldering remains of my home, the fire chief told me extinguishers are set with pins. *You have to pull them,* he said. *They won't work with the pin still in it.* Under the wide brim of his hat, his eyes were kind and free of judgment. But I judged myself. I was so stupid. And I'd paid a steep price for my ignorance.

The fire chief placed himself between me and the vultures who prey upon the bereft. Contractors and insurance adjusters. They all lined up waiting to shake my hand while two fire companies tore holes in my roof.

"Sorry for your loss, ma'am," each one said. "Is your husband home?" They were soft-voiced and patient. Their tone conveyed concern, but the content of their message was this: *You need me. More than you need this other guy behind me. Or the one who just left. Please, sign here.*

I blinked at them, one by one, but I couldn't cry. The smoke had sucked up my tears. After a while, the fire chief told them, "She's had enough tonight. Come back tomorrow."

Tomorrow, I thought? *By tomorrow this will be over.*

Harold brought me a blanket. It was warm and smelled of Downy. I wrapped the blanket around me and closed the edges until I was enveloped like a cocoon. But there was no rebirth for me. Just smoke and labored breath. Disbelief.

"Do you want me to call Jake?" Harold asked.

I dropped my chin. "He doesn't live here anymore."

"Let's go inside, then. I'll put on some coffee, and you can use my phone to make some calls."

"There's no one else," I said. "No one I want to talk to, at least."

After the flames were out, several firemen stayed to pick at the smoldering remains, digging in the attic to be sure all the hot spots had been extinguished. The chief with the kind eyes approached, and I saw his nametag read Chief Wright. He told me an arson investigator from the city needed to ask me a few questions. I shook my head to clear the fog, and for the second time in a matter of months, I wondered when I'd wake up from this nightmare.

"It'll be quick," the chief said. "Don't be nervous."

"Mr. Wright? Will you stay with me?" He looked over his shoulder at what was left of the bungalow, blackened bones calling out accusations. "Sure," he said. "Call me Kenny."

Frederick Jones, the arson investigator, had a face like a hawk and a handshake to match. Like everyone else, he apologized for my loss, then he walked me through the scene. I told him I'd been gone all night at the hospital. That I'd returned just before sunset. Then, when I opened the front door, I smelled smoke. And the wind blew in, and the flames ignited. Just like that.

How long before the room was engulfed? Where did you see the first flames? Here? Are you sure? And then what? And after that?

I don't remember my answers. Not exactly. Despite Chief

Kenny's assurances, I was afraid. *What had I done wrong?*

Mr. Jones asked if I'd tried the extinguisher, and I said I didn't know to remove the pin. So I ran to the bathroom, but I couldn't find the cleaning bucket. By then the mattress and the bags of clothes and the drapes were on fire. And all my books.

"How much time had passed?"

"I don't remember. Maybe a minute or two. It felt longer."

"And that's when you exited the premises."

"I wanted my computer, but it was in the guest room. I mean my office. I was afraid I'd be trapped."

"Did you take anything with you?"

"No," I said. "Just me."

Mr. Jones went to his car then to fill out his report. Afterward, he didn't talk to me, he just left a copy with Fire Chief Kenny. The exact cause of the fire was inconclusive, but they all thought it was electrical, the point of origin in a back corner of our living room.

An old cord, maybe. The floor lamp.

A picture flashed in my head of Jake and me last night, and my blouse tossed over the lampshade. I'd been so caught up in him, and then so desperate to get to Nora, I couldn't remember if I'd turned the lights off.

"You OK?" asked Chief Kenny.

"I don't know," I said. I meant it. "When can I get back into the house?"

He took off his hat, and his salt-and-pepper hair was ringed with sweat. "Not for a while," he said. "I'm sorry."

While the other fire trucks pulled away in a quiet caravan, sirens turned off, Chief Kenny stayed to help me choose a contractor to board up my property. A crew got to work with boards and caution tape, and Kenny offered me his big flashlight. "Just in case."

"Are you leaving?" He squinted at me, and a lump gathered in my throat. I felt suddenly alone despite the men working behind me.

"Thanks for everything," I told him.

"It's what I do," he said.

"Still." I thought I would cry then, but I didn't.

Chief Wright was climbing into his truck when Stephen Stashik, my insurance agent, called. He told me how sorry he was for my loss. Then he said, "I've got a temporary room for you and Mr. Townsend at the Comfort Suites. I tried to reach Mr. Townsend but—"

"Thanks," I said. "I'll handle it."

"Then you're all taken care of, Mrs. Townsend."

"Lia."

"OK, Lia. When you arrive, tell the front desk you're the ones from the fire."

I looked down at my soot-stained clothes. "I think they'll know," I said.

They knew.

I brought nothing with me to the hotel except my purse and the clothes I was wearing. Everything reeked. My tank top and jeans. My bra and underwear. Even Harold's blanket. I didn't realize how bad it was until I got out of the shower. I stood in the hotel bathroom, shivering above the pile of my stinking clothes. I couldn't put them back on. I didn't even want to touch them, so I kicked everything into the hallway. Then I shut the door on the smoky remains of my old life.

I thought about calling someone. Jake. Maren. Regina. But my brain was fuzzy, and I couldn't find the energy. Instead, wrapped in a plain white towel, I curled up on the hotel room's stiff couch. I didn't bother to get into bed. I figured I wouldn't sleep anyway.

At two o'clock in the morning, my phone battery died. There were several chargers at the bungalow—*there had been several*—but not anymore. And I'd given the one from my car to Maren to use in the hospital. I had the vague idea that being unreachable should bother me, but my mind was numb. Important business awaited me. In the morning there would be more papers to sign. Wait. It was the morning.

Get it together, Lia.

I'd have to tell Jake at some point. But I wasn't ready to explain what had happened. To me. To us. Not yet. I'd wait until I could figure out what I wanted to do.

What did I want?

It was an absurd question. I was sitting in a towel on a couch in a Comfort Suites with nothing but a dead cell phone. What else could I possibly need?

I started laughing until hot tears streamed down my face. Maybe being alone wasn't healthy. I glanced at the hotel phone on the nightstand. I could call someone. Or ask the front desk if they had a charger I could borrow. But I did neither of these things. Instead, I threw my still-wet towel on the floor, crawled naked into bed, and slept for the first time in two days.

Twenty-Six

When I finally woke and poked my head into the hallway, my smelly clothes still lay there in a heap. A part of me wished they'd been taken, but I couldn't very well wear a towel. So I slipped back into the outfit I'd first put on Wednesday night. Hours of airing out hadn't dampened the stench, and a charge went through me like flames through my old mattress. I tied my hair into a knot, then scrubbed my face one more time. But below the skin, I still felt dirty.

Like I'd never be clean again.

A breakfast buffet was finishing up in the lobby. A tray of scrambled eggs the color of dead grass sat at one end. Beside the eggs were shriveled bacon strips in an open serving dome. My stomach lurched. I turned my back on the food and hurried to the parking lot. I was halfway to Manhattan Beach Middle School before I realized it was summertime, and I had no classes. I had to go home, to witness what was left of it.

When I pulled onto my street, a half dozen insurance adjusters stood behind the caution tape toting clipboards and serious expressions. Harold was also there, pacing in his bathing suit and flip flops, but now he wore a sweatshirt zipped to his chin. As soon as he spotted me, he hurried to my car, slid into the front seat, and slammed the door.

"Where did you disappear to last night? I went to make a pot of coffee, but when I came out, you were gone." He splayed his hands as if he'd just made a rabbit disappear. I shifted my focus over his shoulder to the strangers milling in my yard.

"Oh, them," he said. "These jokers started lining up at the crack of dawn. I've been watching from my window. Keeping an eye out as I do. That guy in the red jacket? He's been here the longest. Keeps trying to step over the caution tape to get a better look. At what, I couldn't tell you."

"Harold?" It was the first word I'd spoken since last night. My voice sounded creaky and distant, as if returning from miles away. "Could you maybe lend me something to wear?"

He glanced at my filthy jeans and the tank top I'd been wearing under the blouse that probably set my house on fire. "I can't promise you'll be a fashion plate," he said. "But I'll find you something."

As I followed Harold up his walkway, the line of strangers with clipboards looked on. The man in the red jacket took a step toward us, but Harold lifted a palm, and the man stopped. A pale woman with jet-black hair stood behind him, the only female on the scene. She was reed thin, almost skeletal. She made eye contact with me and nodded.

I can wait, her nod seemed to say. *Take your time, Lia. Take your time.*

"That one seems nice," Harold said over his shoulder. "I'd go with the lady if I were you."

"Go with her where?"

"Beats me. I don't know what those people are here for."

When I was in kindergarten, a fireman came to speak to our classroom. We still said *fireman* back then, not *firefighter*. I liked the man's moustache and his uniform. It was bright yellow like the highlighter pens on Ms. Murphy's desk. I don't recall the name of the fireman, but I do remember my excitement turning to unease and finally terror as he asked us about our family's plan for an emergency. It was our job, he explained, to make sure our loved ones were safe. We needed escape routes and ladders. Twice a year the batteries in our smoke detectors should be checked. I was pretty sure we didn't have any smoke detectors, and I knew we didn't have a ladder. My grandfather was gone. My grandmother was sad. It would be my fault if what was left of our family died.

Regina was annoyed by my nightmares. She insisted I was safe, that she'd sacrificed a lot to make sure of it. The only reason she was stuck in this place was because she'd wanted what was best for me. Eventually, when my bad dreams continued, Regina told me a secret:

Our house is special. It can't burn. It's made of stuff fire can't touch.

When I pointed out that wood burns, she explained our wood was magic. Called *siding*. I believed her because I was tired, and I wanted to sleep again. I'd been sick with fear, but I turned it off. Like a light switch. Maybe I hadn't been worried enough.

I used to get frustrated when Jake left lights on. I told him he was being wasteful, but he brushed off my concern. "People walking by will think someone's home," he said. "So what if it costs us a few extra pennies each month? Leaving on a light or two keeps us safer in the long run."

Maybe.

But two nights ago, when I rushed to Cedars, I must've left my blouse draped across the lampshade. I'd been determined to get to the hospital before Maren. Determined to prove Jake wrong. In my eagerness, did I forget to turn the lights off? Had I ignored a whiff of singeing?

"Lia."

I blinked.

"More coffee?" asked Harold.

I nodded. I was wearing a pair of his cotton drawstring pants tied tightly at the waist. He'd also loaned me a long-sleeved T-shirt from a Rolling Stones concert decades ago. *Keep it*, he said. *And the blanket. I've got plenty. Won't even miss it.* And as he refilled my mug, I let myself wonder for the first time if I'd let Jake's bungalow burn on purpose.

Until the fire, I'd never heard of an insurance adjuster. But that day, I met six people who assured me I needed to hire one. "If not me, then someone," said the man in the red jacket. His name was Tony Robinson. "You'll want an advocate," he explained. His voice was deep and gentle. "A person to serve as mediator between you and your insurance company."

"That's the main difference between an insurance agent and an insurance adjuster," said Jean Mortimer, the rail-thin woman. According to her, our agent, Stephen Stashik, worked for Farmers. "But if you hire me, I'll be working for you." Her smile was friendly enough, but her eyes were cold. By that time, I'd talked to five other adjusters and the conversations had begun to blur. It took me a while to figure out what Ms. Mortimer was admitting: She'd oversee all the details of the rebuild and the replacing of lost items. For this service, her company would receive ten percent of my insurance settlement. "Of both the contents and the structure," she added.

"What does that mean?"

"Your home is the structure," she told me. "Your things—whatever's burned or been irreparably damaged—that's the contents." At the word *irreparably*, her eyes traversed the space that once had been my living room. "Most of your stuff here's a total loss. You'll need money to replace it. I have a guy who comes to make a list."

"A list of what?"

"Of everything."

"Oh." *Everything.*

"Your insurance company will research the price of lost items and cut you a check, but I can get you more."

"More than what?"

"More than Farmers." She licked her lips. "They want to give you as little money as possible. I'm the opposite. The more I get for you, the better it goes for me." What did she mean by *the opposite*? Was that even legal? I sucked in a breath, and for a moment, I wished Jake would walk through the door. Well. What used to be the door. Now it was cheap particle board secured with metal bolts.

I took Jean Mortimer's card and said I'd be in touch. But when I got back to my hotel room, I called Tony Robinson and hired him. He said he'd be right over. I met him in the lobby. He brought a phone charger and hugged me.

We sat together in two large chairs across from the reception desk. Tony answered all my questions and was patient with my fogginess. After I signed the contract, he handed me a check. "This is to tide you over while we get started on the process."

I looked at the check and gasped. "Ten thousand dollars?" It was a terrifying sum. Exactly how much had I lost? The number made my disaster seem even worse.

"It sounds like a lot," Tony said, "but believe me. You'll need more than that. And you'll get it too." He told me to use the money to replace anything that couldn't wait a few weeks. Like my computer. And emergency clothing. "Have you done any shopping yet? New socks? Underwear? Pajamas?"

I looked down at Harold's drawstring pants. "No."

"When you do, hold on to the receipts."

Caleb Stone's face appeared before me then, as he paid for Regina's sink.

Keep the receipt, I'd told him that day. Had she ever paid him back?

Tony left, and I went up to my room to charge my dead phone. I had no missed calls. No new texts. *Fine.* I didn't want to talk to anyone anyway. I silenced the phone, left it on the nightstand. Afternoon sunlight streamed through the window, and I smelled a wisp of smoke. Was the scent real or in my head? Either way, I needed rest. I shut the curtains and put the *Do Not Disturb* sign on the door, then crawled into bed. I was exhausted, but unlike my phone, my inner voice couldn't be silenced.

How come you haven't called Jake yet? Or Maren. Regina?

What makes you think you can handle any of this on your own?

After a sleepless hour, I checked my phone again. Still no missed calls or texts from Jake or the Hollisters. Maren and Danny were busy worrying about Nora, and they had no reason to think anything major had happened to me. As for Jake, I was glad he hadn't tried to contact me again. He'd sounded so strange when he called me at the hospital yesterday.

Was that only yesterday?

I could hear it in his voice. Guilt. Indecision. The sex had sent him reeling.

I scrolled through my contacts, and my finger hovered over Maren's. Already, I'd waited too long to reach out to her. I could predict the questions. The confusion.

Why didn't you call me sooner?

Are you all right?

Seriously, what the hell is wrong with you?

Maren would be hurt, maybe even angry; but did I care? Right now I felt nothing but hollow space between us. She was on the other side of a chasm with her husband. Her daughter. My ex. She and Danny had chosen Jake over me. I couldn't imagine ever bridging that gap. But I couldn't imagine severing our thread either.

Snip snip, Lia. Don't look back.

I shook my head. That was too much like Regina. Too self-centered and dramatic. *All about me.* No matter what, I couldn't let my friendship with Maren turn to ashes. The frame of us would stand. Just like my house.

Twenty-Seven

I drove to the bungalow at sunset, the exact time of yesterday's fire. I couldn't call it home any longer. It was a movie set. An illustration. With my newly-charged phone, I took a picture from the front yard and sent it to Maren. Then I looked at what the shot revealed.

The bungalow was a black yawn, toothless and tired, with patches of roof caved in. Harold's home, a slice of it, was on the left side of the picture. On the other side was the bungalow owned by Sol Dempsey. Each summer he rented it by the week to families who wanted a beach-adjacent vacation. Now, the place would be fire-adjacent, sharing space with a construction zone.

Sol will be so pissed.

The street was quiet as I unlocked the padlock on the temporary front door. Already, I recognized the smell. It probably lived inside my nose now. In the entryway, my bags of clothes were a soup of soggy blackness. Gnarled beams stretched overhead. My couch and loveseat had been shoved against the walls. The mattress and books were mostly dust. Room by room, I moved in slow motion taking a mental inventory.

Where was my wedding dress? Had my grandmother's china survived? And those damn Calphalon pots and pans from Ivy. Which things would be a total loss?

Maybe all of them.

My bed was flipped on its side, pillows heaped on the floor. Through the soot-streaked window I could see Sol's house. Was I supposed to call him? Would our insurance agent do it? Or Tony Robinson?

As the sun set, the space grew darker, a cave with no electricity. I found Chief Kenny's flashlight in the kitchen and turned it on. When I held the light up to my chin, the plastic felt warm against my skin. I pictured the effect, a ghoulish skull lit from below. I was still standing there frozen when Maren texted.

WTF?

Instead of replying, I set the flashlight down on the table. Its light beamed across the kitchen into the living room. I wiped my hands on Harold's shirt, grateful for the hand-me-downs. His clothes were comfortable, and my brain was too numb to care about how I was dressed. Besides, a part of me liked that I looked different on the outside now. Underneath, I'd felt like a stranger for a long time. My phone rang, and I didn't answer it.

WTF.

Maren was right.

୨୦୧

I was sifting through soaked photo albums when a car door slammed and I heard footsteps crunching on the walkway. "Lia? Holy shit! Where are you?" Coming through the makeshift front door, Maren picked her way across the ruined hardwoods. When she saw me, I thought she might rush to my side. Offer comfort. A hug. But she just stood there, her head tipped to one side. "I don't even know what to say to you," she said.

"That makes two of us."

"What the hell happened?"

I shook my head. The question was too big.

"Holy shit, Lia." She lifted her hand to cover her mouth. "I'm so sorry."

"I know you are."

"I mean for everything."

I nodded. "How's Nora?"

"Oh God. She's already begging for ice cream and complaining about bedtime. I was so damn scared, but she's completely unfazed. Like, completely. Danny's home with her now. Slightly less unfazed but still good."

"I'm glad."

Maren looked around the room as if suddenly remembering what we were standing in the middle of. "Oh my God, Lia. I just can't believe this. It's unbelievable." Her fist was back at her mouth again, and she bit her knuckle. "What can I do?" she asked. "Please. Tell me."

"When I figure that out," I said, "I will."

"Have you told Jake yet?"

"That's why I sent you the picture. So you could show him and break the news for me. I figured he'd be at your house." I paused. "Since he lives there now."

She shook her head. "He was gone when we got home from the hospital."

"Good," I said. "I almost told him to leave, but then I figured that was your job. Yours and Danny's."

"Well." Maren shifted her gaze from corner to corner, trying to take it all in. "Thank goodness you weren't hurt."

"Was that supposed to be a question?"

"No," she said. "It was dumb. I feel so dumb right now. And helpless. I guess regular words don't cut it. Maybe I should just shut up."

"Just be here with me," I said. I managed a weak laugh. "Anyway, it's only stuff, right? At least that's what everyone keeps telling me." My hand swept the length of the room. "Damaged things can be replaced. But not damaged people. I'm alive. I should be grateful."

"Bullshit."

I stared at Maren.

"No, seriously, Lia. That's total bullshit. People have no right to tell you how to feel. You can be pissed off. At the world. At the whole universe! Hell. Be pissed at me if you want. I can take it, and I'm not going anywhere. No matter how bad it gets. Even if you hate me."

I swallowed hard, but I didn't cry. "I don't hate you."

"I know," she said. "I mean I hoped not."

"We'll get through this."

"We will," she said. "In the meantime, let's get some goddamn coffee, and we'll figure this shit out together."

"Give me a minute," I said.

"Take your time. I'll check in with Danny. Make sure Nora's still doing OK." While Maren went out to the porch to call Danny, I made one last pass through my house. It smelled like failure. The dead ficus mocked me from its corner. *I couldn't even save a stupid potted plant.*

Maren poked her head inside. "Ready?"

I sighed. "No."

"Good. I'm not either." She came toward me until our foreheads touched, and we stood there for a moment.

"Enough?" she asked.

"Enough."

Maren looped her arm through mine. And as she led me out of my ruined home, I didn't bother to lock the door. There was nothing left for anyone to steal anyway.

ৎ৵

For a Friday evening, Peet's was crowded. The line at the counter stretched almost to the entrance, and Maren held the door while I slipped inside. Around me, the air was warm and sweet with cinnamon. A chorus of voices made a comfortable hum. Scanning the room, I worried we'd find no free tables. Then someone stood and motioned us over.

"Danny?"

Chewing my lip, I walked toward him, and he folded me in his arms. My tears came fast, and he patted my back. "Shhh," he murmured. "Shhh." He smelled like shampoo, and his hair was damp.

I pulled away from him. "Who's with Nora?"

Maren came up from behind me. "Veronica's over at our house," she said. "She's been really sweet since we tore out of book club, worried about Nora and all. She'd just called to check in on her when you sent me that picture, so I asked her to come sit for us. Danny stayed until she got there."

"You didn't have to do that," I said.

"But Nora's fine, and you're definitely not! I hope you don't mind that I told Veronica what happened. I swear she's the only one."

"I don't mind." My brain felt numb.

"Everything's going to be all right," Danny said gathering me in for another hug.

But what if it's not? I thought. *What if nothing is all right ever again?*

Closing my eyes, I surrendered to the memory of the night Danny and I met. I'd tried to shake his hand, but he went in for a bear hug. Then he lifted me off my feet in the middle of Hennessey's. Maren stood there shaking her head, apologizing for her husband. She told him he was acting like a fool, so he set me down and pulled her in close. *On the contrary,* Danny had said while sandwiched between us. *I'm the most brilliant man in this bar.*

The rest of the night, they'd teased each other. Traded insults. Acted miffed. Over time, I learned this was their ruse, a repeat performance for the outside world. Underneath the show, they loved each other deeply. Even Jake saw through their bickering and said he preferred it to sticky-sweet displays of affection. I thought about how well Jake understood the Hollisters, how close he'd grown to them. Closer than I was?

I stepped away from Danny.

"You all right?" His eyes moved over my face. "Hey. How about some lattes?"

I nodded.

"It's about time you offered," Maren said. She put a hand on his shoulder and pushed him toward the counter. While Danny ordered us drinks, I took a seat at the table he'd saved for us. On the floor beside the chair sat a large shopping bag from Nordstrom.

"What's this?"

"I asked Danny to bring some of my clothes over for you," Maren said. "I would've brought you something last night, but you didn't call me. I had no idea…" She appeared wounded, and I opened my mouth to protest, but she was right. I had been punishing her. She and Danny had been kind to Jake, and I'd been hurt by it. I'd wanted her to hurt too. But that wasn't helpful or fair to her, I realized. It wasn't fair to any of us.

"Mare." My eyes brimmed, and she took my hand.

"Anyway, that was before," she said. "You'll come live with us now."

I dropped my eyes. "I don't think so."

"Why? Because of Jake?"

"No." I withdrew my hand and fiddled with a stack of napkins. "It's going to take months to rebuild," I said. "And my insurance company's paying for a rental."

"But Lia—"

"It's already arranged," I said. "A real estate agent is showing me places next week. Gwendolyn something-or-other. It's already set."

Maren shook her head. "If I were you, I'd want to be in familiar surroundings."

"But you're not me," I said. "And nothing about my life's familiar anymore."

ജ

We were finishing our lattes when my phone rang.

Jake.

I held up the phone so Danny and Maren could see the screen. They both claimed they hadn't told him about the fire. I wondered if this was true, then I decided it didn't matter. At the last second, I accepted his call. "Hold on a minute," I told him. "It's loud in here."

"Where are you?"

"Just wait," I said, making my way outside. At the door, a man and woman on their way in smiled at me. What must I look like to them? A pale woman with bedraggled hair in a pair of dirty drawstring pants. The smell of baked goods wafted over me. I laughed out loud. The sound was a trill in the cool night.

"Lia, what's going on?"

I sat on the curb. "Where are you?"

"At my parents' house," he said. "I couldn't stay with

Danny and Maren anymore." I nodded as if he could see me, as if he understood what I was feeling. "I've been thinking about you," he said.

"I've been thinking about you too."

"You wouldn't talk to me yesterday, but—"

"Tomorrow night," I said, cutting him off. "Meet me at the bungalow."

"Eight o'clock?" he asked.

"Looking forward to it," I said.

And I meant it.

Twenty-Eight

When I was twelve years old, I ran away from home, trudging three miles in a mismatched pair of flip flops to the cliff above Boarshead Beach. There, steep stairs made out of abandoned railway ties offered a narrow passage down to the sand. At the cliff's edge stood a railing, and I leaned against one section, testing its weight with my body.

I had no real curves—hadn't started to develop at all yet, honestly—but Dawn Martin had been wearing a bra since third grade, and the month before, Celeste Clark told everyone she'd started her period.

Menarche she called it. Menarche?

I spoke the word out loud three times into the wind, and still it sounded strange to me. My hip bones pressed against cold metal. To my left, a yellow warning sign cast a shadow in the afternoon sun. *Steep Drop.* On the other side, the city had posted a sign designating this as a "Scenic Spot." Hey, tourists! Take pictures here!

Enjoy breathtaking views!

But this seemed illogical to me then. Why would anyone want to draw people's attention away from their goals, tempt them to stop on their way to somewhere else? Beauty beside danger. *A risky prospect*, I thought.

I peered out over the endless ripple of waves trying to see the end of the world. It was the hour when the sun dipped closest to the water, just before disappearing entirely. Even if

someone were to survive a fall from the cliff, other dangers
lurked below. Everywhere. To someone like me who hadn't
been raised to believe in heaven, death meant the absence of
everything. Eternal nothingness. Huge and fearsome.

Still, I thought, maybe easier in some ways than the terror
of living.

I set down my bag then, an old backpack with a broken
strap I'd repaired with duct tape. Holding up my hands, I
made a square box with my fingers like I'd once seen a
professional photographer do. I arranged the shot, what would
be in my picture. A jagged rock. Protruding cypress branches.
White caps in the distance.

I didn't own a camera, of course. Everything I had of
value—which wasn't much—I'd packed in my bag: my two
favorite outfits; a battered diary; Grammy's bracelet which
Regina told me wasn't real gold; a week's worth of clean
underwear. I'd been checking mine daily for blood stains.
Nothing yet.

I climbed the first five steps down. Where was I going? I
had no idea. Maybe I'd walk up the coast for a mile or two,
then resurface on a stretch of highway and hitchhike to Uncle
Quentin's. I'd copied his address into my diary. But would
some stranger be willing to drive me there? I thought I might
be raped or even murdered, but at least then I'd be someone's
story to tell. I was tired of being nobody.

Taking a seat on a railroad tie, I imagined my own funeral.
The stench of flowers and the wail of an organ. Kids from
Crestfield Elementary would be crying, the girls wishing they'd
invited me to their birthday parties, the boys wishing they'd
kissed me in a game of spin the bottle. In small groups, they'd
talk about me. Hushed whispers at first, growing louder, so
that those standing nearby could hear and realize they weren't
as special. They'd pretend we'd been good friends, argue that
they knew me better. That I liked them more.

The year before, Grady Denton had died of leukemia, and
everyone pretended to be his best friend. School
administrators brought grief counselors in so stricken students
could talk about their feelings. I hadn't been really sad then,
only curious, wondering what Grady was feeling in his coffin.

Was he aware? Where was his soul? Who first discovered that he'd stopped breathing? Was it his mother? His little sister? Had they dropped to their knees, sobbing, convinced they couldn't go on?

Not without Grady. No!

These questions haunted me at night and nauseated me during the day. Who'd find me if I were lost? If I fell to the rocky beachfront, would anybody care? I shook my head, climbed the five stairs back up to the cliff's edge, and walked home. It was fully dark before I realized I'd left my backpack under the warning sign. I didn't go back for it. I could start a new diary, and my grandmother's bracelet wasn't real gold anyway.

ᔥᕞ

When I got to the bungalow the following night, Jake's Subaru was at the curb parked behind Harold's VW, and the front door stood open, a black grin inviting me in. Stepping over the wreckage, I steeled myself for another round of questions. Would I even tell Jake about the blouse? What could I say?

This is our fault.

It was my fault.

I found him in the office sitting at my desk in his pilot's uniform. The ashes on the chair would ruin his pants, but this was no longer my concern. I wondered who ironed his shirts for him. Ivy? Maybe their housekeeper? I used to love taking care of Jake, wanted him to need me as much as I needed him. I cooked his meals, balanced his budget. Picked up his dry cleaning.

He left me anyway.

"The door was unlocked," he said. Without looking at me, he took off his hat and set it on the desk. I figured he was in shock. I mean, I still was, so why wouldn't he be?

"Sorry I didn't call," I said, "but there was nothing you could do. And you gave the place to me, remember? So. This isn't your problem, Jake."

"Jesus, Lia."

I waited for him to ask what had happened, but he simply stared at the wall. How could a man sit in the husk of his old home and not ask a single question?

"They said the rebuild will take four months," I told him. "Maybe five. But you know how these things are. They always go longer than anyone estimates. Contractors are overly optimistic to win the business and all that." I leaned against the wall. "I hired an insurance adjustor."

"We have an agent." Jake's voice was robotic.

"Stephen Stashik," I said. "I know. But I wanted my own advocate. Someone to fight for me." *Like you didn't*, I thought. *Why didn't you fight?* "His name's Tony Robinson, and not that it matters, but I think you'd like him. He got me some emergency money until he can arrange a settlement. He's got an agent helping me rent a place."

Jake looked at me. "Where are you staying now?"

"Not with the Hollisters, if you're worried."

"That isn't why I asked."

"What did you want to talk about, then?"

"Not this." His eyes traversed the room. "I guess I came here to discuss what happened with us."

"Overall, or just three nights ago?" *Had it been only three?*

"Yes," he said. "Both."

I shook my head, looked around the office. "There's nothing left to talk about. Literally. Nothing."

He stared at me in stunned silence. He'd not yet absorbed this fact.

"So I'm saying you're free to go, Jake. For real. End of story." In my mind, I pictured a thin blouse draped over a lamp. A slow smolder. Our lives burning down.

He looked at his hands, then back up at me. "I'm sorry. I thought maybe we still had a chance to—"

"A chance?" My laugh was a yelp. Like a kicked dog. "I waited two months for you to come to your senses."

"We were together seven years, Lia."

"And you walked away from all of it."

"But I'm here now. And I'm asking for more time."

My throat tightened. "More time?"

"Come stay with me for a while," he said.

"Stay with you?" I took a step backward. "Where?"

"I was thinking… maybe… Portland?"

"Ha!" My face burned. "You have to be joking."

"I know it sounds insane."

"Yes," I said. "It does."

"Think about it."

I lifted my arms, spread them wide. "Look around you, Jake. My life's in ruins. Our lives. You ruined us."

"I'm not promising I can fix anything. But I guess I'm not ready for everything to be over, either. Not completely. I thought I could move on, that a clean break would be better for you—for everyone." He lowered his voice. "But I miss you."

"You miss sex with me."

"I miss *you*. The companionship. You're my best friend, Lia."

"How sweet," I said.

I saw his fists clench, then release. "Don't be mean."

"All right," I said. "So you miss me. You want me to move to Oregon to be your *best friend*?"

"Why not? It's a start."

"A start."

I dropped my head. Why was I arguing with him? If he couldn't see already why a relationship between us was impossible, I wouldn't be able to explain it to him. The truth was, I didn't have a clear answer to the *why* myself. He was suggesting exactly what I'd wanted to hear for the past two months: time together. To see what the future might hold. A glimmer of a chance to work things out. In April, even in May, I would've done anything for this sliver of hope. I would've sold my soul. Traded it all. I would've burned my whole house down.

"Can we at least try?" Jake let the offer hang between us like a precious gift.

"No," I said.

"Lia. Please."

"Just lock up when you leave."

◦◦◦

Two days later I met Gwendolyn Walters, a real estate agent who specialized in temporary rentals. She was low to the ground and sturdy, a bulldog of a woman with a neat cap of hair.

"Nice to meet you, Ms. Walters."

"Gwendolyn," she said. "Or Gwen." Her handshake was a swift pump. "It's nice to meet you, but I'm sorry about the circumstances." Next came the lines I'd come to expect by now: that what I'd lost was only stuff, but people couldn't be replaced.

Gwendolyn squeezed my hand. "Thank God you weren't hurt."

Who said I wasn't hurt?

She took me through three potential rental options that day. First was a condo off 4th Street that was small but newly remodeled. It had granite countertops, Pergo floors, and a view of the parking lot. Then we saw a three bed/two bath in Redondo. The place was spacious, yes, but old, and it smelled like kitty litter. Finally, we visited an attached townhome with a lovely community center. This was her favorite, and it also came with the largest commission.

"They have a clubhouse with tennis courts," she told me. "And a golf course. And two lap pools."

"I don't swim."

Gwendolyn smiled. "You could learn."

"I'll think about it," I said.

Later that week, Tony introduced me to Kurt Lutz, the contractor handling my rebuild. I was wearing a pair of shorts and a T-shirt from Maren, and I felt like a stranger touring someone else's home. Kurt Lutz had pockmarked skin and a smoker's cough. His baseball hat was sweat-stained. But I liked his easy, loping gait. His face seemed trustworthy.

I needed to trust him.

Between the two of us, Jake had been the one with the eye for design. He'd picked out all the furniture and most of the paint colors. Our kitchen tile and hardwood floors. My sole contribution to our original remodel had been keeping the popcorn ceilings. In my previous life, I never scanned *Architectural Digest* or *Better Homes and Gardens*. And I wasn't about to start now.

Kurt Lutz and I began his survey of my place out front, then I showed him the rest of the damaged bungalow. He said little at first, just took copious notes. When we got to the bedroom, he addressed the hole in the ceiling, a gash in the bumpy popcorn texture. "All your ceilings'll need to be redone," he said.

"Smooth," I said. "I'd like them smooth. Like paper. White. Clean."

"We can do that," he told me. "Not a problem. We can do anything you want."

After we'd covered the entire property, Kurt stood beside me leafing through his estimate. "This is a lot of work," I said. Not a question.

"Yep." He kept his focus on the clipboard. "But in the end, this place'll be great. Maybe better than before." When I asked if there was anything else he needed me to do, he took off his hat and wiped at his forehead. "Yep," he said, finally meeting my eyes. "A lot." He explained that for the next several months, he'd be calling me multiple times a day.

"Can't I make all the decisions now? Like from a list?"

"Questions are gonna come up," he said. "You make a choice, then bam! Some city inspector shows up and says, *no good*. So you gotta be available. Or I'll be making choices on the fly, and you might not like 'em."

"But I don't know what I like."

"Better start figuring it out."

After my meeting with Kurt Lutz, I went back to the hotel and curled up in an armchair in the lobby. Over the past week, the Comfort Suites had grown on me. This hotel had become familiar, if not luxurious. Cozy and unpretentious. I couldn't imagine beginning again in yet another place. In my lap I held flyers for the three potential rental properties. Gwendolyn had been encouraging, but none of these places felt right to me. I didn't want to start over from scratch. Rented furniture. Loaned forks and bowls and sheets.

"They'll even give you a vacuum cleaner," Gwendolyn told me. "And an ironing board. Toothbrush holders. Dust pans. The works."

She'd sounded excited, but I could barely breathe.

I felt like a foreigner visiting my own life, a tourist trading one hotel for another temporary space. I crumpled the flyers and threw them in the trash next to the lobby's newspaper stand. Then, back in my room, I called Maren.

"Lia?"

"How's Nora?"

"Oh, she's great." Maren snorted. "Already back to her old self, for better or worse. How did those shorts fit?"

"Fine," I told her. "And thank you. But anyway, I have an idea."

Twenty-Nine

The alarm felt especially early today, a jangle in my ear. I'd slept in my sweatpants and a sweatshirt so I wouldn't need to change. I slipped on shoes without untying the laces. Everything I wore these days was comfortable and purposeful—either hand-me-downs or stuff I'd bought with that first insurance check from Tony. In the bathroom Regina saved for *guests*, I gathered my hair into a bun, securing it loosely with two chopsticks. This was Regina's trick, and I wondered how much I resembled her these days. I had new auburn hair and lonely eyes. My pale face was slightly dazed and confused. When people ran into me up here in Santa Cruz, what did they see? A younger version of her, perhaps. Familiar and yet strange.

Coming here for the summer wasn't the worst plan I'd ever hatched though. Not when the alternative was navigating the rebuild of the bungalow on my own. After my first talk with Kurt Lutz, I'd felt unequal to the task. Overseeing contractors. Design decisions. Inspectors. Budgetary constraints. I was way out of my depth, but I knew Maren would be right in hers. When I asked her to handle the rebuild, her shriek pierced through the phone.

"Yes! Yes! Yes!" she said. "Hell yes! Does this mean you trust me, Lia?"

"I do," I said.

"To make all the decisions? For real?"

"I do," I repeated. "Yes."

"Damn!" she said. "It'll feel *so good* to stretch my professional muscles again. Not that raising Nora isn't rewarding," she added. "It is, of course. A mother's challenge and all. But, oh my God! I can't wait! Thank you thank you thank you!"

That was more than a week ago.

Since then, each day at dawn, I'd walked the hills through town, taking the steep path down to the shoreline. Once my shoes came off, the wet sand sucked at my toes and gleamed around my feet. I'd look back over my shoulder at the evidence behind me. Small prints in regular intervals. The weight of my existence.

On my way back from the beach now, I breathed the air—sharp and cold. *Inhale. Exhale.* I took one long stride, then another, feeling lean and strong and purposeful. Cresting the hill on Marview Lane, I took the gravel road that led to Regina's. The morning fog hung thick here all the way through the end of June, and the streets still wore a mask of gray. In the mist, a hooded figure jogged my way, his breath a frosty gust. "Caleb?" I called out. The man stopped a few yards from me and bent at the waist.

"Hey," he said to the ground. Then he straightened and swiped off his hood.

"It is you," I said. "Hi."

"I heard you were back."

"Did you hear why?"

He shook his head. "I don't listen to other people's stories much."

I nodded at him, but Caleb lived next door to Regina, and by now she would've told him what had happened whether he wanted to listen or not. "I've been out walking every morning," I said.

Caleb squinted. "Yep."

"Surprised I haven't seen you yet."

"I usually finish my runs earlier."

"But not today?"

"Nope," he said. "I sleep in on Sundays."

"Is it Sunday already?"

"It is."

"No church for you then, I guess?"

"None for you either," he said. "I guess."

I laughed, and it sounded good in my ears. "Regina always said I was too practical for religion. She likes to describe herself as spiritual." I put air quotes around the word.

"I think a person can be both," he said. "Spiritual and religious."

"Are you both?"

"Nope. I'm neither."

We were both quiet for a moment. Then I said, "Thanks for being nice." He glanced up, tilted his head, an unasked question. "The last time I was up here, I thought you didn't like me."

He shrugged, kicked at a rock beneath his shoe.

"I mean, you spoke about four words to me the whole time."

At the edge of his mouth, there came a hint of a smile. "That's about what was called for."

"Well." The cold air was making my nose drip. "It made me wonder if I'd done something wrong. Now. Or maybe back at Grant High." I sniffed and wiped my nose on the sleeve of my sweatshirt. "In the end," I told him, "I decided it wasn't me. It was you."

"Huh."

"That's it? Huh?"

"I'm not one to talk much without a reason."

"And today you have a reason?"

"Maybe."

I wondered what Caleb knew about me, what he'd heard since I was here last. Did he feel sorry for me now? Anyway, I didn't want his pity. He regarded me evenly, gave no hint of what he was thinking. A breeze brought with it the smell of pine. A taste of salt. I brushed a strand of hair from my mouth and licked my lips.

"I should head back," I said. At this, Caleb turned and strode up the path he shared with Regina. I walked behind him, trying to match his pace, and my breath came quick. When we reached the fork separating the two properties, he paused. One road curved toward Regina's. From here, I could almost see the rooftop, its shingles damp and mossy. The other road looped back to his place, a distant structure of wood siding and brick. Caleb looked back at me and lifted an eyebrow. "Coffee?" he asked.

"Sure." I followed him down the path to his house. I'd never been inside.

When I was a child, Regina's warnings about Mr. Nelson had kept me from exploring past the hedges. What I remember from my rare glimpses of him: a pale flash behind his windshield. A drawn face. Unshaven. Haunted. Mr. Nelson, I decided sometime later, wasn't dangerous, but lonely. He might've welcomed a knock from the child next door who carried loneliness too.

Still, this was Caleb's home now, the exterior obscured by trees, ground covered with fallen leaves being browned by summer sun. Against the garage he'd propped a yellow broom, oddly bright in the morning grayness. I made a mental note to discuss garage door choices with Maren while Caleb opened his front door. He'd left it unlocked. A trusting man. I smiled and stepped inside.

I expected Caleb's house to be sparsely furnished. Clean, or at the very least, tidy. I imagined a few sturdy chairs gathered around a kitchen table. Maybe one long couch in the living room. So when we walked through the front room into the kitchen, I was unprepared for the clutter. Paint cans and brushes lay strewn across stained tarps. In what I would've called the family room, Caleb kept a workbench heaped with tools. Crooked nails lay scattered about the floor. A ladder leaned in one corner covered with peeling wallpaper. In the other corner sat a sign that read *Stone's Way Construction*.

This man was a contractor?

Scanning the room, I was reminded of the adage about the cobbler's children going without shoes. Caleb said nothing about the mess. Then again, the man said little about anything. I pulled a stool from under the kitchen counter, while Caleb removed a bag of ground coffee beans from the freezer. As the water gurgled and hissed in its pot, he rescued a mug from the sink, then hunted for a second mug in a cabinet above the refrigerator. He washed and dried both mugs, and without asking, poured me a cup. He must've noticed that first morning at Regina's that I took mine black. A man who paid attention.

Neither one of us spoke, which historically would've made me uncomfortable. But sitting here at Caleb's counter, I felt myself relaxing. Ropes of steam curled toward the ceiling, and I breathed in the scent of dark roast. I'd quit drinking coffee when I returned to Santa Cruz, although I'd not thought much about why. Probably a part of me didn't want to ask Regina to make a whole pot again. Not to accommodate me. Not if she didn't do it on her own.

For three days, fatigue and headaches from caffeine withdrawal had sidelined me, and I'd spent most of my time lying on Regina's couch. I brought the mug up to my cheek now, and the heat of the coffee seeped through me. Lips to stomach to bone.

Why had I given this up? Just to be stubborn?

I sighed, and Caleb heard it. "Good?" he asked. I bobbed my head. Then the quiet settled between us again. While Caleb drank his coffee, I itched to ask him questions. *What brought you back to our hometown? How many times have you been deployed? Do you still have faith in humanity? Have you ever been very afraid?* But I bit my tongue. I wouldn't break the silence or risk saying something stupid. If I had learned anything about Caleb Stone, it was that he didn't welcome inquiries about his past. Or his present, for that matter. Whatever he might reveal would have to be initiated by him. I set down my mug.

"What?" he asked. I paused before answering. Caleb wasn't the only one who could be mysterious.

"I was just thinking about your brother," I told him. No questions, simply a statement.

"Ezra," he said, and I laughed.

"You have another brother I don't know about?"

He flinched, and I immediately regretted my words. Of all people, I should've known better than to make that kind of joke. "Sorry," I said. "I was kidding."

From over his coffee mug Caleb studied my face. "The way I figure it, no one ever knows for sure."

I nodded. "You got that right."

When I thought of Caleb's little brother, I pictured his hair—a great dark mop of it—obscuring the gleam in his eyes. Ezra Stone wasn't a troublemaker, necessarily, but he didn't like being told what to do, either. He was fond of skipping school and exceptionally good at it. Our senior year he was voted *Guy Most Likely to Ditch*. As for me, I didn't win any yearbook superlatives, and the one time I tried to cut class resulted in my getting Ezra caught.

That day I'd decided to leave the school grounds after lunch without permission. What was the worst that could happen? Either I'd be discovered and the resulting punishment would prove to Regina I could be rebellious, or I'd escape and spend the afternoon at the beach instead of history class. Halfway across the student parking lot, I spotted Ezra creeping behind a row of bushes.

"Ezra?"

"Shhh!" An arm stuck through the hedge and pulled me through. "Are you an idiot?" he hissed. *Yes*, I thought. But I didn't say it. Instead, I dropped my head.

"Where's your car, Lark?"

Ezra Stone knew my name? I dragged my shoe along the dirt, but I didn't look up. "I don't have one."

"Bus?"

I shook my head.

"What the hell, then?"

"I walk?"

He spat at the ground and missed my sneaker by an inch. "Come with me," he said, "and for Christ's sake shut up." I tried to play it cool while I followed Ezra to his truck, but Bunny Tittle, the head noon-aide, had already spotted us. Her golf cart hummed across the parking lot. "Let me do the talking," muttered Ezra.

At first, he tried to convince her we both had permission to leave. "Lia here doesn't have a car, you see. And she forgot her medicine at home. Please, Bunny. It's an emergency." Ezra grinned, and I shivered, but Bunny was unmoved by Ezra's charm.

Her eyes twitched, and she looked at me. "What's it for?"

"Huh?"

"The medicine. What's it for?"

"Oh." I searched my brain and came up empty. Ezra's shoulders sank.

"That's what I thought. Let's go kids. Hop on. I'm turning you in to attendance." Ezra and I waited together outside the assistant principal's office at the back of the administration building. My heart raced, not with fear but with excitement. Sure, I'd failed at my first attempt to ditch school, but now I was sitting next to Ezra Stone. His fingers drummed against his knees.

What would he say to Mrs. Kershaw to explain our joint transgressions? Ezra's storytelling was legendary, and soon I'd be able to witness him in action. This was, perhaps, the most thrilling thing that had ever happened to me. When the story got out, I'd be famous in the lunchroom. At least for fifteen minutes. Of course, this incident might be exceptional only because Ezra Stone had never gotten caught before.

Not until I entered the scene.

The door to the AP's office opened, and Mrs. Kershaw called Ezra in. "Just you, Mr. Stone." She glanced at me. "You," she said. "Go back to class."

Apparently, Lia Lark was an afterthought, too boring and unimportant to be punished. I blushed at having believed—for even a moment—that someone might've cared. Later I learned Mrs. Kershaw had, in fact, called my house. After school I erased the message from the answering machine. I blinked back tears, grateful the assistant principal hadn't been able to reach Regina. Not because Regina would've been angry, but because she probably would've been proud. I'd attempted to buck the system, after all. This was something she lived for. She would've lied to confirm Ezra's story. But I didn't want to be like her.

I wasn't like her.

I'd failed to be a failure.

Thirty

When my coffee grew cold, and my stomach started rumbling, I thanked Caleb and headed back to Regina's. I thought maybe we'd have breakfast together, but she was nowhere to be found and hadn't left a note. No hint of when she might return. *Just like the good old days.* My heart sank, realizing nothing had changed. I'd most likely be spending the rest of the day alone. Or the rest of the week. Maybe even the entire summer.

I hated being lonely.

The next morning, however, I found Caleb at the fork in the road between the houses once again. He was wearing the same hooded sweatshirt and stretching against a white picket fence. As I approached, he squinted at me in the early light.

"Hey," I said. "What's up?"

"Thought I'd walk with you," he told me. "It's not safe out here alone." I looked down the deserted path to where it curved toward Main Street.

"That's nice of you," I said, "but I've been fine so far. And besides. Aren't you a runner?"

He shrugged. "I'm good with going slower."

"Are you good with conversation?" He looked at me and said nothing, but I caught the hint of a smile. "Guess I'll do all the talking," I said. "And I can protect myself."

From then on, we walked together each morning—across town, along the beach, then looping back home. Sometimes we talked, but usually we were quiet. And it was comfortable, for the most part. Fresh air. Exercise. Peace. One day, when the silence was too much for me, I told Caleb about the fire. I left out the part about my blouse—about Jake—focused instead on the rebuild. He listened without any questions, so I asked him about his work. On this subject as with most others, Caleb had little to say. He did tell me that instead of contracting these days, he was employed by Greenway Construction. It was a job to him. Paid the bills. Enough said.

For him at least.

Although Caleb never asked about Jake, eventually I told him. I needed to get the broad strokes out, if only to make sense of it myself. I explained that Jake had left me to raise his daughter, a child I didn't know he had. My throat caught on the name Addie Barrow. And Josie.

Would they ever be easy for me to say?

"Oh, and my in-laws have this big party every year for the Fourth of July. But this time, Jake won't be there, so I might show up. Yeah, I probably will." Out of the corner of my eye, I saw Caleb shake his head.

"What?" I asked. "You think it's a bad idea?" He shrugged and jogged up a wet sand dune. I scrambled up behind him wondering who he thought was crazier: the Townsends for inviting me or me for attending.

From there we kept walking along the coast, back to his place, to another pot of coffee. Caleb always drank his, and I pretended to drink mine. Then we'd go our separate ways. And the next morning he'd be at the forked road again, same sweatshirt and same squint. I'd say *Hey,* and he'd nod at me.

This was beginning to feel comfortable.

ço⌢ç

A week later, Regina's hens stopped laying, and she grew frustrated, unused to being refused. Squatting beside her in the garden, I examined them through the wire of her homemade coop. "It could be a seasonal thing," I said. "A summer vacation for chickens? Or maybe their diet. Did the books say anything about nutrition and laying cycles?"

"What books?"

"The ones you read about hens and eggs," I said. "Please tell me you didn't think you could just *intuit* your way into being an urban chicken farmer."

Regina shrugged. "This place is really more rural."

"In other words, you did no research on raising chickens."

"How hard could it be? I raised you just fine without consulting a single book."

At this I smiled. "Excellent point." The rooster strutted toward us across the dirt. "Hey there, Bertram," I said.

Regina grunted. "You named him?"

"Bertram," I repeated. He was beautiful, with his bright red comb and feathered wings.

Regina eyed me from the side. "You were being sarcastic, weren't you?"

"When?"

"When you said I was an excellent mother."

I turned to look at her straight on. "Please. Let's not fight."

"You think I'm horrible."

I sighed. "Regina, you and I are who we are. Leopards in our own way. And changing our spots isn't very likely."

"I hate it when you wax metaphorical."

"So do I," I said. "So do I." I sniffed and caught the stink of manure in the air. Above us, the evening sky was a spectacle of pink.

"Anyway, you've been acting strange all afternoon," she said. "I know you've got something on your mind. So out with it."

For a moment, I considered lying, then I decided I'd rather shock her. To hell with not riling her up. I'd spent my whole life placating Regina. "I'm driving down to the Townsends' tomorrow. You know. For the Fourth."

"So." She sucked in air through her teeth. "They invited you?"

"I'm invited every year."

"Things change," she said.

"Yes, they do." I settled down beside her cross-legged on the ground. "Except for the fact that you don't approve of them. That never changes."

"I'm just curious," she said. "What does Ivy want from you now? You've got an insurance payment coming your way. Think she'll ask for her money back?" I looked up at her surprised, and Regina frowned.

"I'm not clueless," she said. "I know good ol' Chucky-Boy and Ivy gave you the down payment for that precious bungalow of yours. Now that their son's not living there anymore, they might want a cut of the action."

"Maybe."

"Don't kid yourself. The Townsends are all about the bottom line. That's how people like that get to be who they are. It's in their blue blood," she said. "And leopards don't change their spots." She smirked. "So I've been told."

"Charlotte will be there," I said. "I'd like to see her."

"I thought you just did."

"It's been a while. And who knows what'll happen, going forward? I may be out of all of their lives. Forever. Maybe this'll give me the closure I need. Anyway, I've always hated that word. *Closure.* But there it is." I drew a line in the dirt with my finger. "And if Ivy Townsend wants her money back? Fine. She can have it." My gaze cut back to the rooster. "But she'll have to look me in the eye when she asks."

"You're gonna get hurt," Regina said.

"I'm already hurt."

"True enough. It's just..." her voice trailed off. From inside the coop came a rustling.

"Go ahead. Say it, Regina."

"I don't trust them."

"I see," I said. For a while, neither of us spoke. "So this has nothing to do with the fact that you're jealous."

Regina squawked. "Of the country club set? Of their Bermuda shorts and L.L.Bean sandals? Hardly." The rooster lifted its head and bobbed toward us on its spindled legs.

"No," I said. "Of course you wouldn't be jealous. Not when your life's so perfect."

She plucked a blade of grass from her bare foot and slowly split it in two. "There you go again," she said. "Sarcasm is unattractive on you, Lia."

"I'm aware of that," I told her.

She glanced at me. "And yet," she said. The words hovered between us. On the other side of the fence, the bobbing rooster stopped to peck at a spot of dry earth. From where I sat, I could identify no goal for his efforts. The dirt was clean. There was no feed there and nothing to be gained. But still his neck moved in swift spasms, the sharp beak attacking bare ground. We both watched him for a minute, silent.

Regina snorted. "Men."

I stood and went inside.

১৯৯৩

On my way out the next morning, I found Caleb crouched behind my car. The sun wasn't up yet, and I could barely make him out in the too-early light. "Hey, there." I set my overnight duffel down, and it crunched on the gravel. "What's going on?"

Caleb unfolded himself from his crouch. "Just checking your tires," he said. "The back one's low on air."

"So it is," I said.

He ran a hand over his dark scalp. It looked freshly shaved. "Probably needs replacing," he said.

"Which one?"

"Honestly? All four."

"Well." I sighed. "Aren't you the bearer of bad news."

"Bad is relative." He squinted at me. "I was about to go for a run," he said. "Thought I'd say good luck to you first."

"With what?"

"The party," he said.

"Right." Between us there was less than five feet of space.

Caleb placed his palm on my hood, looked down at my bag. "When'll you be back?"

"I'm not sure," I said. "I'm going to the party, then spending the night at Mare's. That way we can go to the bungalow in the morning to check it out in the daylight. She wants to show me everything she's done so far. Get my approval and all that. But I'm sure it'll be great. Better than anything I could come up with. Design's not my thing."

"Mare's?" Caleb said, regarding me quizzically. Maybe I was talking too fast for him again.

"My best friend? Maren Hollister? I told you about her. She's the one who's been handling the rebuild for me while I'm up here."

"But you will be back," he said. Not a question.

"Like I said, I'm not sure." I dropped my gaze. "If Maren seems overwhelmed by all the work, or if I start to feel homesick when I'm there... I don't know. I might stay awhile."

Caleb waited a beat. "Stop at a gas station before you hit the highway," he said. "Check that tire."

"Right."

He shifted his focus away from me, down the gravel path that disappeared around the corner. From here, the main road was out of sight. "Caleb. I—"

"Good luck," he said. Then he began to run.

Thirty-One

When I arrived at the Townsends', I parked in front of the Tow Zone sign at the edge of their property. Ivy had it installed—illegally—to save a space for family members only. Since the spot was still open, I figured Charlotte hadn't arrived yet or she'd parked her rental car in the circular driveway. Either way, I seized the opportunity. After a quick glance over my shoulder, I headed up the walkway toward the party already in full swing.

Above me, white lights hung from tree branches in lazy swags. The bulbs weren't illuminated yet, but I knew from previous experience that after nightfall, the effect would be dazzling. As I climbed the porch, my heart hammered along with the cover band playing Toby Keith in the Townsends' backyard. In the air hung the smell of cotton candy and roasted peanuts.

What am I getting myself into?

Just inside the door, a butler I didn't recognize sat in a chair he must've dragged over from the dining room. Surprising. Either Ivy and Charles were lightening up, or this guy was risking his job. Beyond the seated butler, a row of French doors had been flung open at the back of the house. American flags snapped in the wind. Children swarmed in and out of an enormous bounce-house. Across the yard was a ping pong table, a bocce ball court, a game of croquet in progress. I wondered again why Jake hadn't brought his daughter. Was he avoiding me? Had his relationship with Addie grown deeper? Maybe he was so happy in his new life, he didn't want to dip back into the old.

Stop it, Lia. Josie isn't your concern.

I showed my invitation to the butler and asked him if the Townsends were in the backyard. He nodded without making eye contact. My gaze shifted then to the spiral staircase across the entryway. *This might be your last chance to visit Jake's room.* After another glance at the butler, I began to climb the stairs. The bannister was cool, its iron scrollwork intricate. Expensive. At the landing, I paused beside the pictures. Ivy and Charles. Jake and Charlotte. The four of them together. Then the portrait of Jake and Addie.

I searched their faces for clues of their impending bond. Had they known even then they'd be in each other's lives forever? In Addie's smile, I saw only the same lovely confidence that had always greeted me. As for Jake, he needed a haircut, but this was hardly a surprise. Ivy told me once that as a child her son had hated going to the barber. *It was a battle. He threw terrible tantrums.* This she'd whispered behind a raised hand, the two of us playing at being confidantes.

Teeth gritted now, I continued to the second floor where Charlotte's bedroom door stood open. As I stole inside, I felt suddenly nervous, worried I might dry heave on her rug. In the corner sat a canopy bed, queen-sized and flocked with pillows. I sat on the edge of the mattress, the place where Jake had kissed me the first time I'd visited here. The walls of the room were mostly bare and had been painted a delicate blush. A few generic prints hung there and a single shelf that held only an empty vase. Maybe Charlotte had preferred her room to be sterile and spare. Maybe Ivy had stripped it down years ago after her daughter left for college.

By contrast, I knew already that Jake's room was a bona fide shrine and still personalized. His walls were cluttered with team pictures and old jerseys preserved in matted frames. On the desk sat display boxes protecting precious, autographed balls. There were pennants. And bobble heads. Fat books of trading cards. Trophies lined the bookshelves and his dresser. When Jake gave me my first tour, I remember thinking, *The museum of boyhood lives here.* Over dinner that night, Ivy had told me teenaged Jake *showed such promise.*

"He was the MVP on his baseball team, always dreamed of playing professionally. But hoping to play for the Angels was impractical, to say the least. So we figured, law school. Naturally." She pursed her lips. An awkward smile.

"Then they found out I wanted to fly," Jake said. "What a profound disappointment."

"Jacob. You know your father and I couldn't be prouder of you." Across from me, Charles nodded, while Ivy patted Jake's hand.

Sitting in Charlotte's room now, I felt a wave of sadness for young Jake, raised with all that pressure to please. Self-imposed or otherwise. For her part, Regina hadn't wanted much from me—had probably wished only that I'd been a little more rebellious, that I'd defy expectations like she had. Instead, I'd been tirelessly conventional, a constant stranger to my mother. As it turned out, Jake and I weren't so different from each other, both of us letting down hopeful parents. This had been, in the end, his number one reason not to have children:

We'd stop the legacy of disappointment.

Or so he thought.

Leaving Charlotte's room, I crept to Jake's door for a final glimpse of the boy he'd once been. Inside, I found Charlotte looking out the window at the teeming yard below. I was so quiet she didn't hear me, so I cleared my throat, and she spun around. Her cheeks were pale, and her lips were a slash of red. Her expression made me nervous. Something felt off.

"Sorry," I said. Two quick syllables, although I wasn't sure what I was apologizing for.

"He wouldn't come," she said.

"Who?"

"TJ. He refused." She moved away from the window, ran a hand along a baseball bat mounted on the wall. Charlotte's fingertip came away clean. Some housekeeper had been dusting Jake's memorabilia for decades. "TJ told me he wanted to stay with Tim for the summer." She sighed. "How could I say no?"

I had no answer for her, so I said nothing. I simply looked around the room with its rich navy blues and cool grays. The corduroy bedspread. A single model airplane suspended from the ceiling. The space smelled of wood and leather. Peppery and warm.

Like Jake.

"Do you think I did the right thing?" Charlotte asked. "Letting TJ stay with his father?"

"I don't know," I said.

"Tim told me a boy needs his dad." Charlotte laughed, but it wasn't a happy sound. "After all this time, the guy suddenly wants to be involved? Now that TJ isn't such a nightmare? Where was Tim when the kid had colic? And during that ADHD diagnosis? Nowhere. He was nowhere. So yeah. Thanks a lot, Tim. For nothing. Asshole."

I dropped my eyes.

"I meant Tim's an asshole. Not TJ."

"I knew who you meant," I said. "I was just thinking."

"About?"

"About everything Jake's missed."

At this Charlotte nodded absently. She'd been sharing her pain with me, and I'd flipped the topic back around to Jake. To me. Ugh. I stumbled over my words, embarrassed by the self-centeredness, but I couldn't help myself. "I meant what Jake's missed with Josie. It must be hard."

Another nod from Charlotte. "And just like Tim, my idiot brother thinks he can swoop in and make up for lost time. Jake's going to make things worse for her, you know. Worse for all of them. Worse for you, of course." Her tone was sharp, and I could taste her bitterness. Like vinegar on my tongue.

"I shouldn't have brought Jake up."

"Maybe not," she said. "But whatever. I guess we're all still figuring this shit out."

I squirmed then, shifted my weight. If being here was this uncomfortable already, seeing Charles and Ivy felt impossible. I needed to get this meeting with them over with and get to Maren's. The sooner the better. "Are your parents outside?" I asked.

"Ah. You haven't seen the king and queen yet."

I swallowed. "Nope."

"Well then." Charlotte lifted her brow. "Let's go find them together."

৵৵

On our way to the backyard, Charlotte took a detour, steering me toward a temporary bar set up outside the kitchen. "Fortification," she said, and I nodded. Maybe one drink would make this easier. At least it couldn't hurt. On display at the bar were a series of cocktail options, each crafted in patriotic shades. Charlotte ordered a gin martini, but I skipped the liquor and asked for chardonnay. A baby-faced bartender with a crew-cut poured a glass for me, then waited for my approval. The wine was buttery. Smooth. Cold. I told him it was perfect, and he shifted to Charlotte's drink. The martini was blue, of course. The guy was working so hard he was sweating.

Then again, I was sweating too.

Charlotte led me to the Townsends' library and shut the door behind us. "We'll have our drinks in here," she said. This wasn't a request. We settled across from each other in high-backed leather chairs. Charlotte took a long sip and leaned back. "Shit, Lia. I just realized I was so busy rambling about TJ, I forgot to say something about your fire. Jake told me. I should've reached out sooner, but I've been… preoccupied."

"It's fine. I have too."

"Did you lose a lot?"

"Just stuff," I said, the practiced answer. "It can be replaced."

"Maybe." Charlotte's eyes shined with sympathy, a glimmer of the sister-in-law I missed. "Some things just stay lost though."

Oof. I felt a knife in my heart at the thought of eventually losing Charlotte. I'd expected to lose the Townsends, but then they sent the invitation. That was what I was here for, after all. "So your parents must've heard, then," I said. "About what happened. The fire."

"Honestly, I have no idea. I got here and went straight upstairs to spy on everyone." Charlotte smirked. "That's what you were doing too, wasn't it? Spying? In Jake's room?"

"That was less spying and more stalling," I said. I gulped my chardonnay. It was served in a real glass, not plastic like most people I knew used for big parties. Even the stem was thick and sturdy. In the end, there was nothing fragile about the Townsends. "I have to admit," I said, "I'm a little scared to see your mom and dad."

At this Charlotte laughed. "To be fair, no one truly likes seeing them, do they? They're like marble statues wheeled out for show."

I smiled and sipped more of my wine. Charlotte was trying to relax me, and I'd do my best to relax. Outside, the band kicked off an upbeat version of *America the Beautiful*. A female voice giggled through the first line of lyrics.

"Oh dear." Charlotte cringed. "It appears the karaoke has begun."

"At least Jake's not here to try to force me to sing again," I said. "He used to beg me at every party."

Charlotte frowned. "And he usually won. What was that song he made you do last year? *Proud To Be An American*?"

I laughed. "Who knows? I tried to forget."

"Yeah, I think we all did." She paused then. She seemed to be studying me. "You look different," she said.

"Oh." I raised a hand to my hair. "It's the color. But you were there when I did this, remember? You're just not used to it yet. For a while, whenever I saw myself in the mirror, I thought I was looking at a stranger."

Charlotte continued to appraise me, her face free of judgment. "No. It's not the hair." *What was she talking about, then?*

"Anyway, I might go back to blonde," I told her.

"Do what you want, but the auburn suits you. It brings out the blue of your eyes."

"Really?" I shook my head. "I think it brings out the Regina."

"Ha!" Charlotte polished off her martini, then set the empty glass on the table. "I'm curious," she said, leaning forward. Conspiratorial. "Have you seen that man again?"

"What man?"

"That dad of your student. What was his name?"

"Oh."

"Declan?" Charlotte tilted her head. "Am I being nosy?" I considered how to respond to the question. Could I trust Charlotte completely? Was there even a small chance she could be fishing for information for her parents or her brother? For that matter, did any of the Townsends know Jake had asked me to go to Portland with him?

Charlotte sat back. "I take it from your silence, the answer is *yes*."

"Yes, his name is Declan." I managed a smile. "And yes, your question was nosy."

And yes—I drained my chardonnay—*I have seen Declan McKinley.*

Still, better safe than sorry. I'd be stupid to tell Jake's sister the details. But it did happen, and I couldn't forget it. I didn't want to.

Maren and I had met up at the bungalow to talk about the rebuild before I left for Santa Cruz. Although I offered to pay her, she was insisting on doing the work pro bono. "You're my best friend, and I'm a designer," she said. "I've been out of the game so long, this can be the start of a new portfolio." Then she'd fired off a slew of questions about what I wanted or didn't want. I had few answers. That was why I'd needed her help in the first place. I told her I trusted her judgment and put the project entirely in her hands.

"Thank you," she said, taking my hand. "I need this, Lia. Maybe more than you do."

I'd managed a laugh. "Let's call it even."

Maren left to go home to her family then, but I wasn't ready for the Comfort Suites yet. I was getting too used to the hotel bed and the four walls. To the loneliness. So I took a walk up Manhattan Beach Boulevard. The air was damp and briny that night, a sweet blanket from the ocean. When I reached Aviation Park, I found a bench tucked back in the shadows. The track was lit, and someone was running laps. My pulse raced.

Declan McKinley.

He was working hard, breathing in swift, short puffs. And as he came around the bend, I almost called out to him. I needed the company. Badly. And I wanted to tell him about the fire. He'd once jokingly offered to help with any future "tequila emergencies." And even though that night seemed so long ago, we could still talk, couldn't we? I opened my mouth, then shut it again. Declan wasn't interested in connecting with me. He'd made that clear enough that morning at the Coffee Bean when he'd jump-started my car.

Luke and I are fine, he'd said. *I hope you are too. Let's leave it at that.*

Still, my heart beat hard as I watched him run. I found myself trying to memorize his shape. His movements seemed so easy, so free and beautiful, his body reacting to the track. With each curve and straightaway, he shifted. Adjusted.

Changed.

In that moment, I resolved that I could be changed too.

"Lia?" My name jarred me back to the present. I was in the Townsends' library with Charlotte who was staring at me.

"Right." I set down my wine glass. "Let's go find your parents."

Ivy and Charles were standing under the gazebo talking to a table full of equally tidy couples. Above them, festive streamers wove in and out of wisteria. Paper lanterns dangled at precise intervals, colliding in the breeze. The weather was almost perfect for a party, but even the Townsends couldn't control the wind.

When Ivy saw us, she hoisted her mouth into a smile. She ignored Charlotte and moved on to me. "Hello, dear," she said, kissing me on one cheek, then the other. Charles bowed at the waist. *So we're being formal*, I thought. *I can do that.* "I'm so glad you could come," Ivy said. "Charles and I weren't sure." Then my mother-in-law addressed her guests.

"Everyone? You remember my daughter, Charlotte." There came murmurs of assent, and nods. A man called out,

Hey, Charlie! Then Ivy lifted an arm to me. "And Lia, Jake's wife?" she said. "Lia, this is everyone." Ivy turned back to me and smiled. A smudge of coral lipstick marred her teeth.

A young woman at the table asked, "Where *is* Jake?" She was younger than everyone else and stunning. Before I could answer, Ivy stepped forward, placing herself between me and her company.

"Oh, Jake would've loved to be here," she said, "but sadly, he's away for work."

Behind me, Charlotte snorted. "Away. Right. Sure."

Ivy turned and touched her daughter's wrist. "Have you run into Maggie yet, darling?"

"I just got here," Charlotte said.

"Well!" Ivy beamed. "She's been asking for you. I think I spotted her on the grass playing croquet earlier. Why don't you go find her?" Ivy gestured across the yard toward the group playing croquet. Between us and them was a row of charcoal grills and buffet tables with platters of barbecued meat.

"I think I'll get a bite to eat first," Charlotte said. "I'd never forgive myself if all the deviled eggs were taken before I had one." She turned to me. "Coming, Lia?" Charlotte grinned at her act of treason, but Ivy reached for my arm.

"Allow me to borrow Lia first."

"Fine." Charlotte shrugged. I waited for someone to ask if this were fine with me, but no one did. To me Charlotte said, "Guess I'll see you later." I nodded at her, but she'd already moved away from us.

Ivy said, "Let's go have a chat." I nodded, too nervous to speak. *So this is how it will be,* I thought. *Ivy is taking me to some private space to discuss my home. The future. Their money.* As we walked together toward the house, the sun beat hot on my face. Her linen pants swished with each brisk step, and the sleeves of her blouse were sails on the wind. I noticed she kept glancing over her shoulder as if I might disappear.

When we reached the French doors that led into the side of their house, I stopped. "Where are we going?" I asked. Without answering me, Ivy continued down a short hallway, and I followed her into her private office. I'd never been in the room before. Of course, she'd feel powerful here. In one corner sat an armchair and a side table with an antique rotary phone. In the opposite corner loomed a filing cabinet. Atop her desk were three bins, each with neat piles of envelopes awaiting her attention labeled *Letters. Bills. Miscellaneous.*

I was well aware—because she liked to tell me—that the various charities headed by Ivy Townsend required constant monitoring. "So much to be done," she would cluck, and I'd imagine her lips pursed while she filled out thank-you cards. Addressed party invitations. Composed personal notes. Like the one she'd sent to me: *There's something we need to discuss in person.*

I took a deep breath when Ivy shut the door behind me. I turned, and we locked eyes. "Lia," she said, and I held her gaze. If she was going to take the bungalow, I wanted her to feel every word of her demand. "Charles and I appreciate your discretion in this matter."

This matter. Charles and I.

"You know we've always loved you," she said.

But, I thought. *There's always a but.* I steeled myself for questions about insurance money. How much would I receive? Would there be enough to cover the down payment I owed them? *Dear, I think the bungalow might belong to us now.*

"We are," she said, "absolutely devastated by what's happened between you and Jake. We didn't raise our children to behave like this." She sighed. "My daughter and her failed marriages. Now Jake. We just can't have it. The way he's treating you. It isn't right."

"Oh." For a moment, I pondered what part of Jake's *treatment* Ivy was referencing, but she continued before I could ask.

"You must understand this has all been a terrible mistake." She cleared her throat. "You do understand, don't you?"

I shook my head, bewildered. "No, I'm not sure I do."

"It seems our son has veered off course," she said. "Terribly. And Charles and I are hoping—we expect, really— that you'll be able to set him straight again." I felt my knees buckle, just an inch. This was not the discussion I'd planned for. The Townsends wanted *me* to make things right? What did they think had been going on with Jake? I squared my shoulders, gathered my strength.

"It's too late," I told Ivy. "There's nothing I can do."

"We disagree," she said. "Charles and I. And we're asking you not to give up."

"But Ivy. Jake gave up on me."

"That's not entirely true, now, is it?" Her mouth wrinkled, and I wondered what she knew. Maybe Jake had told her about his invitation to Portland. Maybe she knew I'd turned him down. "My son is a Townsend, and Townsends don't quit."

"Charlotte quit," I said. "Twice."

Ivy grimaced. "Yes, that was a disappointment. But neither of those men was right for her."

"And you think I'm right for Jake?"

"I know you are. And my son knows it too. There's still a chance for you, Lia. A chance you two can be together. It's all up to you."

"So, wait." I cocked my head. "You didn't bring me in here to talk about the bungalow?"

"What about the bungalow?"

"I assumed you wanted your money back. From the down payment."

Ivy gaped at me. "That home belongs to you and Jake," she said. "There were never any strings attached."

A lump formed in my throat. "But it isn't ours anymore. There is no *ours*. There's his. And mine. And I'm not even living there. Not since..." My words fell away, like pebbles off a cliff.

"Oh yes, the fire." Ivy waved a hand in front of her face as if batting away a fly. I was distracting her, apparently, from the real reason she'd brought me here. "We did hear about the fire. Charles and I were very glad no one was hurt. But it must have been horrible for you."

Tears gathered in my eyes. "I swear it was an accident."

"Of course it was."

"Anyway, everything's being rebuilt now. I put my friend Maren in charge. She's a designer and really talented. She'll make the place even better than it was before."

"I'm quite sure." Ivy nodded grimly. "You're very responsible, Lia. Charles and I always thought you were a good influence on our Jake."

At this I dropped my gaze. Maybe I was the one who'd been misjudging the Townsends all along. For so many years, I'd felt like an outsider. I'd acted like one. I became one. "I'm sorry," I whispered.

"Don't apologize," she said. "Just promise you'll keep trying to make things work with our son, Lia. Jake needs you."

"No. You're wrong." My heart rattled in my ribcage. I couldn't listen to this any longer. "Jake needs his daughter." *There. I'd said it.* The silence stretched like a tightrope between us.

"There is no daughter," Ivy said.

"I'm talking about Josie."

"I know who you're talking about." She crossed the room and pulled apart the brocade drapes. A burst of light illuminated her face.

"I'm confused," I said.

"So is my son."

"But my friend saw her. Maren *met* Josie. At Easter."

"Maren met a girl," Ivy snapped. "That doesn't make her Jake's daughter."

"But." My vision tunneled. I put a hand out to steady myself against the desk. "Josie looks just like him. Maren told me."

"Because the girl has black hair and dark eyes? So does most of the world's population." Ivy moved to her desk and collapsed into the chair. "If Jake hadn't run into Addie at the Coliseum, he never would've known that child existed."

"The Coliseum?"

"Yes," Ivy said. "Jake didn't tell you?"

"No. But I remember the expo there. It was on Valentine's Day, wasn't it? Jake only went there to support your charity."

At this Ivy flinched. "Which is why I cannot allow this to happen. I simply refuse to be the reason for the disintegration of another Townsend marriage."

"Maybe that's not up to you."

"Well, Jake isn't meant to be with Alexandra Barrow, either. And he is not that girl's father."

"You think Addie's lying to him?"

Ivy swiveled to face me, and her jaw shifted. "I think DNA doesn't make a family. Commitment does. And history." She'd regained herself and was calm now. She sounded patient. Gentle, even. "Jake made vows to you, and he should be honoring them, not chasing some ghost from his past."

"I thought you liked Addie. That picture on the staircase—"

"I keep it because Jake looks handsome, and the colors match our paint quite beautifully." Ivy leveled her gaze. "But that woman wasn't right for my son. She never loved him the way you do. She clearly didn't want Jake then. And now, suddenly, it's become convenient for her."

"It doesn't feel convenient," I muttered.

"Maybe being a single parent was harder than she thought," Ivy said. "Perhaps she hopes to benefit from our extensive family connections. The reasons don't matter to me. If Addie Barrow wanted her daughter to be a Townsend, she should've started ten years ago."

"But Jake loves her now," I said.

"Who? Addie or Josie?"

I looked down. "Maybe both of them."

"Either way, Charles and I will not allow our son to play the fool." Her eyes clouded, and I was afraid she might cry.

"That isn't your choice anymore," I said.

"But it can be yours, Lia." Her voice was a wheeze. Ivy Townsend was unaccustomed to begging. "Win him back," she said. "Make your marriage work. Then you and Jake can have your own baby."

But Jake never wanted children. Maybe Addie knew that then.

I swallowed hard. "I know you mean well, Ivy, but this is beyond your control."

"No." She stood and reached for me. I took a step backward.

"I loved your son. I did my best to make him happy. And he left me anyway."

"Jake doesn't know what he wants."

"You're wrong. He knew. He knows."

"This will break him, you know. My boy will end up broken."

I smiled. "Well. That makes two of us."

"But you're his wife."

"No," I said. "I'm not."

Ivy's reply was stony silence.

"Goodbye," I said. "And thank you."

Ivy looked away from me toward the window. As I left her office and closed the door behind me, I decided I would, in fact, repay the Townsends every cent of that down payment. Not today, but as soon as possible. Only then would I be free.

Making my way back down the hall, I thought about finding Charlotte. I wanted to steal a hug and wish her well. No matter what. But I kept walking. I couldn't face her now. Maybe I never would again. What did we have in common anymore besides our shared disappointment in Jake?

The butler who'd greeted me in the foyer was no longer in his chair. Alone in the entryway, I climbed the Townsends' staircase one last time. Pausing in front of the framed picture of Jake and Addie, I examined their smiles up close. Were they happy then? Were they now? How many smiles between us did we all fake?

Ivy claimed Jake and Addie didn't belong together, and yet the portrait still hung on her wall. Maybe she needed a fresh start too. My hands shook as I unhooked the picture, held it to my chest, and walked out the door.

Thirty-Two

I didn't go to Maren's. I just couldn't. My guts were churning, and I needed to get out. To get away. During a gas stop in Santa Barbara, I texted her: *Can't meet after all will call tomorrow to explain please don't be mad.* While I drove, fireworks exploded in displays all the way up the coast. It felt a little bit like I was celebrating my own independence day.

By the time I reached Marview Lane, even my bones were tired. The sky was moonless, and the tree branches overhead added to the canopy of darkness. One low branch shrieked along the car's hood like fingernails on a chalkboard. I shivered and checked the clock again.

At this hour, would he still be awake?

I cut the engine, took two deep breaths, then trudged to Caleb's house. I stood on his porch and felt the silence button up around me like an old coat. I knocked, listened, waited. No one came to let me in. Of course he could've been sleeping, but I felt a hole in the space that Caleb usually filled. I checked the carport at the edge of his property. His truck was gone.

Chilled now and officially exhausted, I returned to Regina's house and crept to her room. She was in bed snoring under the homemade blanket she'd given me the night I found out about Josie.

I knelt by her side and shook her arm.

"Wake up. Please." When I flipped on her lamp, Regina rolled over and moaned. On her nightstand sat an uneaten bowl of soup with no spoon anywhere I could see. After some grunting, Regina managed to prop herself up on an elbow. We blinked at each other in the light.

"Well. This is a surprise," she said.

"Where's Caleb?" I asked.

She rubbed at her eyes with a fist, and when she dropped her hand, a speck of crust clung to one corner. "What's the matter?" she asked. "You in some kind of trouble?"

"No."

"OK." I heard a note of skepticism in her voice. "When did you and Caleb start keeping track of each other's whereabouts?"

"Anyway, sorry I woke you," I said, standing. "Go back to sleep."

"Are you all right?"

"I'm not sure," I said.

"What's going on, Lia?"

I looked at her, breathed the scent of sleep. The air in her bedroom was cold and stale. "The thing is," I said, "Jake and I never got married."

With the words out there, I felt a gush of relief. Besides Uncle Quentin, Regina was the first person I'd told, the one I promised myself I never would. But what was the point of keeping the secret now? It never had held the weight I thought it did.

She blinked at me again. "What's that you say?"

"Jake and me. We didn't really get married."

"Oh, Lia." Regina sighed. "No one ever really does."

When she settled back against the pillows, I couldn't tell if she'd understood me. Her eyes were closed again. Was she even fully awake? I supposed it didn't matter. I'd spoken my truth. Lying had worn me out.

"I just thought you should know," I said.

I switched off the lamp, shut her door, and went to bed alone.

Thirty-Three

The wall clock read nine o'clock. Already the sun had broken through the mist to bathe the guestroom in light. I sat up and stretched, took a few deep breaths. Then I picked up my phone to finally call Maren. Never before in our relationship had I been afraid to talk to her. I'd been frustrated or annoyed, sure. Even deeply hurt. But these emotions were rare and overshadowed by the goodness we usually brought out in each other. Next to her silliness, I seemed calm and wise. With Maren, I'd always felt hopeful. Less heavy in the world. But I worried that by not showing up last night, I'd rearranged the room of our friendship.

Maybe forever.

In my head came a restless thrumming, and I stuck a finger in my free ear. Below me the quilt felt lumpy, so I shifted my weight. Cleared my throat. Counted the rings waiting for an answer. *One. Two. Three.* Then, from what sounded like a million miles away, came Maren's familiar voice.

"Lia?"

She answered like this every time, even though my name always came up on her phone's screen. Each call began with *Lia?* as if she were surprised to discover I was still a part of her life.

"Great timing," she said before I could apologize. "I'm at the bungalow now, and you wouldn't know it by looking at the place, but we've made a whole lot of progress. Most of the big decisions have happened already, and all the major orders are placed. But don't worry. I'm saving the receipts and keeping good records of everything."

My heart skipped a beat. Maren sounded so normal. *Wasn't she mad at me?* I'd been ready for her to be upset—even straight-up angry—that I'd bailed on her last night. But maybe she didn't care that I hadn't stayed after all. "Everything, huh?" I said. "That sounds like a lot."

"The big stuff, yeah," she said. "Flooring. Roof. Garage door. I picked out a dark wood one like you asked. There are still little details to figure out, like crown-molding and door handles. Light switch plates. Things like that. Oh, and I didn't love any of the stone samples Kurt Lutz sent over for the bathroom. But don't worry. I'm meeting him at some quarry-type place downtown today to look at travertine. Tony has a guy he says will give me the best price. And there are some granite slabs we can check out there for the kitchen counter too. I mean, I can check it out, since you're not here."

"I'm sorry."

"Don't be," she said quickly. "So, should I send pictures of the options once we've got them narrowed down?"

I shook my head, even though I knew she couldn't see me. "I trust you to decide."

"I think you're going to love the paint I picked out. You've always been timid about color, but I chose an accent wall in every room for a big pop. To give some contrast, you know?"

"Thank you," I said. "So much." Maren was being so nice, the nerve I'd built up to explain myself was shifting to guilt. I felt a little sick.

"By the way," she said, "Did Tony send you those papers to sign?"

"He did," I told her. "And I will."

Two days ago, Tony had emailed me a preliminary list of contents lost in the fire. I was supposed to check the list item by item, adding anything the insurance adjustors might've missed, then send it back to Tony. But the stack of papers, once printed out, was intimidating. Thick. The truth was, I'd barely scanned the document. Anyway, what did it matter now if I wasn't compensated for a ruined wedding dress?

"I know my thing's design, not the content settlement," Maren said, "but there's some overlap. Like, I convinced them you need a new refrigerator. Your kitchen's going to be gorgeous, Lia."

"Right," I said. "Gorgeous."

Maren began to gush again about how much she appreciated my faith in her. She actually sounded chipper, more alive than she'd been in years. As she spoke, I stared at the sheer fabric of my nightshirt, my legs poling out like pale sticks below the hem. These limbs belonged to me, yes, but I felt detached from myself. Undone. Raking my fingers through a snarl of hair, I held the auburn strand out for inspection. Was I still Lia? Where had she gone?

Did I even want her back?

"Lia?"

"Sorry. I'm here."

"Good," Maren said. "Because the next hurdle for me will be picking out all the new furniture. I'll have at least a month to worry about that, but my budget's pretty healthy. I'm so excited."

"Me too," I said. "I guess."

"It took the workers a whole week to sort through your place to figure out what needed replacing. They'd show up and put on these gloves and ugly blue face masks, which was a good thing because the one in charge—her name's Cindy— she had a face that was kind of hard to look at. Not because she's ugly. I'm talking about her expression, like she was at a funeral every day."

"Yeah," I said. My voice sounded flat, like my emotions. It would take a toll on someone, I figured, sifting through the ashes of other people's lives, witnessing what they had and who they were and what they lost. *Total loss.* The words echoed in my head. Tony used the phrase all the time, as if, without this reminder, I might think I still had something.

"Apparently, Cindy had a fire once too," Maren continued. "She told me her whole place burned to the ground, and after she saw how much Tony was able to help her, she wanted to do the same for someone else. So she started working for him." Maren paused then, allowing room for me to speak, but I said nothing.

"It's kinda sad," she said, "but it makes sense. I mean, why else would a person want to spend her whole life doing such a horrible job?" I didn't answer her because the question was rhetorical, and I wasn't shouldering my weight of the conversation anyway. I hadn't been prepared for Maren to be so kind. Was she being kind? I almost couldn't tell.

I swallowed and said, "So, I'm sorry about yesterday."

"Huh," she said. That was it.

"I meant to come," I told her. "I was planning on it."

"We waited, you know. Danny and Nora and me. For a long time."

"Didn't you get my message?"

"We did, but not until after," she said. "I left my phone charging at home."

I imagined the three of them, the Hollisters gathered at the beach to watch the fireworks. They would've brought a basket of bread and cheese and grapes. Maybe a bottle of wine in their cooler and a six-pack buried under ice.

"I'm sorry," I said. Again.

"I mean, it was stupid of me to not bring my phone," she said. "But I had a feeling you might cancel, and I figured if you couldn't get ahold of me, you'd have had to show up."

So this was how it was now. We expected to be let down by each other.

"Being at the Townsends' again knocked me off my axis," I told her.

"I'm sure it did," she said. From the open window above me, came the sound of a hammer next door. A steady pounding, dull and rhythmic. Caleb must've come home.

"Are you there?" Maren asked, dragging me back to her.

"I'm sorry," I said for the third time.

"Don't," she said. "Please. In the past few months, we've both been disappointed in ways neither of us saw coming. So we might as well stop apologizing to each other. There's no need to pile fresh mud on the corpse."

"Mare."

"Listen. Kurt just got here," she said. "I should go." I pictured the straight line of her mouth, heard the sadness in her voice, tasted my own hot tears, and smelled the ruins of my home. Ash. Smoke. *Corpse.* Maren was right.

Our old lives were dead.

♋

After the call, I lay in bed listening to Caleb hammering, trying to think about nothing. From the kitchen came the smell of coffee, the half-pot Regina still brewed for herself. I'd hoped Regina would make room for me on her own, that she might include me in her life without needing to be told. But she didn't, so I gave up drinking coffee. The saddest part was, I don't think the woman even noticed. I suspected Caleb did notice. But for a month of mornings, he'd been making a fresh pot and pushing a cup toward me. At first, I'd pretended to sip. Once. Twice. Three times. I put on a good show. But eventually I stopped faking it and just let my cup cool while we talked.

I thought maybe these weeks with Caleb were at least partly responsible for the growing chasm between Maren and me. With Maren, our discussions always circled back to her. Or to Danny. Or Nora. Jake. The focus almost never stayed on me, and I'd always been comfortable in the background. With Caleb, though, I'd felt like I was emerging from a cocoon. I wasn't wrapped up anymore, protected and buffered. I'd opened up.

And it was nice.

The hammering stopped, and I wondered what Caleb was up to now, if he'd already gone for his run. So I dressed in my workout clothes and went next door. The garage door was halfway open, suspended in midair. I held my breath as I slipped under it. Like an intruder. A trespasser. Thief.

The place smelled of gasoline and engine oil, and I had to pick my way around a rusty car propped on blocks. In the darkest corner sat a narrow workbench lit by one bare bulb. There, Caleb bent over a pane of glass and two pieces of a broken frame. Watching him study the seams, I thought about the picture I'd taken from the Townsends.

At the time, I had no great plans for it. I'd felt only that this portrait—a moment frozen between Addie and Jake—no longer belonged above their stairs. I wanted to free Ivy from Jake and Addie as much as I wanted to free myself. My throat flushed with the realization that I still cared. That I might always.

"I came to see you last night," I said into the silence. Caleb lifted his head, but he didn't look at me.

"I wasn't here."

"So I discovered." He said nothing more. I watched while he rummaged in a drawer and retrieved a couple of nails. "I thought I'd be gone for a couple of days," I said, "but obviously things changed."

Was that a nod?

Caleb set down the nails and turned to face me. "What can I do for you?" he asked.

"I missed our walk this morning. Did you go for a run already?" He shrugged. Of course he'd gone. Daily exercise was his routine, and our long, slow walks had been a temporary sacrifice.

Last night, I'd rushed back here prepared to tell Caleb everything, a purging of details I still hadn't shared with anyone. About what happened between Jake and me the night of the fire. About how I'd treated Declan McKinley. About me and my non-marriage. The baby I lost and Josie. The portrait of Addie and Jake I stole straight off the Townsends' wall. But the moment had passed. Maybe it never existed. Maybe there was less between Caleb Stone and me than I'd let myself believe.

"OK, then." I ran a thumb along the hood of Caleb's old car. "I'll let you get back to it."

I turned to leave, and Caleb said, "Lia." It was the first time I'd heard him say my name. "You want some coffee?"

"I don't really drink it."

"I know." He tipped his head.

❧

For someone so gruff and sparse of speech, Caleb was surprisingly soft, all smooth lines and warm skin. My head rose and fell with his chest as I lay there listening to him breathe. His heart beat against my cheek. He ran a hand over my hair. I thought of Jake, a flicker only, then I pushed the image away.

"Hey." I stroked Caleb's arm, asked him to say my name again.

"Lia," he repeated. "Lia."

Through the window streaked a hazy light, the sun high in the sky. There were no curtains, and I pictured Caleb in his bed at night, lying here gazing at the stars. For a long while, we said nothing. Then, without my prompting, he began to tell me a halting story about a phone call and his mother on the line miles away. Sobbing. Hysterical.

Ezra, his baby brother. Dead.

As Caleb spoke, my throat tightened like a tourniquet. I opened my mouth, then I shut it again. If I said *I'm so sorry*, would he stop talking? I couldn't risk it. I settled more deeply into his arms, my signal for him to continue.

"It was his own fault," Caleb said. "Ez was drunk, driving on a suspended license. He already had a DUI." Caleb's words were like raked leaves, dry and crumbling. He paused, took a breath. I twined my fingers through his and squeezed. "He killed two people," he said. "This young couple. They had a little kid at home with a babysitter." Against my cheek now, Caleb's heart beat faster. "I've never told anyone, but a part of me was glad Ez died that night. No trial to suffer through. No more fear about what he might do someday to other people. He'd already done the worst." Above us, the ceiling shifted, my mind playing games with my eyes. "Sometimes I think about finding that little kid," he said. "The one Ez made an orphan. He'd be a teenager now, probably living with his grandparents. I'd apologize. Tell him I should've done a better job. Set a better example. Yeah, it was Ezra's fault. But he was my little brother."

Inhale. Exhale. Another rise and fall of his chest.

Did Caleb want me to argue with him? Give him reasons why other people's tragedies weren't his burdens to bear? I could've told him about personal responsibility. That each one of us makes our own choices. That in the end, our decisions were all we had. Instead, I raised Caleb's hand and pressed my lips to his palm. His skin tasted of sweat. I pulled him to me.

Caleb was done talking.

ৡৣৡ

Our time together stretched out then in a long, slow blur. Misty walks at the shore. Hot mugs of coffee in my hands. We made love under warm sheets, watched the sun rise in his window. Then we'd go our separate ways, face the business of our separate lives. This wasn't the real world, and we both knew it. We were just two souls afloat seeking an anchor. Each morning we met at the crossroads to greet the day again.

For the first time since my childhood, I felt comfortable in silence. Caleb and I spent much of our time together wordless. Not that we had nothing to say. We simply waited, patient and generous, for the right time. For each other. We spoke in bursts, then surrendered to the quiet. Caleb listened when I finally told him about my visit with the Townsends. About Josie and Addie Barrow. He nodded when I swore I'd find a way, someday, to pay back my in-laws every penny they'd loaned us. And when I admitted how much I still liked Declan McKinley—how often I thought about him—I blushed.

When it was his turn, Caleb shared a few stories, dark and short, about his deployments. About friends injured or lost altogether. He wouldn't tell me much. I don't think he *could*. But in his eyes, I saw pain beyond description, and I might've understood why he'd come home. For a while, he'd made a go of his own construction company, Stone's Way, a lifelong dream. But civilian life felt like squeezing into boots three sizes too small. Then he lost Ezra, and the rest of him unraveled. Stone's Way became too much. So he took the job at Greenway Construction. It was under the radar and easy. He worked the overnight shifts. That's where he'd been the night of the Fourth.

For her part, Regina never asked about Caleb and me. In fact, she acted surprised each time she noticed I was still around. Then again *Caring for Lia* never had made the list of projects she embraced. No, Regina Lark couldn't be my mother. She was too busy painting, sculpting, or scribbling ideas for inventions on napkins. I told this to Caleb one morning as we lay on his bed. I wondered aloud what might've become of Regina if she hadn't inherited my grandparents' house. "She'd have nothing," I said. "She'd be nothing without the constant support of Quentin."

I heard my own words, then caught my breath.

For years I'd relied on Jake. Both financially and emotionally. When he left, I looked to be rescued first by Maren, then by Declan. Now I was here with Caleb, staying in Regina's house, living off insurance money. The fire had been a terrible, necessary accident. A purging of my old life. But if I continued this way, what would become of me?

Escaping. Hiding. Denying.

My name on Caleb's lips.

"Lia," he said.

I pulled the sheet over our shoulders, touched his cheek, then closed my eyes.

The next morning, in my inbox, I found this message:

Hi Lia.

I got your email address from Ivy Townsend. She called me last week and wow. She had a lot to get off her chest. I can't stop thinking about what she said, and I need you to know I didn't plan any of this. Josie and Jake. None of it. Which is to say running into him was a coincidence. I hope you will believe me.

You probably already know it happened at a charity expo at the Coliseum. The woman in charge of our booth got food poisoning, and I had to step in at the last minute. Of course, I had Josie with me. And we'd barely gotten set up when Jake appeared next to the display of my mother's books. She was a writer, my mother. Maura Barrow. (You've probably never heard of her.) The plan was to sell her books and donate the profits. Anyway, I was as shocked as Jake when we saw each other.

Then he got a look at Josie and…

I expected him to be furious, to never want to speak to me again. But he couldn't walk away from her. From Josie. He's been so good to her. So good for her. I'm sorry if that's hard to read. And believe me, I've made none of this easy for him, either. And I don't know why I'm telling you that now.

I guess my point is, Jake's not the same man I used to know, and I'm thinking you must be the reason. When we were together, he was pretty much all about himself. Don't get me wrong: We had fun, and we cared about each other for a while. But we wanted different things in life. By the time I found out I was pregnant, I knew where Jake stood on kids. Should I have told him? Maybe. Yes. I should have. But to be honest, I didn't trust myself. Jake could be pretty persuasive back then, and I wanted to keep my baby.

Anyway. I'm off topic. This happens when I'm nervous. I don't expect a reply from you, but I'm here if you wish to respond. Just please know this: Jake is a better man now. Maybe because of you. He was yours, and he still can be if you want him.

Sincerely,
Addie Barrow

Delete.

Thirty-Four

The first of August brought with it a morning rainstorm, and then later that day, my Uncle Quentin. He arrived as the sun broke through the clouds. Earlier that week he'd called to say *hello,* and I heard Regina on the phone fielding his questions. About her. About the rebuild. About me. I wasn't eavesdropping—not exactly—but I couldn't help overhearing. At least I didn't try to. Most of Regina's answers were vague at best and at worst completely wrong. To hear her tell it, I was in a downward spiral.

I think Lia's forgotten how to be happy, she said. I thought this was pretty funny coming from Regina. When had she started noticing other people's happiness? Did she even know what her own happiness looked like?

So that afternoon when Regina told me Quentin was planning to visit, I wasn't surprised. Even a little bit. He was worried, and he genuinely wanted to see me. This I knew. I also knew this meant another awkward meeting like the one at Uncle Bill's Pancake House. Yes, Quentin loved me. Yes, I loved him back. But there was always this small distance between us. Like a swaying bridge we couldn't quite cross. I think to him I'd always be Regina's little girl, another person he loved and couldn't save.

When Uncle Quentin arrived, our hug was tight and longer than usual. I couldn't help wondering just how worried about me my uncle had become. Hoping the fresh air would lighten the mood, I led him to a table in the backyard. Around us hovered a few rogue bees and the fragrance of wet honeysuckle. I wiped off two chairs, and we sat down opposite each other. He removed his glasses, polished them on his shirt, and I waited until our eyes met to speak. "Regina's finishing up a portrait for a friend this afternoon," I told him. "She promised not to be long. But you know how that goes with her."

"I do," he said. "And it's just as well. I'd like to talk to you first, anyway." I noticed the hard set to his jaw, like a brick in the wall behind him. That's when I suspected Quentin hadn't come here simply to check on me.

"All right then," I said. "I'm ready. Spill it."

He chuckled, shook his head. "You don't beat around the bush, do you?"

"No sense playing coy." I offered a tentative smile. "I've wasted too many years pretending not to see the signs."

"Are we talking about us? Or Jake? Or have we skipped right to your mother?"

"Yes," I said. "Yes and yes."

Quentin laughed out loud, then scanned the yard, taking in the changes since he'd been here last. His brief survey ended at the chicken coop, and he shook his head. "She really did it, huh?"

"I take it you don't approve."

"Hardly. But I don't think it matters. Let's talk about what does matter. How's my favorite niece?"

"I'm fine," I said, although my *fine-ness* felt unsteady, like planks over a shallow river. I was afraid of putting my weight on it, of cracking the boards and falling in.

"How's the bungalow?" he asked.

"Coming along," I said.

"Even with you here?"

"My friend Maren's been handling the rebuild. She's a designer—well, she was—and I think it's been good for her, this project. She's saving me, but I'm also kind of saving her too. She's given up a lot of herself in the past few years. We both have."

Quentin nodded, but I wasn't sure he understood. What

did my uncle know of real sacrifice? As much as he'd helped Regina and me, he never had to rearrange his life for us. There'd been lovers in his past and some girlfriends even qualified for the adjective "long-term," but very few of his relationships lasted longer than six months.

"You need anything?" he asked.

"I'm good." I smiled at him.

"You'd tell me if you weren't?"

"Nope. Probably not."

"At least you're honest." His smile was gentle. "How about Jake? Have you moved on from all that yet?"

All that. I shook my head, then realized there wasn't a better way to put this. "It's a work in progress," I told him.

My uncle cleared his throat, looked down at his hands. "Progress is good," he said. A breeze kicked up and raised the hair on my arms. Or maybe I sensed something big was coming.

"Anyway, how are things with you?" I asked. "How's Simone?" At the mention of her name, Quentin lifted his face. His eyes softened at the edges. This was the face of a man in love.

"We're getting married," he said.

"Well, well!" I smiled again. A full-on grin. "That is huge news."

"Yes."

"I'm so happy for you. Both."

"Really?" He exhaled now. "That's a relief," he said. "I was worried."

I tilted my head. "Why?"

"Because you… aren't," he said.

"Married?"

He dipped his chin. "Not anymore."

"Ha! You mean *not ever.* I haven't forgotten that I told you."

Quentin cleared his throat again, and a hummingbird in a nearby jasmine vine skittered away. "Sorry," he said. "I'm a clumsy old bastard."

"You're not old."

"You don't think so?"

"I do not."

"Thank God," he said. He leaned back in his chair. "Because there's something else." He rubbed his chin.

"Ah. A banner day for you." I perused his face, noted the looseness of his neck.

"Can you guess what it is?"

I laughed. "Based on your face," I said, "I'm not sure I want to!"

For a moment, he laughed with me before growing serious again. "I'll save you the trouble," he said. "Simone's pregnant."

"Oh. Wow." Above us, the leaves rustled, a lullaby in the breeze. I felt heat on my cheeks and wondered what tale the rest of my face was telling.

"We weren't planning this, I can assure you."

Of course you weren't, I thought. *Forget what I said before. You are too old.* These words danced on my lips, but I didn't say them. "What a wonderful surprise."

"The better word for it is *accident*."

"Maybe." I took in his pale face. I'd never seen him look scared. "Listen," I said. "Accidents don't have to be bad. Some of the best things happen to us when we least expect them. At least that's my mantra every morning when I wake up. Most days, I even manage to believe it."

Quentin met my gaze. "You're pretty wonderful, you know that?"

I chuckled. "I wish that were my other mantra."

"No, seriously. I'm sure it hasn't been easy staying here," he said. "My sister can be... challenging. You two getting along?"

I took a beat, measured my response. A teaspoon of reality would be enough. "Regina and I coexist," I said. "She rides her own wave, and I try not to knock her off. Not that I could if I wanted to."

"Can I ask you something?"

I nodded.

"Why did you keep visiting her, all these years, when you didn't have to?"

"Hmmm. That's a good question. Why did you?"

"Regina's my sister."

"I'm her daughter," I said. "And I know how it feels to be lonely."

Quentin peered at me over his glasses. "It's not your job to mother her."

"Sure," I said. "But if I don't do it, no one else will."

"When do you think you'll go back home?" he asked.

Home. I glanced at my lap, then back at him. The concern in his voice made my nose sting. "Soon," I said. "School starts again in a couple of weeks."

"Will your place be ready by then?"

"Probably not," I said.

"What's your plan?"

The Plan. Even when I thought Jake and I had one, well, it wasn't in stone, anyway. Since returning to Santa Cruz, I'd tried not to think too much about the future. This summer had been a respite from real life, but it was ending. Caleb and I would end too. I just wasn't sure yet what our ending would look like. I wasn't sure I was ready to see it.

"I'll figure that out when I have to," I said. "Regina's always telling me I'm too much of an organizer. She might be proud of me for winging it. That is, if she even notices I've left."

My uncle and I shared another smile. "You'll be fine," he said.

"Anyway, why are we talking about me when we could be talking about your baby?"

"Oh. That." He ran a hand through his thinning hair and squinted. "You will help me break the news to Regina, won't you?"

"Don't worry," I said. "She'll be thrilled."

"She definitely won't be." He laughed. "My sister's rarely thrilled for anyone else. She forgets other people exist. You should know that better than most of us."

"You're right. I do."

"Besides. There's the touchy subject of her inheritance."

"What are you talking about?"

"My substantial fortune, of course." Uncle Quentin smirked. "I'm kidding. I'm hardly rich, but I had been

planning to leave everything to you and Regina. Now I'll have
to change the will. What a heartbreak."

"Don't be morbid," I said. "And you're younger than she
is. You'll probably outlive us all."

"No." He touched my elbow. "I wouldn't want to do
that." We were both quiet then, listening to the hens clucking
in their coop. He closed his eyes, and for a moment I thought
he might've fallen asleep. With his eyes still shut he asked,
"Do you know how old I'll be when this baby's eighteen?"

"Stop. I hate math."

"Over seventy." He opened his eyes. "After that, I think
I'll stop counting. Who wants a seventy-year-old father at his
graduation ceremony?"

"I think you'll make a great dad. And you'll be seventy-
three."

He smiled. "You did the math."

Despite his reservations and demurring about his age, my
uncle was clearly pleased by the words. *Father. Dad.* He sniffed,
and I studied his face. Were Quentin's eyes growing wet? This
was, without a doubt, the deepest conversation we'd ever had.

"I'm going to be a father," he said. The swaying bridge
between us steadied.

"That's amazing," I told my uncle. And it was.

❧

Quentin broke his good news to Regina as soon as she
returned home, but instead of congratulating him, she said she
needed to go wash up in her new kitchen sink. She came back
out with a bottle of wine and three glasses, then led us to the
living room where she launched into a discussion of the latest
portrait she'd been commissioned to paint.

"It's for Beverly Swanson's husband's birthday," she told
us. "She's surprising him with a nude. Remember, Lia? I told
you about it months ago. We've been working on it since
May."

"I remember," I said. "So what do you think?"

"About what?"

My uncle rolled his eyes.

"Uncle Quentin's getting married," I said. "Simone's having a baby. Any of that ring a bell?"

"Oh yes, he told me. Come on, Lia. You were here! Have you forgotten already?" She glanced over her shoulder at the kitchen. "Has anyone started dinner yet?"

The meal we threw together was a long, noisy affair. The scrape of fork against plate was drowned out only by Regina's endless, embellished stories.

Did you hear about the time I wrote a poem for President Reagan? He wanted to use it for his inauguration, but Nancy was jealous. As if I'd date a Republican!

And Lia, you were the worst sleeper with all your constant nightmares. It's a wonder I ever survived with so little rest when you were young.

Once I woke up in the passenger seat of my car, and I was parked in front of the police station. You were in the driver's seat. I'll never know how we got there!

After we finished eating, I cleared the table and offered to wash all the dishes. I was hoping to give Regina and Quentin some privacy to talk. But it wasn't long before my uncle came to join me at the sink. "Well, that was pointless," he said. "She kept changing the subject whenever I tried to talk about the future."

"Hers or yours?"

"Both."

I sighed. "Give her time. You know Regina. She needs to process how this situation affects *her*."

"Situation. Right."

My uncle found a dish towel shoved behind the toaster and dried the plates after I washed them. When I'd scrubbed the last pot and left it to dry in the rack, he said he had to go.

"It's a long drive home, and Simone will be waiting."

"Of course," I said. "Thanks for coming. And just so you know, I'll be fine." He pulled me in for a hug that was even longer than the hug when he'd arrived. When I stepped back, he took my hand and spun me around like we were dancing. "Why, Uncle Quentin! You've got some moves. Who knew you were so dapper?"

"Don't tell Regina. She'll launch into the story about the

time I failed a square-dancing unit in P.E."

I laughed. "Should we go find her?"

Quentin shook his head. "We already said our goodbyes."

I walked him to the door, and on the front porch he paused. "You really think I'll be a good father?"

"You're going to be there," I said. "That already puts you ahead of a lot of dads I know."

୬∘ঔ৶

I found Regina back out in the garden, on her knees pulling weeds in the dark. She wore new dungarees and a white T-shirt. *An interesting choice for the work.* Her favorite red bandanna swept her hair back, the length of auburn trailing down her spine.

"Hey," I said, and she looked up. In the moonlight, her face was luminous. She could've passed for half her age. She could've been me. Without a word she returned to her work, so I knelt beside her on the damp earth. In the juniper bushes, crickets chirped. From farther away came the crash of a wave, then its long withdrawal. Eternal and relentless.

"Well, that was a good visit," I said, another way into the conversation. From Regina came a stifled grunt. Her shoulders lifted in a shrug.

So this is how it would be.

"He's pretending to take it in stride," I said. "The pregnancy. Marrying Simone. But I think Uncle Quentin's beside himself."

She paused then, weeds hanging from both her hands. "Your uncle's a foolish man," she said. "Oh, that poor, poor kid." I watched the pile of weeds grow and considered who *the poor kid* might be. Was she talking about the new baby? Uncle Quentin? Maybe she meant Simone, who was two decades younger than he was. Anyway, the answer didn't matter. Regina's focus had already returned to her weeding.

I lifted a handful of mud to my nose and inhaled the richness of the soil. "What are you going to plant?" I asked.

"Brussels sprouts. Cauliflower. Cabbages." I heard a familiar *tsk*. Regina hissed through her teeth when she was annoyed. "I try every year, and every year the cabbages wither. Anemic little bitches."

"Ha!" I laughed out loud. This was perhaps the first time she'd admitted any project of hers had failed, and I wondered if she counted me among the wasted fruits of her labor.

"He's going to be a terrible father, you know. Quentin's far too selfish. A baby will wring him dry," she said. At this I shook my head. I was half-amused by this prediction and half-angry. In all my life, Regina had never expected success from anyone but herself.

"I need to ask you something," I said. When she glanced at me, her lips were pursed. She looked almost afraid.

"Well?"

"Where did you go?"

She sighed. "I told you. I had a portrait commissioned. For Bev Swanson. Maybe you should write these things down, Lia."

"Not today," I said. "I mean after Grammy died."

"What are you talking about? I didn't go anywhere. I was stuck here with you, remember?"

"I know you didn't move or anything. But you'd leave, Regina. And I'd be here alone for days at a time."

She picked up a trowel. "Don't exaggerate."

"It's true," I said.

"Hmph."

"I never told anyone."

Regina began to make tiny holes in a neat row. "You were very mature for your age, Lia."

"I was ten."

"Exactly. And I was an adult. You and I had nothing to say to one another. So I had to get out sometimes. Find stimulation. Be with my people."

"Your people?"

"Yes." From a small paper packet, she shook seeds into her palm, then pressed them one at a time into the earth. She covered them up gently. Lovingly. "I needed to be around creators, Lia. Thinkers. Innovators like me. Otherwise, I was surrounded by sheep. All the time. My parents. And Quentin."

"Me," I said.

She wiped her hands on her dungarees. "I never belonged here," she said. "And that wasn't my fault."

"It wasn't my fault either."

My voice was soft now and gentler than I'd intended. But rage would do neither of us any good. Regina and I were the same people we'd always been, the same people we'd always be. For us, change came like a wave over the sand, a temporary shock. We'd be soaked for a while, wet and smooth. Cohesive. Then we'd return again to our natural state, separate grains no longer glued together.

"So," Regina grunted. "Why didn't you ever tell anyone?"

"That you left?" Her nod was grim and tight. Perhaps she'd always hoped she'd be caught. Maybe she'd wanted to be released from the burden of raising me alone. "I didn't want you to get in trouble," I said, although this wasn't the whole truth. A part of me had been guarding a secret: *My mother didn't want me. I wasn't good enough.*

She frowned. "You were always so scared."

"Of being abandoned?" My voice was getting louder. Finally. "I was a child!"

"You were scared of taking risks or getting in trouble. Scared of punishment. Scared of being wrong. As if being wrong is the worst thing that could happen to a person."

"Maybe I was," I said. "But is that an unforgiveable flaw? Wanting to do what's right?"

Regina narrowed her eyes, which betrayed her answer. To her, being afraid was the worst sin of all.

"Well," I said. "I guess I'm over that now, anyway."

"Are you?" Regina patted the mounds of dirt over her seeds. Overhead, moths beat their dusty wings against the bulb of a patio lamp. My grandfather had loved that lamp. It was made to look like an old-fashioned streetlight, one you might see in New Orleans. *Flutter. Thump. Flicker. Thump.* The moths never gave up. They kept skirting the halo of light.

A futile dance.

"You're being reckless with him," Regina said, her focus still on the ground.

"With who?"

She straightened and squared her shoulders. "Caleb."

I could tell by the bend of her neck that Regina knew about Caleb and me. My heart beat fast with the thought that she cared about my feelings. "It's OK," I told her. "I won't get hurt. Don't worry about me."

"I didn't mean you," she said. "I meant Caleb. Aren't you hurting him?"

She was staring at me, and I saw it in her eyes. Regina was actually jealous. I was on the verge of becoming the person I was meant to be, while she was still a hollow shell, some ghostly moth beating against a streetlight in the dark.

Despite all her big dreams, Regina Lark wasn't a famous artist, a published author, a sculptor, or poet, or superstar. She was an aging woman, a faded beauty, her brightness dimmed by her own dissatisfaction.

I felt something dislodge in my chest then. This shift. A kind of knowing. Regina would never fully be on my side.

"No, Mom," I whispered. "I'm not hurting him."

"Be sure you don't," she said. "I have to live next door to the man, you know."

I closed my eyes, breathed in and out.

It was time for me to go.

⁌⁍

I sat in my car for a long time, perhaps an hour, while the windshield fogged with my breath. With my frustration. More than once, I flicked the keys dangling from the ignition. I listened to them chime against each other, considered the possibility of flight. I ached to start the engine, to ease down the driveway in a slow crunch of gravel, with nothing but the soft glow of taillights to suggest I'd ever been here at all.

Two months. Less than that, even. And I was prepared to run again without a goodbye.

This is what you do, Lia. What you've always done. You run. And you've surrounded yourself with other runners. Other people who give up.

I'd found Jake, a man who ran so hot and cold I couldn't gauge his temperature. I sought the push and pull of him, the *all in but not quite*. He wanted to be something he wasn't. Like me. A slippery slope.

I fled from Maren and the stretch of our friendship. *Why try? Why risk the strain?* Better to abandon her first than stick around to watch our tether snap. Then after the fire, I left my home and the dark suspicion I might've let it happen.

Although I hadn't chosen Regina, she was the first runner in my life, the one who set the pattern for all the others who came after. Each time she left, I wanted her back so badly. I'd hated being the one who'd been rejected. So tonight, I picked a fight with her, then headed to my car so I could leave her first.

Through the vents came a whisper of smoke, some neighbor probably stoking a backyard bonfire. Waves of white ash floated over the rooftops. At least I thought it was ash. It might've been dust from my brain, the creeping denial finally escaping. Here I sat, ready to start the car, to drive off without looking back. But the voice inside me grew louder than the throbbing in my head.

You can be strong, Lia. Make this time different. In the morning, you'll find Caleb. You'll say goodbye and wish him well. You'll hug Regina and thank her. You'll hold them both close, and you'll feel the release, light and silent, when you let go. Then, after you've scattered these bread crumbs, you will safely leave this place. And like a grown-up Gretel, you can one day find your way home.

Thirty-Five

The next morning on our walk, the streaks of sunrise cut through the clouds. Side by side Caleb and I trudged together, clumsy in the sand. Heavy steps, bumped elbows. We brushed against each other, then moved apart. In the air was a sting of salt. The breeze pulled at my hair, wet strings across my cheek. It was too early for shadows yet. Only our footprints trailed behind us.

Instead of talking, we listened to the ocean. When the waves rushed at us, we scrambled up the bluffs. I tripped, and he caught me. He tripped, and we laughed. Each time the water withdrew, a line of foam remained to mark its reach.

At a low cement wall, we both stopped and took a seat. Caleb squinted, focusing on the gray horizon. What would it feel like to step with him into the ocean? To keep wading until I could no longer stand? I imagined being lifted by a surge of water, his hand under my back, a buoy as he taught me how to float.

"I think you should try again," I said.

Caleb blinked, but he didn't reply.

Through the cotton of my sweatpants, the cold seeped up to my skin. "I mean starting your own business," I said. "Stone's Way. You should give it another shot."

To this he said nothing.

"I know these past few years have been hard on you," I continued. "With good reason. And working for someone else is less risky. But—"

"It's not about risk."

"Oh."

"I'm content with the way things are," he said. "You get what I mean?"

"But—"

"You want more for yourself. I get it. But content's a good place too."

"I'm con–"

"No," he said. "You're not."

"Stop interrupting," I told him. He nodded, and I shifted my body, dragging one leg up the wall to turn and face him. "You're right about one thing. I do want more. I *need* it. I just don't know what *it* is yet."

"Not knowing's fine. Takes more work, is all."

"You got that right," I said. We stayed quiet for a while, the ocean air skimming my face. Along the strand, a man ran past us, swift of stride and panting hard. His clothes and shoes were technical. Expensive. I smiled and called after him. "Nice pace!" The man lifted a hand in acknowledgment, then he kept running, each footfall a soft slap.

When he was out of earshot, Caleb said, "Slow's OK too, you know."

I laughed. "I've seen you run. You're the opposite of slow."

Caleb regarded me for a moment, then he smiled.

Oh.

He wasn't referring to speed. He meant living. And I wasn't sure I wanted to have this kind of talk with Caleb Stone right now. Today was supposed to be about saying goodbye and thanking him for the company. *It's been a rough summer, and you made it a little better. I'm grateful. Please be all right.*

"I like my life, Lia," he said. I opened my mouth to tell him I liked mine, but the words froze on my lips.

"I'm glad," I told him.

Another nod. "You'll get there too. You're going to be happy someday. Maybe very happy. Maybe soon."

"You think so?"

"I do. I think you could be very happy."

"Good," I said. I lifted my eyes to his. "Now, could you tell me what happy looks like?"

Caleb chuckled. "No, I cannot." After a moment, he returned his gaze to the ocean. "Ezra loved the beach," he said. I hadn't expected this. I waited in silence for him to continue. "When we were kids, we'd come here every day. At first, we dug holes, made our own tide pools. Then we built sand castles. I taught him to surf."

I swallowed hard. "I didn't know your brother very well. Hardly at all, really."

Caleb shrugged. "Nobody did."

Overhead, a seagull flapped its white wings and descended in a graceless flop onto the sand. The bird bobbed its narrow beak, appraised us for food, then hopped off in search of other prospects.

"What made you come back here?" I said. "After."

Caleb's shoulders pitched upward then sank. "All my life, I couldn't wait to get away. Enlisting seemed like the quickest way to get gone. Then I saw what the rest of the world looked like, and home didn't seem so bad."

"So this is home to you?"

Caleb nodded, and I knew it was time.

"I have to leave," I told him.

"I figured," he said. "When?"

"I don't know." I took a beat. "Tomorrow, I think."

He rose then, reached out his hand. "I'll walk you back."

"Not yet," I said. "There's something I need to do."

I slid off the wall and peeled away the top layer of my clothes. They dropped in a pile at our feet. He met my gaze, and my skin rippled with goose bumps.

"Caleb. Swim with me."

Thirty-Six

Regina was in her studio when I came to say goodbye. She'd left the door open, and the room was awash with light. I took this as an invitation to enter. In the past, when she'd wanted to tap into the deeper parts of *the artist within*, Regina would close the shutters and stuff towels against the bottom of her door. I once discovered her wearing earplugs and eyeshades while she painted blindly onto pieces of found driftwood. But today she stood under the window, an old soldering iron in her hand. A ribbon of heat hissed at its tip. Colored glass winked in sections on the table. Regina pretended not to notice I'd come into the room, but her eyes flickered my way when I knocked on the wall, an announcement of my presence, and she dropped the iron to suck at her index finger.

"Shit," she muttered. I ignored the injury, waited for her to turn her head.

"What are you up to in here?"

She lisped over her finger. "Take a guess…"

"Looks like an interesting new project."

The finger dropped from her mouth. "Hardly new, Lia. I've been working with stained glass for years."

I forced a smile. "You must really enjoy it then."

She sighed. Maybe frowned a little. "Being an artist isn't about enjoyment."

"Ah." I nodded. "I guess I'm not creative enough to

understand."

"No," she said. "You're not." Rather than respond, I kept right on nodding. Regina's eyes turned to slits. She was probably annoyed I wasn't fighting back. That was her problem. Not mine. "Anyway," she said, "I normally shut the door because visitors disturb the flow."

"I didn't mean to interrupt, I just came by to tell you I'm leaving." Regina lifted her chin but said nothing. "Maren's been great," I told her, "but I think I need to get back to help her with the end stages of the rebuild. Also, school starts again in a few weeks, and I've done absolutely nothing to prepare." When Regina remained silent, I continued. Did I want her to protest or let me go? Either way, I knew for sure I should go now. But a part of me had hoped she'd ask me to stay. "Anyway, I should look into tutoring. Going forward, I might need the extra income."

Regina turned to the piles of stained glass on her table. "Artists can't afford to worry about money," she said. "We'd never get anything done."

Under my breath, I said, "Too bad we don't all have a brother like Quentin."

Regina bristled. "What was that?"

"Nothing." My gaze moved to the soldering iron, the pieces of glass in front of her. "It's just… you're lucky to make a living doing something you love."

She shook her head. "Art isn't about luck or love. It's about being my authentic self."

"Of course it is." I smiled. "Take care of yourself, Regina. And take good care of Bertram too."

Regina pursed her lips. She looked confused.

"The rooster," I reminded her. "I like his moxie."

"Oh. Bertram. Yes. Sure." In that moment she sounded vulnerable. Chastened. Almost sad. Her arms dangled at her side, and my throat grew thick. This would be my most recent memory of her, the proof of what we'd always been to each other: strangers with opposite views of the world who happened to share blood.

"Tony, my insurance adjuster, arranged a rental for me," I said. "Sol Dempsey's place. It's the house next door to mine, so it's convenient. His bungalow's usually booked solid this time of year, but no one's lining up to live next to a construction site. Even if it is near the beach."

Regina shifted her focus out the window toward Caleb's house. "You'll get used to the noise," she said. "Pretty soon, you'll hardly notice it."

"Maybe." I thought of Caleb and the clutter of his house. The chill of the ocean. His arm beneath me as I floated.

Regina shrugged. "I'm sure you're anxious to get out of here," she said. I opened my mouth to reply, but she put up a hand to stop me. This was good because I didn't know what to say. "I'm not mother of the year," she admitted, "but I'm not stupid, either." A shadow moved over her face. I took a step forward, and when she didn't back away, I took another. Closing the space between us, I gathered my mother into my arms.

"I admire you," I whispered. Her hair smelled of green apples and dust.

"No you don't," she said. "But that's all right."

I pulled away, met her gaze. "I suppose it has to be."

Her shoulders were stiff, like a coat hanger was hanging from her collar bone. "When will you be up here again?" she asked.

"It might be a while," I said. "Things will be hectic with the bungalow and school and tutoring. I can't be sure—"

"Thanksgiving?"

"Maybe."

She turned away, picked up the soldering iron again. "I'll invite Quentin to come. And Simone if they're still together."

"They're having a baby, Regina."

She stared at the wall. "That doesn't mean anything."

I nodded. "You might have a point."

"I always have a point. And I'll make a ham," she said. "For Thanksgiving." Then she bent once more over her table.

"That sounds nice," I told her. "Very nice."

Thirty-Seven

In one oversized duffel bag, I was able to pack all the clothes I currently owned: a couple of outfits for working out; seven pairs of underwear and socks; two bras; one pair of running shoes; three hoodies with matching sweatpants; five T-shirts and four pairs of jeans. These were the things I'd purchased after the fire, and they were new, and more importantly, comfortable. Along with these, I still had Maren's hand-me-downs, mostly sundresses and shorts, plus Harold's drawstring trousers, his Rolling Stones T-shirt, and his blanket. These had all been washed so many times by now, they always smelled of detergent.

When school was back in session, I'd have to supplement my wardrobe, but I didn't particularly want to, and I couldn't explain why. Except to say this: I loved the unexpected simplicity of having almost nothing to choose from, an excuse to wear the same pieces of clothing over and over. And over. These days, I gave my appearance little thought and fashion even less. I knew that people who ran into me around town or at school might've heard what had happened to me. The end of my relationship. The fire. I didn't care either way. It was freeing.

I felt free.

After a hot shower each night, feeling deliciously clean and warm, I'd crawl under my cool, white sheets—the single set I'd bought the last day I spent at Regina's. Everything else in Sol's bungalow belonged to him, not me. But I didn't care. I figured the rest of my life had changed. I might as well embrace the new normal.

Rather than sell any of my stuff that had been salvaged after the fire, I called Safe Haven and arranged to donate everything. Restored furniture and knick-knacks. *His pots. Hers pots. Yours pots.* All of it. The donation trucks would go directly to the storage unit for pick up. I was glad to donate. Happy, even. But I didn't want to meet them there or watch my old life packed up and taken away.

"You can have everything in the storage unit," I'd told the woman on the phone at Safe Haven when I called to make the appointment. "And whatever you can't use, please just throw out for me." The woman was silent for a moment, and I began to stammer. "So, is sorting through all my things too much? Is asking for that not OK?"

"No, ma'am," she said. "I mean yes, it's OK. It's very generous."

I swallowed then, relieved.

"Can I get your name and address, so we can send you a tax receipt?" she asked. "Or do we already have you on file?"

"It's 588 Morningside Drive. In Manhattan Beach."

There came a click-clack of fingers on a keyboard. "Yes, we've got you. Mrs. Townsend. I see you've donated before."

"It's been a few years, but yes. That's me. Except it's Lark now. Lia Lark."

"I understand." She paused, and I wondered if maybe she did understand. Maybe she was already changing my name in their system. "Ms. Lark?" she said. "Our trucks will be at the storage unit on Tuesday, September 12th, in case you change your mind."

"No, I'm sure I want to donate."

"I meant if you decide you want to oversee the collection of your goods."

"Oh, I won't," I told the woman.

She thanked me again, and I smiled.

౿⌁౷

The following week Pauline brought bagels to my classroom. She knocked twice, our agreed-upon signal, and I rose from my desk to let her in. I'd been keeping the door locked and the lights off while I prepped for the start of school. I wanted to avoid other faculty members for now. I wasn't ready for their curiosity.

In June, a local newspaper had printed a story about the fire, and according to Pauline, rumors regarding me had rippled quickly throughout the summer school staff. She'd promised to keep the details vague when anyone pressed for information, but I still felt sick when I imagined the speculation. *In the wake of her collapsing marriage, did Lia Townsend pull a Fatal Attraction and burn the place down for revenge?*

Maybe.

Bagel in hand now, Pauline squeezed into a student chair next to me. "So. I've got good news," she said. Her expression was inscrutable. Was she being sarcastic? "Around here, you're kind of a hero, Lia."

I choked on my sesame bagel. "Hero?"

"Yep." Pauline smiled, apparently pleased with herself. OK. She wasn't being sarcastic. "On Monday I talked to Hannah Morgenstern—we all know whatever Hannah hears, everyone hears—so I was pretty sure she'd share whatever I said about you with the rest of the faculty. And I was right."

"So?"

"So… I might've let it slip that even though you'd already lost so much—you know with the fire and Jake and everything—that you volunteered to give up the rest of your things to Safe Haven. In other words, freakin' hero!"

I frowned at her. "Pauline."

"What?" Her eyes widened with feigned innocence. "We've all seen you this week sneaking around school in that white getup." At this Pauline glanced down at Harold's drawstring pants. "Hannah herself said *Lia Townsend looks like some kind of angel.* So I got to thinking. Why not make you one? For real."

"I'm hardly an angel," I protested, but my heart swelled at Pauline's kindness. "And I don't want that kind of attention. But thank you for thinking it anyway," I told her. "Also, I want to be Lia Lark now."

"Good for you!" Pauline chuckled. "I'll let Hannah know that too."

"Perfect."

From outside the building came the sound of laughter, and I gazed out the window. Boys and girls were traveling in bunches, mapping out the stops on their new schedules. Would any of them be in my classes? I hadn't gotten my lists yet. Tori Zilkin ran past my room, and I wondered if she'd found her birth mother yet.

As the kids jostled around each other, I couldn't help thinking about Luke McKinley. He'd be starting eighth grade this year, another September without his mother. That meant Declan would be shopping for his son's school shoes again and buying him fresh notebooks and pencils. A backpack. I pictured Declan, towering and playful, poking his son as they walked the aisles at Staples. Every time I imagined them together, Declan and Luke McKinley were grinning.

"Lia? You OK?"

I turned back to Pauline who now had a smear of cream cheese above her lip. "I'm fine," I said. "How's Eddie?" I wanted to shift the subject to something other than me.

Pauline chewed and swallowed a bite of bagel. "He's good," she said. "Better than good." She moved to take another bite, but her mouth twitched, and she set the bagel down. "Actually, we're talking about moving in together." At this, she lifted her face to mine. Her eyes were shining. Hopeful and happy. I nodded, and my throat began to ache.

"That's wonderful, Paul."

She sucked in a breath. "Is it?"

Once more, I nodded.

"I was afraid you'd be sad," she gushed.

"Why? Just because I'm probably going to die alone?" I laughed then, willing her to get the joke, but Pauline dropped her head and brushed stray crumbs into her lap. Then, without looking up at me she asked, "What's going on with him, anyway?"

"With who?" I asked, pretending nonchalance.

She blew out a breath. "Jake."

"Nothing," I said. She studied me, quiet for a moment.

"You don't have to tell me," she said. "But I'm here if you want to talk."

"Well, I don't want to talk about Jake," I said. I peered out the window again at the now-empty schoolyard. August sunshine poked through tree branches, dappling the ground. I knew the air smelled of fresh-cut grass and jasmine, the hint of beginnings and endings at the same time. I turned back to Pauline. Her cheeks were flushed. "There is something I could tell you," I said. "But no one else knows."

"Ooh." She leaned toward me, her breasts spilling over the desk. "I'm all ears."

I swallowed hard, then said it. "I'm going to take a sabbatical." Pauline's jaw dropped, a trapdoor on a hinge.

"What?"

I nodded. "When the new contracts come around in January, I'm putting in a request for next year," I said. "And I'm going to apply to nursing school." The idea had been nibbling at the edge of my mind like a mouse with a wedge of cheese. But as I spoke the words, they became true. I'd told someone. Now it would happen.

"Wow." Pauline shook her head, and my pulse raced. This was why I didn't want to tell anyone, or even admit this dream to myself. I dreaded her arguments, considered my own. How would I explain this choice? I felt unprepared. "That's what you really want?" she asked.

I nodded again, tears gathering in my eyes. Of happiness. Maybe even joy. Or hope. Yes, hope. That was it. "I really do."

"Oh my God, Lia!" Pauline unfolded herself from the desk and came over to wrap her arms around me. "I'm going to miss you so much." Her breath was hot, and I heard her gulp. If she cried, I would cry too.

Endings and beginnings.

I edged away from her, and we both were quiet, working on our smiles. "You're just full of surprises," she said.

"Yep." I blinked at her. "I guess I am."

Returning to her seat, Pauline looked dazed and confused. I figured we both did.

"So," I said.

"So."

"When you move in together, is Eddie going to live with you in your castle, or will the princess be moving to his bachelor pad?"

Pauline laughed. "Smooth change of subject." She dabbed at her eyes with a napkin, wiped the cream cheese still smeared above her lip. "We're in negotiations," she said. "But we're thinking we should find a neutral location. He's got his place, and I've got my place. We want to find one place that's ours."

Again, I heard my mother-in-law's words as I opened up their Calphalon wedding gift.

His pots. Hers pots. Yours pots.

Ivy had tried hard on our behalf, but Jake and I were never fully committed to the *yours*. We played at marriage, said the lines, moved around the stage—without embracing our roles.

"If you're going to do it," I said, "Go all the way."

"Ha!" Pauline snorted. "We have no problem with that."

"Oh, man." I shook my head. "I walked right into that one, didn't I?"

She laughed harder. "I am who I am," she said. "People never really change." For a moment I took this in, then I decided Pauline was wrong. Jake had changed, and I had too. How much still remained to be seen.

"Did you two start looking yet?" I asked her. "For an *ours* place, I mean."

"Nah. We're waiting for the school year to start. We want to get settled. Let everyone talk about us for a while behind our backs."

"Perfect again," I told her. "That'll take the heat off me."

Her smile swept into a grin. "So you're not going to talk to me about Jake? Or the fire?"

"I'm not ready. But when I am, you'll be the first to hear."

"Deal," she said.

"And speaking of ready, when the time comes, I might have a place for you and Eddie."

Thirty-Eight

I never could sleep the night before the first day of school. Even when I was a girl. While most kids mourned the end of their summers, I lay awake, eager for my good days to start up again. It was not the cusp of a new beginning I looked forward to. It was bidding good riddance to ten weeks of loneliness. Ten weeks of uncertainty. Ten weeks of the unknown.

When I was at school, I knew exactly what to expect. For eight hours we'd read and learn and think. I found comfort inside the four walls of a classroom helmed by an adult I could trust to be there. After my grandmother died, this feeling grew stronger. Close to all-encompassing. I was desperate to believe someone else was looking after me. My teachers meant so much to me, I doubted they could feel the same back. In seventh grade, I began to wonder.

Did any of them truly notice Lia Lark?

As a test, I went almost totally quiet in class. I stopped raising my hand and whispered answers to the teacher's questions when I had to. I stopped turning in work, and no one seemed to care. Math became a bore. Science provided little mystery. I still looked forward to English though. I loved reading books and writing stories. I loved language in my ears and on my tongue. I got worried my intentional slacking had taken its toll in Language Arts. So I visited Mrs. Sewald at the end of the first semester. Weak-kneed and trembling, I approached her desk. What would I say to her? How would I explain my plummeting grade?

"Cou—could you," I stammered, "please tell me… how I'm doing in this class?"

Mrs. Sewald glanced over the wire rims sliding off her nose. "Oh. You have an A," she said. "Congratulations."

An A?

For months, I hadn't turned in my homework, although I'd completed it every night. I'd stopped studying, participated little in discussions. Maybe I was just that good. My heart thrummed with pleasure. I believed her.

Later that night, I told Regina about my A. She might've been painting. I know that I blushed. "That's fine," she said. "Go to bed."

The following week, when I received my report card, I was shocked by the C from Mrs. Sewald. She added no comments. Not even a satisfactory in citizenship. Just a C. Average achievement. She'd lied to me.

Emboldened by anger, I went to see her again. Mrs. Sewald didn't look up. I cleared my throat. "Can I help you?" she asked.

"It's my grade," I said. No stammer.

Her focus was fixed on a paper calendar in front of her. "What about it?"

"You told me I had an A."

At this, she lifted her chin. "And?"

"You gave me a C," I said. "On my report card."

Mrs. Sewald nudged her glasses up and peered at me. Then she opened her roll book, skimmed the names with the tip of her finger. "Oh, yes," she said. "I see what happened. I thought you were someone else."

"Who?"

"Genevieve Pinkerton."

And that was it. That was my moment. Standing there in Mrs. Sewald's classroom, I decided to become a teacher. I also promised myself I'd *stop* teaching the moment I was no longer moved by it. When I started at Manhattan Beach Middle School, I vowed that I'd learn every single student's name on the first day of school. And each year I did. All of them.

Sometimes more than a hundred.

Period by period, I'd walk the rows putting strange names to strange faces. I repeated. Practiced. Memorized. *You are seen. I know you. I promise.* Long into the night, I'd study the seating charts—repeating, practicing, memorizing—until I had every one of their names seared into my brain. I wouldn't break their hearts.

The next day, excitement danced on their faces, although they tried their best to hide it. The students glanced around the room, waiting for me to reach their desks, fidgeting nervously.

What if she forgets me?

One at a time, a pair of eyes went wide as I said the correct name.

Arjun Patel. Samantha Hu. Nat Dwyer.

And on and on and on. No stammer.

∽∾

Yes, the first day of school was always my new beginning, and it got to me every year. The excitement. The nerves. This was our chance—mine and my students—to erase our pasts and embrace fresh starts. Clean slates all around! That's how school worked, right? So this year, on the night before school started, I truly believed I could face my new life for the first time since April 1st. And for the first time *ever*, I believed that, just maybe, I no longer needed the first day of school to feel like this anymore. Maybe I didn't have to wipe out everything that happened to me *before* to handle my *after*.

Voicemail

Lia? It's Veronica. I got your message. Please don't worry about not being able to host the September book club meeting. You know I'm nothing if not flexible, and Bets Farinelli said she's happy to step in! I think her son Cam is going to be in your class this year. What a hoot! Anyway, I've already called everyone personally to let them know about the change in location. I hope you've been enjoying Love in the Time of Cholera! *I'll bring extra post-it notes if you need them, although I'm sure you have plenty. It's not like you live in a cave now.* ☺ *Well. See you at book club!*

Save.

Hello, Ms. Lark. It's Fran Clarkson from Safe Haven with your confirmation call. Our trucks will be coming to Warehouse Storage on Tuesday, September 12th between 8 a.m. and noon. If you need to change your appointment date or time, please contact us as soon as possible to reschedule. Thank you again for your donation and have a safe day.

Save.

Lia! I'm sorry I missed your call, but you know I'm always in the garden at night. Try me during the day next time, and you'll be more likely to catch me. Anyway, I'm fine, thank you for asking, and so is Bertram. At least I think he is. He can't tell me. If you want to know, you should come up here and ask him yourself. Anyway, I'm glad to hear your classes are going well. Those kids are damn lucky, and I raised one helluva daughter. Call me back when you can. I've met someone special. I think you'd like her.

Save.

Hi, Lia. I was visiting Jake when he got your text, and I realized it's been a while. Too long. Have we really not talked since July? I hope you're well. If you have a moment, I've got a question about TJ. No rush to get back to me. Just whenever you have time to chat. Until then, kiss kiss. From TJ and me. Bye!

Save.

Hey. I got your text, and I can come by Wednesday, sometime late afternoon. Let's say 4:15? I've got a layover at LAX, and I'm not flying out until early Thursday. Call me if that time doesn't work. Looking forward to seeing you. Oh, and Charlotte says hi. So. Hi.

Save.

Thirty-Nine

I sat on the floor of Sol Dempsey's house in a patch of afternoon sunlight. Beside me were two boxes just dropped off by a guy who worked for the restoration facility. On the outside of each box was a large white label. One read 113, the other 114. I could barely wrap my brain around the numbers, each one a cube of my past life. The rest of the boxes had been picked up by Safe Haven, but I'd requested these two be set aside. The delivery man smiled when I signed for them. And as I had been on the day of the fire, I was impressed by the generosity of strangers.

Three months ago, when my life was in ruins, I'd felt irrevocably broken. But this morning Kurt Lutz had estimated his construction crew was more than "halfway to the finish line."

Halfway to the finish line. I thought. *Sounds about right for me too.*

Hunching over the boxes now, I inhaled long and deep. From inside the cardboard came a sweet, clean smell. The delivery guy told me that was the ozone treatment used to save smoke-damaged items. When I'd read through Tony's extensive salvage list, I'd discovered these boxes of Jake's things. Number 114 contained several plaques and awards he'd received from his airline. And in 113 were the following items:

letters, cards, invitations
yearbooks

loose pictures
photo albums
The day he left, Jake told me to keep everything, but I was sure he wouldn't want his personal items at a women's shelter or in a dumpster. At some point these things had mattered to him. At some point I'd mattered to him too. If he didn't want these boxes, maybe Josie would.

Someday.

Alone on Sol's floor, I almost dug through box 113. For years, when Jake was away for work, I'd write something to him daily. Poems. Letters. Cards. I'd leave them on his pillow for him to read when he returned. He kept them all in his nightstand. The top drawer. Always the same spot. I didn't ask if he liked what I'd written, and I tried not to mind that he never wrote me back. *Writing's not my thing,* he said. We had an understanding.

While I labored over each message—careful with each adjective, noun, verb—Jake preferred to talk to me in person or on the phone. I saw now that in many ways, his communication style was better. He didn't curate his thoughts, never edited or revised. He said what he meant in the moment, sometimes changing his mind in the next.

But not me.

I deleted and rewrote, word by word, sentence by sentence. I worked until I'd gotten down exactly what Jake wanted to hear.

For this reason, I left the box sealed now. I couldn't bear to face this spillage of my heart, my thoughts scrutinized and manipulated. I knew the words weren't honest or real. They were sculpted. Works of art. I guess, in that way, I was Regina's daughter after all.

What if I'd let Jake read the first drafts? Would he have appreciated the rawness, my insides flying across the page? Would he have been able to decipher the chicken scratch? Maybe he would've seen the real me, the truth of my love for him. Maybe it would've saved us.

Maybe I didn't want the "us" to be saved.

From outside Sol Dempsey's house came the slam of a car door. I checked my watch. 4:13. *Right on schedule.* Jake was never late. When his footsteps reached the porch, my throat began to clog. I'd left the door propped open, and there he was, suddenly, his body framed by the sun.

"Hey, Lia."

The rest of his face was in shadow, but I could see his mouth curved in a smile. "On the floor again?" He shook his head. "We have to stop meeting like this." When I frowned, he asked, "Too soon still?"

I smiled. "Too soon always."

"So. What are you doing down there?"

"Thinking," I said, because it was the truth.

"Join you?"

I swept my hand toward the space beside me, and he took a seat on the floor. He'd changed out of his pilot's gear into typical beach wear. Shorts. T-shirt. Flip-flops. This close to him, I grew warm. He smelled like sandalwood.

Unfamiliar.

A bead of sweat trickled down his neck.

"You got a haircut," I said, and I was glad. It hurt a little less to see these small changes in him. Jake looked at me, and his eyes were soft. I wanted to kiss them. To pluck them out. To never see them again.

"You look good," he said.

"Do I?"

He nodded. "You do."

I hadn't been fishing for the compliment, but a part of me hoped he meant it. I worked so little on my appearance these days, I imagined what he saw when he looked at me. Wild auburn hair in need of a brush. Blue eyes free of makeup, fine lines fanning at their edges. The afternoon light probably betrayed every bit of my thirty-five years. And I was glad of it. I was sick of trying to be something I was not.

"What are you thinking about?" he asked.

I stared at him. Exhaled. "Well… I was thinking we should get married. For real this time. What do you say?"

Jake's mouth went slack. "You're kidding."

"Yes," I said. "I am."

He threw back his head—I assume to laugh—but his skull cracked against the wall. "Aw, shit!" He reached around to rub at what was sure to be a bump back there. "Ouch," he said.

"Good," I said. "Now we're even."

We both began laughing then, on the floor together, side by side. I waited until I saw his shoulders relax, and I hoped the ice had broken. We turned to face each other, our legs folded, birds huddled in a nest.

With a bend of his head, Jake indicated the two large boxes. "What are these about?"

"They're yours," I said.

"Mine."

"Yes. Everything else is gone."

I thought he might remind me that I was supposed to keep everything. This was his penance, after all, the price he felt he should pay for leaving me. But he didn't. He reached out, wrapped my hand with his. "Thank you." He squeezed my fingers. After a beat, I withdrew my hand.

"I thought maybe Josie might want your old yearbooks."

"Maybe." He smiled, eyes wistful, probably thinking about her now. "Would you like to see a picture of her?"

"Oh." My pulse raced because I did. I wanted to see the woman Jake had left me for, even if she was his daughter. I wanted Josephine Barrow to be beautiful. And sweet. I wanted not to hate her. Not too much.

Jake sat back, unlocked his phone—*he'd always kept his locked*—and scrolled through his photo library. "Here," he said, deciding on a picture to share. "This one's from last week. We finished a whole pizza, just the two of us."

I took the phone from him and held it up to peer at her small face. In the shot, Josie was alone, but Jake might as well have been in the picture. The girl was an exact match. Full lips. High cheekbones. Long lashes below a sweep of black hair. Ivy Townsend was crazy if she thought Jake could turn his back on this girl. I wondered for a moment what might compel her to reject her granddaughter. Then I stopped myself. Those were someone else's demons, and I'd stick to managing mine.

I opened my mouth to say *she looks just like you,* but I couldn't get my tongue around the words. Instead, I squeaked, "She's pretty," an understatement of immense proportions.

Jake's daughter was lovely beyond description. His chest swelled, and I could tell he knew it too.

"Maybe you'll meet her someday," he said.

"No." I shook my head, mouth full of cotton.

"Lia." He inched closer. "If you and I are ever going to—"

"We aren't," I said. "Jake, I can't."

He leaned back again, eyes fixed across the room. Opposite us slumped Sol Dempsey's couch and an old coffee table. On the floor stretched a large, worn rug. One edge lay within my reach, and I picked at a loose thread, felt it unravel between my fingers.

Jake was watching me.

"Addie and I aren't together, you know."

"I didn't know," I said. "But it doesn't matter."

His exhale carried the sting of frustration. "I panicked, Lia."

I nodded. "You did."

"When I ran into Addie that day at the Coliseum—the two of them together there—well, I took one look at Josie and—" His eyes dropped to his lap. "I should've told you, but I was in a fog. I didn't know what to do. What to say. I couldn't think about anything except making up for lost time with her. Lia, please. I never wanted to hurt you. I just—"

"I understand," I said. "I do."

"Really."

"I've done my share of not being honest."

"But you can't forgive me," he said. A statement, not a question.

"It's not about forgiveness. It's about who I am now. Who I've become. You don't want her."

"What if I do?"

I was quiet for another moment. In the silence, a second hand ticked. I had no idea where Sol kept his clock. "At the Fourth of July party," I said, "your mother begged me to give you another chance."

"I didn't ask her to do that."

"I figured. That's not your style." I smiled at him. It was small, and my teeth felt tight. "Do you know why she thinks we should still be together?"

"Because my parents love you."

"Because they loved the Lia Townsend I pretended to be," I told him. "You all did. Even Charlotte."

"You're wrong," he said.

"Maybe." I got to my knees, stood my ground. "But I can live with that."

"So this is it, then?"

"It has to be." I walked to the door. When I reached it, I turned and found Jake still cross-legged on the floor. He averted his eyes and ran a hand over the box closest to him.

"What's in here, anyway?"

"Letters. Cards. Things people wrote to you over the years you must've saved."

"You sound surprised."

"I am."

He raised his head, and we smiled at each other. "Guess you don't know the real me, either."

"Maybe," I said again. An echo. A realization. "But I can live with that too."

Forty

"Damn, I wish you'd been my teacher," Maren said. She was sitting in my swivel chair while I mounted a new crop of poems on a *Welcome, October* bulletin board. "Are you sure you want to give up teaching?" she asked.

"Nope." I aimed my staple gun at a fall poem by Kyra Jones. "Not sure at all. But it's just a leave of absence." *Punch. Punch.* "I can always change my mind."

Behind me, Maren muttered. "Hard to come back once you've been gone."

"What?" I'd heard her fine, but I had my own agenda.

Maren raised her voice. "I said *nothing ventured, nothing gained.*"

"Yeah. That's what I thought." *Punch. Punch.* "Speaking of ventures, have you given any more thought to contacting LeBlanc? I'm sure they'd love to hire you again."

"That was your idea, not mine."

"Nothing ventured, nothing gained!" I used my sing-song voice, and Maren snorted.

"Nora's only been in full-time preschool for a month. Can we all slow down?" She made a sound not unlike the groans I heard for hours on Nora's birthday. *My baby's four*, she kept repeating. *How the hell did that happen?*

"I'm not pressuring you," I told her. *Punch. Punch.* "I'm complimenting you. When it comes to design, you've still got it. That's all I'm saying." Maren spun in the chair, a full revolution, legs in front of her. When she reached me, she bumped the back of my knees. Not hard, but I turned around.

"Don't look at me like that," she said.

"Like what?" I returned to my bulletin board. *Punch. Punch.*

"Like you're disappointed in me."

"Never." *Well, sometimes.* But no one gets through friendship without a little disappointment.

"Anyway, I'm the one who should be mad," she said. "You're bailing on me tonight."

"Sorry, but I'm not bailing. I'm choosing something else."

"*Something else.*" Her foot bumped the back of my knee again. "Just admit it. You won't have as much fun with Pauline and those other girls."

"You're right," I said to the wall. "Sari and Helen are great, but you're more fun. For sure."

"I'm not jealous," she said.

"Of course you aren't."

Maren was quiet for a moment. "What if Danny let me go dancing with you?"

"Ha! Like you've ever asked his permission in your entire life!" *Punch. Punch.* "But sure. You're welcome to join us. Pauline adores you."

"And so do you."

"Yes." I looked over my shoulder at her. "So do I."

Maren shrugged and handed me the final poem to mount. "Thanks for the invite, but I read the damn book. All 800-million pages of it. *The Count of Monte Cristo.* Sheesh. What a slog. And you thought *Love in the Time of Cholera* took a long time."

"See? Now you *have* to go to the meeting just to show Veronica you followed through." *Punch. Punch.* I took a step back to survey the bulletin board. "There. Is that good enough?"

"Yep," Maren said, but when I faced her again, she was staring out the window. "Look," she said, and I turned. A flock of birds was making its nightly migration across the sky. We were both quiet for a moment, then she said, "Anyway, I should get going."

"It's not that late," I said. "It's just getting dark earlier now." Soon we would come off Daylight Saving, and the other teachers were already lamenting the change of clocks. I played along, grumbling with them in the lunch room. But this year, I welcomed the passage of time.

"You want me to stay?" she asked.

"A few more minutes. Please."

"Fine." She sighed. "A few more minutes. But don't expect me to have a good attitude."

"Don't worry." I smiled. "I'll keep my expectations low."

"Wise choice," she said, smiling back. This was how things went for us now, a barb here, an apology there. We were still circling the friendship a little, waiting for our seas to calm.

"Have you packed for Napa yet?" I asked. Her in-laws were flying in to watch Nora so Danny and Maren could finally take that vacation. Maren always perked up when I mentioned their trip.

"Packing is impossible. You can't imagine." She shook her head in faux annoyance, but her eyes were wide and bright. "This time of year, the weather's unpredictable. You have to bring jeans and boots and sweaters, but it could also be hot. So I'll need sundresses. Sandals. Tank tops."

"For three days?" I considered my limited wardrobe, how much I liked not worrying about being stylish. When I was a nurse, I'd have an even easier time of it. I couldn't wait to wear scrubs to work.

"Danny's mad about the extra luggage," Maren said. "But he owes me. This is our first trip since—"

"Nora was born. Yeah. I've heard that."

Maren sucked in her lip. I figured she was thinking the same thing I was, about the birthday weekend she'd pushed for. How differently things had turned out.

"I've been reading up on the harvest," she said. "The vineyards are in a stage they call 'crush'? Apparently, this is the best time to go." She smiled at me. "I'm lucky."

"Yes," I said. "You are."

Since Nora could walk and talk, the child would toddle up to me, a cracker or cookie in her hands. "Two pieces or one?" she'd ask, holding the cookie up for inspection. I was allowed to look but not touch the broken sides she'd pressed together. Although it was there, the split was invisible to the naked eye. I always pretended her cookie was whole. It was the first rule of the game, the reason she kept playing. Maren and I played by those rules too.

And for now, it was enough.

All my relationships were shifting and settling like aftershocks following an earthquake. Charlotte and I had spoken a few times since the new school year started. She said TJ's English teacher was a jerk and she needed confirmation. What Charlotte wanted to hear was that her ex-husband was a bad father. My last text to her was *Good luck!* Neither of us had picked up the thread since.

After the Townsends' party I'd made no attempts to contact them, and neither of them had reached out to me. As if Charles Townsend would call. Maybe Ivy would send a Christmas card. I did wonder about them sometimes. If they were happy or at least healthy. And about how long it took them to notice the portrait missing from their stairwell.

I gave the picture to Jake the evening he met me at Sol's. While he loaded the boxes into his car, I hauled the heavy frame from the trunk of my car. "Here," I said, handing it to him. After a moment spent staring at the glass, Jake burst out laughing. He thanked me, and I almost asked him *what for,* but he set the picture on his passenger seat and drove away.

Since his move to Portland, his car has been parked in the Hollisters' cul-de-sac. Was the picture still inside? I refused to ask Maren or Danny. I knew Jake visited them during his layovers, brought Nora gifts, shared stories about Josie. I heard very little, requested only the broadest strokes of his schedule to avoid crossing paths. Whatever Jake did, whatever the Hollisters did with him, that was their story now, not mine. I'd been a part of it once, an important chapter. But despite Jake's half-hearted attempts to invite me back in, it was too late. I'd started my own book.

I was still working on the title, and I'd be OK with that.

Maybe forever.

On Halloween, Quentin called me. He had no idea what night it was. "How could you not know?" I asked him. "Candy? Costumes? Nothing?"

"Sounds good," my uncle said.

I'd stayed home to hand out miniature Snickers bars but also to keep an eye on my place from Sol's kitchen. Construction on the bungalow wouldn't be done before next month, and every once in a while, I still spotted kids trying to break in. On those nights, I called Harold, and he headed over with a baseball bat to break things up. *You wouldn't actually use the bat,* I said. *Only if I had to,* he replied. Then he grinned. I'd really miss that man when I moved out.

In December—assuming the bungalow was ready— Pauline and Eddie were moving in, and I'd start renting Eddie's apartment. It was a one-bedroom place across the street from the middle school. The difference in rent would supplement my income, and I could easily tutor there after school. When I told him the plan, Quentin advised me to sell instead. He said it would be smarter to invest the profit and make money off the equity.

My equity. I told him I wasn't ready for such permanence. At least not yet.

"How's Simone?" I asked.

"Nesting," he said. "It's fabulous."

"Do I sense sarcasm?"

"You sense honesty."

"Right," I said. Then, although it was none of my business, I asked, "How does it feel to be married?"

"That's a funny question." He took a beat. "Coming from you."

"Oh, I'm hilarious," I said, and to prove it, I laughed. I couldn't tell if he was laughing with me on the other end of the phone.

"I called your mother," he said, a swift change of subject. "She's leaving for some ashram in New Mexico. Says she needs to get away for a while. Be with her people. Breathe in her chakras. Whatever that means."

"Regina didn't tell me."

"I know." My uncle paused again. "She asked me to."

This shouldn't have surprised me, but still my insides fluttered. Regina in an ashram. Quentin's baby. Pauline and Eddie. It was a lot to take in. I plucked a Snickers bar from the bowl, tore open the wrapper with my teeth. While I chewed, my uncle continued. "She doesn't know when she'll be back. So if you want to come here for Thanksgiving, Simone and I would love to have you."

"Thanks." I swallowed. "I'll think about it." A thought occurred to me then. *Bertram.* "Who's taking care of Regina's chickens while she's gone?"

"Her neighbor's looking after the place. I haven't met the guy, but she said he was trustworthy."

I pictured Caleb roaming Regina's yard, watering vegetables, sprinkling feed into the coop. Bertram the rooster would bob over to him, feathers on display. I smiled at the thought of it. Two men, one territory, neither of them talking.

"Oh, good," I said. "That's good."

There came a rustling on the front porch and a *knock knock knock.* More trick-or-treaters. I told Quentin I had to go, grabbed the bowl of Snickers, and headed for the door. Just outside, a pack of boys jockeyed for first position. From their height I guessed they were teenagers, but barely. The group reeked of Axe spray and sweat. Instead of Halloween baskets, the boys carried pillow cases, and all of them wore minimal costumes: Beanies pulled low on a brow. Backward ball caps. Comical sunglasses. They were restless, trolling for candy and something more. I grinned at them. I'd been thirteen once too and hungry for something I couldn't yet name.

"Help yourselves." I held out the bowl. "Two each." The boys dug in, but they took turns. Almost all of them mumbled a thank you. Behind them, at a distance, a father stood, shifting his weight. *Good man,* I thought. *Good kids.*

The last in line stepped up and ducked his head. His costume looked like a mechanic's uniform. Under the grease paint smeared across his cheeks, I recognized the face.

"Hi, Luke."

"Hey, Mrs. Townsend."

I fought the urge to correct him. To say, it's *Lark. Ms. And I was never a Mrs.* Instead, I said, "Happy Halloween." He flashed me a small thumbs-up, and I nodded. Our little secret. Done with me now, the boys took off down the street, running toward Harold's house.

"Watch out!" I called after them. "That guy carries a bat!" When they reached Harold's door, I turned to shut mine and saw the lone father walking toward me. From out of the darkness he slowly took shape. I took in the broad-shouldered frame and those bright eyes that smiled even when his mouth didn't. But he was. Declan McKinley was definitely smiling.

"Hi, Lia."

I adjusted a pair of pointy black ears atop my head. "I'm a cat," I said.

"Yes." He grinned. "I can see that."

My stomach felt tight, and my whole face burned. "I moved," I told him.

His eyes cut to the bungalow, then back to me. "I heard," he said. "I'm so sorry."

"Yeah. I'm sorry too."

In the wake of our apologies, we were quiet for a moment. A breeze brushed my face, and I felt the ocean in it. "So—" I swallowed hard. My tongue was thick. "This is a coincidence, huh?"

"No." Declan ducked his head. "Not really."

"Oh," I said. *Oh.* The heat from my cheeks spread to my throat. From up the street came the shouts of boys. A stumble of footsteps and cursing and laughter. "Are you supposed to follow them?"

"No." Declan leaned forward, just an inch. "Not really." Under the porch light, his face remained half-shadowed.

Let go, Lia. Dive in. Believe.

I tilted my head. "Want to stay, then?"

"Yes," he said. "I do."

I reached for his hand and led him inside.

Want more from Julie C. Gardner? Check out *Letters for Scarlet*: Corie and Scarlet are each hiding secrets from their high school days. Now, a decade later, can they face their past and rebuild their friendship?

A Note from Julie C. Gardner

Dear Reader,

I'm thrilled you read *Forgetting Ophelia*, a novel several years in the making. The seed of the story took root when I asked myself how a woman in her thirties would handle the implosion of her seemingly perfect life: Could Lia Townsend move forward? Would she remain haunted by her past as Ophelia Lark?

I felt for Lia and wanted her to find happiness; I just wasn't sure what that happiness would look like. Lia answered those questions—for herself and for me—while I wrote her story. I love that at the end, her future is still unfolding.

If you enjoyed the book, please consider leaving a review on Amazon. Reviews help other readers discover authors they might not otherwise find. Even a few sentences saying why you enjoyed the book can make a big difference. And to those of you who've reviewed already: thank you, thank you, thank you!

I'd also like to invite you to sign up for my newsletter to stay up to date on my latest news and special sales: http://juliecgardner.com/newsletter.

Thanks for reading!

All my best,
Julie

P.S. I've got more extras for you on the next few pages: a book club discussion guide and a sneak peek at *Letters for Scarlet*.

Read more from
JULIE C. GARDNER

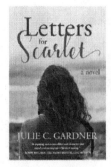  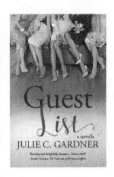

Book Club Discussion Guide

I'm delighted you've chosen *Forgetting Ophelia* for your book club read! If you'd like me to join the discussion via Skype, please email me at juliecgardner4@gmail.com. In the meantime, here are some questions for your group to consider:

1. As readers, we know Lia's anniversary/birthday dinner won't follow The Plan. Do you think Lia suspected something was wrong, or was she in denial?

2. Throughout the breakup, Lia worries about Maren and Danny's loyalties being split between her and Jake. Is this fear justified? Have you found yourself torn between couples after a separation?

3. Jake doesn't want children, and Lia goes along with this decision. Is she partially to blame for Jake's choices before and after Josie, or is Lia merely a victim?

4. Regina Lark is narcissistic and, one could argue, delusional. Why does Lia continually return to her childhood home in Santa Cruz? Is Lia's motivation practical? Emotional? Both?

5. Lia feels an instant rapport with Declan McKinley, but their relationship won't work for several reasons. Were you rooting for them anyway? Why or why not?

6. Caleb Stone is both a comfort and an escape for Lia when she's in Santa Cruz. How did you feel about them being together? In what ways is Caleb right or wrong for Lia?

7. Jake admits he acted hastily and suggests he and Lia might fix things between them. Why is a relationship with Jake the best or the worst choice for Lia? Whom were you hoping she'd choose?

8. What was your impression of Charlotte Townsend? Of

Ivy Townsend? In what ways do Jake's sister and mother influence Jake and Lia? What about Lia's Uncle Quentin?

9. Lia's friendship with Maren is tested more than once. They feel both supported and let down by each other. Could you relate to this type of friction between best friends? Whose side were you on?

10. The ending of *Forgetting Ophelia* hints at Lia's future, but isn't tightly wrapped up. What do you imagine will happen to her? Do you support Lia's choices, or were you hoping for a different resolution?

Letters for Scarlet

a novel

JULIE C. GARDNER

Lavender Press

Corie

I've always liked my nickname and the fact that those who are close to me have an easier time of it, subtracting a syllable from more formal introductions. *Corinna* is a mouthful, but *Corie* is simple, the way things should be when people are friends. Tuck digs even deeper, calling me *Core,* a single word that can be either a noun or a verb. Both imply a goal. Something central. Intimate. Four letters that unite this pair of opposites.

He's all action and go, go, go. I'm content with stillness, the noun of our relationship. Tucker is black hair and lashes like warm silk. I'm blond curls and eyes so icy-blue my sister said I was adopted from a wolf pack. She chanted *See-Through See-Through,* and I hated being pale. So thin. Practically transparent. Then one day Tuck Slater suggested I was *translucent in a good way,* and I began to count the number of times his skin chose my skin, to memorize the way his bones fit my bones.

That was a decade ago when we attended Conejo High, before I landed a job teaching literature instead of writing it. Parking in the faculty lot was uncomfortable at first. So was using everyone's first names.

Hey, John! Not Mr. Pickett.

Good morning, Bev! It still feels strange to call Mrs. Fox by her nickname.

What remains uncomfortable now is wondering what they

see when they greet me in the halls: Corinna the student, the John Keats wannabe, the one from "the terrible tragedy"; or Ms. Harper, the English teacher who scribbles in journals on her lunch breaks.

Today I've barely settled on a couch in the corner of our lounge when the new assistant principal strides toward me, skinny and fresh-faced, a bag of microwaved popcorn steaming in his hands. His cheeks shine with the hope of someone starting his career, and the sleeves of his oxford are rolled up at the wrists.

"Ms. Harper." He nods at me.

"Hello, Mr. Callaghan."

He's wearing glasses of the Clark Kent variety, and his dark hair spikes upward like a head full of licorice. "That smells good." He indicates the frozen meal in my lap. "Chicken parmesan?"

"I think so," I say. "I just grab whatever my husband puts in the freezer." I shove a forkful of mozzarella into my mouth, but after I chew and swallow, he's still studying me, eyes round and quizzical.

"Mr. Harper does the grocery shopping?" he asks.

"Slater," I say. "Mr. Slater. Harper is my maiden name."

"Ah. Progressive choice."

I shake my head. "It's less *progress* and more *I hate going to the market*. Tucker—that's my husband—he's great, but he hates to cook. So he buys the groceries, and I make the food. You could say we take on each other's bigger hate. So to speak." I inhale a chunk of chicken to stop myself from rambling, and Mr. Callaghan smiles at me.

"Sounds equitable," he says. "But I was referring to the fact that you use your maiden name."

"Oh!" I cough on the chicken chunk, and my forehead warms to the point of sweating. "No," I manage to say. "You see, Harper was the name on my credential, and then my dad died, and I decided to stay a Harper. For him. Not that he would have expected me to. I just thought it was the right thing to do. And easier too."

So much for not rambling.

Mr. Callaghan sets down his bag of popcorn and takes a

seat on the opposite end of the couch. He smells like aftershave and hot butter. "I'm sorry about your father."

"It's been a while, but thanks." I picture my dad's kind face, his strong hands. I drop my chin, and my hair is a drape of white-blond curls along my neck.

"Anyway." Mr. Callaghan exhales as if he might clear the awkwardness in one gust. "I came over here for a reason." His voice is softer now but still deep. I lift my head to hear him better and catch Stella Womack and Bart Kominski grinning at me from across the room.

Great.

"I wanted to compliment you on your lesson yesterday," says Mr. Callaghan.

"I got a copy of your evaluation this morning," I tell him. "You were very generous."

"It's not easy to act natural when you're being observed. But your class? It was a pleasure."

"Thanks again, Mr. Callaghan."

"Please," he says. "Call me Henry. We've been working together for a month. I think it's time."

"Has it been only a month?" I ask. "This school year's really dragging." I paste on a smile in case he doesn't have a sense of humor. Henry nudges his glasses higher on his nose.

"I hope you don't mind if I call you Corinna," he says. Behind him Bart and Stella wave and blow kisses.

"Nope," I say. Then I set down my fork and pick up the pencil next to my journal. "But I'd better get back to writing. No rest for the weary."

"No rest for anyone on this couch." His small laugh is reassuring. Henry Callaghan likes to joke. "It should be against the law," he says. "Or at least a health code violation."

"That's funny," I tell him. *A little*, I think.

"It's true," he tells me back. "I'll leave you to your work, then."

I look up at him. "My what?"

"Work," he says again. "I see you writing in that journal every day. Concentrating. Serious. I figure it must be pretty important."

My forehead grows even warmer, and I worry I might

blush. "No one ever calls my writing work. Not even Tuck."

"Then let me be the first."

"Do I have a choice?" My smile is crooked. "After all, you are the boss."

"So I am," he says. "But don't forget. It's Henry."

He pushes himself up off the couch and collects his bag of popcorn. When he stands, I notice his pants could use a decent ironing. Then, as Henry Callaghan walks across the lunchroom and out the door, I watch him go from under lowered lashes.

⚜

For my afternoon classes I write these instructions on the board:

- Read the poem at your desk.

- On the paper below the poem, share what you think the poet implies about IDENTITY.

- After five minutes, pass your poem to the left and repeat the process.

When the bell rings, the students amble into the room in packs and take their seats.

"How much do we have to write?" they ask.

"There's no minimum or maximum," I say. "Just tell me how you feel."

"I feel tired," says Greer Larson. "I need caffeine."

"Trust your instincts," I suggest. "Trust yourself."

"What if my instincts are telling me to go to Starbucks?"

I shake my head. "You have five minutes per poem. Starting now." I check the wall clock and make a mental note of when to tell my students to stop trusting themselves and pass what they have written to the left. I'm collecting the papers from my sixth period class when I begin to feel the ache. It is dull. Familiar. Regular as the tide. A hand slides to my stomach as the kids stack their work in the wire bin next to my computer.

I tell them, "Don't forget to check out your copy of *Inferno* from the library by Friday," although it has been written on the white board for a week. As they exit the classroom, I ask

Troy Solomon to shut the door behind him. A stump of a boy with ferocious acne, Troy waves at me from the hallway.

"See ya, Ms. Harper."

Another cramp tugs at me, emptying my insides without permission. I listen for the click of the door latch and fumble in my purse for a tampon and liner.

৵৵

After dinner Tuck washes dishes while I remain in the dining room with a folder of student essays. I mark them with purple ink instead of red and try to write at least one positive comment for each critique. Sometimes the writing is so bad I'm stuck with *Good choice of college-ruled paper* or *Thanks for removing the raggedy edges from the left side of the page.*

Greer Larson's character analysis of Sydney Carton seems especially awful, but the truth is, I am harboring a negative attitude like a fugitive in an attic. Since leaving school today, I've cradled it, this lump of sadness swaddled in my arms. The failure leaves room for nothing else. It's all I see now, what I look for.

Tucker enters the room so quietly I do not notice him at first. Since my sister and her children moved in with us, Tuck and I have taken to creeping around on tiptoes. But tonight the kids are with their father, and Bets won't be back from her night shift until morning. Tuck clears his throat, and I look up. He has changed out of his work clothes into gray sweatpants and my favorite of his T-shirts. The cotton is faded red, frayed by frequent washings. From ten feet away my husband smells like Tide.

"Almost done in here?" he asks.

"Never," I tell him. "Ever."

"Give 'em all As and take me to bed." He grins, and I imagine I could fit my whole thumb in his dimple.

"I wish. Didn't you bring any work home from your trip?"

"Just a suitcase." He takes the pen from me and sets it on the table. "Come on, Core. These kids won't spontaneously combust if they don't get their essays back tomorrow."

"No," I admit. "They won't." I study my empty hand and

remind myself that Tuck doesn't mean to minimize my career. He values teachers and me in particular. But the way his words erase my goals—even in jest—leaves me feeling hollow. Unimportant. Less than.

Act full, Corie. You have so much already.

"I missed you this week," I tell him.

"Don't you always miss me?"

"Hmm," I say by way of agreement. He pulls out the chair next to me, and I push my gradebook away. I can make room for him. I will.

"I forgot to ask how your evaluation went with the new guy. What's his name? Calloway?"

"Callaghan. Henry Callaghan." I picture his spiked hair and wrinkled pants, hear him calling the words in my journal *work*. "He's on the young side. Not much older than I am." My lips are dry, and they crack on a smile. Tuck shifts in his seat and appraises me.

"He any good?"

I consider the question. "I have no idea," I say.

Tucker prompts me with a tilt of his head. "Come on. What does your gut tell you?"

"Stella and Bart haven't organized a lunchtime protest against him yet. I guess that qualifies as good." Before Tuck can push any deeper, a cramp cuts through the center of me, and a grimace replaces my smile.

"Hey, hey," he says. "You all right?"

"Yep," I tell him, although I'm not.

"Headache?"

"No," I say. "Unfortunately, it's not a headache."

"Oh." Tuck studies my face for the answer he already knows. "I'm sorry, Core."

"I'm sorry too."

He stands and puts a hand on my shoulder. "Guess I'll shower and unpack."

"I'll finish up here soon," I say. "Promise." When he leaves, I stuff the essays in my book bag and grab some Advil from the lidless container above the refrigerator. Throwing away the childproof tops is a habit Tuck hasn't broken.

They're a pain in the ass, and we don't have kids.

Yet, I tell him. *Not yet.*

Filling a glass with water, I swallow three tablets. Then, once I hear the shower running, I pluck my cell phone from its charger. Almost a year has passed since I tried the number, and I enter it quickly before losing my nerve. Eleanor Hinden never answers anyway. Each time, I get her answering machine with the same old message Scarlet and I recorded more than a decade ago. I like to listen and hang up without saying a word. I'm simply being kind, making sure Scarlet's mother is all right. Still, I don't tell Tuck about the calls. He would claim they're motivated by something else entirely.

Tonight the phone rings four times, and I await our giggled greeting. Scarlet's voice with my bright laughter in the background. A bridge across ten long years. Instead, there is a hiccup followed by the robotic sounds of the default message: *No one is available to take your call; please leave your name and number at the beep, and someone will get back to you as soon as possible.*

Truth settles in the pit of me, a friendship replaced by the programmed lines of a stranger. Scarlet has finally left me.

Forever.

Find out what happens next... Pick up *Letters for Scarlet* today!

About the Author

Julie C. Gardner is a former English teacher and lapsed marathon runner who traded in the classroom for a writing nook. Now she rarely changes out of her pajamas, and is an author of Women's Fiction. She lives in Southern California with her husband, two children and three dogs.

Keep up with Julie online:

Newsletter: http://juliecgardner.com/newsletter
Website: JulieCGardner.com
Facebook: Julie.C.Gardner
Twitter: @juliecgardner
Instagram: @juliecgardner

Acknowledgments

For their unconditional love, I thank my parents and sister, the original Christiansons. I'm the luckiest to have you forever and ever.

For welcoming me into their family with open arms, I thank the Gardners. I love you all.

For their critiques of the many drafts of *Ophelia* (and the friendships that inspired such generosity) I thank Diane, Courtney, Jennie, Kim, Charlene, Cheryl, Cameron, Angela, Julie, and Karen.

For their judgment-free commiseration (of both the laughing and crying variety), I thank the Writing Safety Tree: Charlene, Kim, Laurel, Lexi, and Rina. "She delighted herself with her own words." I'm grateful you share yours with me.

For ongoing inspiration, I thank the marvelous and prolific Robin Bielman. (I don't know how she does it!)

For life-support beyond the page, I thank the wonderful Kerry Rider.

For the many ways they enrich my life, I thank my fabulous cousins, aunts, uncles, nieces, nephews, and extended family, everywhere.

For their legendary examples of love and marriage, I'm indebted to my grandparents, Phil and Pauline Christianson, whom I miss dearly; and Knute and Renis Anderson, whom I'm beyond fortunate to still have.

For taking a chance on me in the first place, I thank Vicki and Adria and everyone at Velvet Morning Press. I couldn't ask for a more supportive publishing house.

Boundless gratitude to my online and in-real-life friends and readers whose support I labor to deserve.

I completed the first draft of *Forgetting Ophelia* on April 1st, 2015. (This date is a coincidence that still takes my breath away!) Five minutes later, I headed to my dear friend Jackie's house with a bottle of champagne and a stack of red Solo cups. Already there were Jen, Suzie, Rowena, and Gail. We toasted to friendship, love, life. It was our last week with Jackie, and I thank her for believing in me. I miss you, Jacko.

To the rest of my posse: I adore you more than I can say.

My final (first, last, best, forever) thanks to the great joys of my life: Bill, Jack, and Karly. I love you more than all the words. Still. Always.

Made in the USA
San Bernardino,
CA